"Do you dislike the thought of physical intimacy?"

"No, or I wouldn't have married, would I?" she snapped, looking edgy and defiant.

"Do I repel you?"

"I said you did not," she replied with some of her old asperity.

"Is there something else?" he asked more gently.

She looked down at the bedcovers. "No. Nothing like that. It's only that you startled me. You were disinterested in the past. Or so it seemed. I mean, I didn't think it would be a priority with you. And so I wasn't quite ready."

"Oh, well," he said with relief as he shucked off his dressing gown. "I can do something about that."

Other **AVON ROMANCES**

EDITH LAYTON

TO WED A STRANGER

AVON BOOKS
An Imprint of HarperCollinsPublishers

This is a work of fiction. Names, characters, places, and incidents are products of the author's imagination or are used fictitiously and are not to be construed as real. Any resemblance to actual events, locales, organizations, or persons, living or dead, is entirely coincidental.

AVON BOOKS
An Imprint of HarperCollins*Publishers*
10 East 53rd Street
New York, New York 10022-5299

Copyright © 2003 by Edith Felber
ISBN: 0-06-050217-7
www.avonromance.com

First Avon Books paperback printing: March 2003

Printed in the U.S.A.

10 9 8 7 6 5 4 3 2 1

For Adam and his beloved Jeanne,
the newlyweds,
who married wisely and well,
with love and, of course, with laughter.
Joy to you, and thanks
for making my dream come true.

Chapter 1

"I do," she said, and only then allowed herself to wonder what she'd done.

But there wasn't time to think once she'd said it. The vicar went on, then her fiancé's voice, light and amused even now, said the words he had to say to her to make her his wife. There was still time to protest—to undo it! she thought in sheer panic, which passed as quickly as her new husband's light kiss brushed across her lips.

"Courage," he breathed for her ears only, but even that sounded to her as if it held a world of amusement. He wasn't a fellow who took things seriously, not even his own marriage or the compromise he'd made to be married to her.

Nor was Lady Annabelle Wylde a woman who grieved for what couldn't be, she reminded herself as she straightened her spine and pinned a smile on her lips. Grief didn't matter, nor could it change a thing. It was as useless as tears shed railing against her fate. Good for effect, but effecting no change. She'd learned that, at least.

Annabelle put her hand on her husband's arm and let him lead her up the aisle to the back of the church, where they could greet those few well-wishers who had come—as well as the horde of gossips and curiosity-seekers who thronged the place this morning.

They stood in the gray stone vestry, bathed in color, the morning sunlight pouring down fractured and brilliant through stained glass windows high overhead. The bride wore a long-sleeved, high-waisted white gown with a sheer gold overskirt set with myriad brilliants that caught the light, casting icy sparks that glinted on her fair skin. A wreath of white orchids was wound into her soft sable curls. She was small but her figure was perfect, shapely in all its proportions, from her high breasts to her gently swelling hips. Her alabaster face, justly famous for its beauty, was serene; the long lashes that shaded her cerulean eyes hid their expression.

Her new husband took congratulations; she, at his side, accepted best wishes. She believed none of them. These people were there in the same spirit Londoners swarmed to hangings: to see something desperate, titillating, and decisive. Today they gathered to see one of London's most beautiful women finally wed. Beautiful, and doubtless damned, because she was seven-and-twenty and had never managed to marry a man she had wanted. Instead, today she had wed a relative stranger to them all—as well as to herself.

Nevertheless, the new Lady Pelham smiled as she accepted their good wishes, false or not, because if she knew nothing else, she knew the correct thing to do. She never lost that smile, not even when a gloriously handsome gentleman and his equally stunning blond wife, who was obviously with child, paused to wish her well. The line in back of the gorgeous pair grew hushed. Not a flicker in the bride's celestial blue eyes hinted that she'd ever thought the gentleman would be the man at her side now, instead of merely offering his congratulations. Her smile didn't slip even when she spoke with his wife, who was carrying the child she'd thought would be hers.

The bride greeted the next couple, a redheaded military man and his wife, with the same sangfroid, as though half of London didn't know he'd been the next man she'd set her cap for. Nor did her smile slip as a tall, thin, elegant gentleman took her hand and his lady greeted her, though he'd been another that rumor said she'd aimed her heart at, a year ago.

She'd give no one cause to gossip this day, even though these men *were* the reason she was a married woman now. Not one of them had chosen her; they'd gone to other women. Her birth, fortune, those famous good looks, conversation, and charm had done her no good. Each had rejected her—only because of fate or chance, or so her mother assured her. London gossips said more. None of it was true, but she no longer knew what was, except for the fact that she'd been rejected so often it was a joke to everyone but herself.

But no more. She'd married this morning. They'd have to find someone else to make sport of.

She watched the gentlemen as she accepted their murmured good wishes. They were bland, cool, and as charming as she was. She was grateful for it. She could bear speculation and gossip, but not pity. Which was the reason she'd passed this bright morning marrying a stranger . . . not quite a stranger, she corrected herself. They had, after all, known each other for two months.

Her father had come to her with the viscount's offer two months ago. Then, she'd refused. Until her father sat and talked with her as never before, with solemn insistence.

"I'm a good judge of men," he'd said. "And intelligent enough not to rely on just that. I've had him investigated too. Miles Croft, Viscount Pelham, is entirely eligible. He's recently returned from abroad and newly settled into his honors. He's handsome enough to please any female, only five years your senior, and has a clean reputation. He needs a wife of good standing."

"Why would a fellow of such looks, sterling reputation, and great prospects want to marry a female he's never even met?"

"You didn't always use that tone of voice with me," her father said with a frown.

She'd been honestly confused.

"That note of venom," he explained, "that sly spite."

"But then we don't talk together often, do we, Father?"

He'd looked down. "My fault entirely," he'd murmured.

There'd been a silence. Earl Wylde spent as little time as possible under his own roof. At home in the country, he passed his time outdoors, riding, fishing, or visiting with his cronies. In London, he was busy with politics, his clubs, his mistresses.

The earl was still attractive at fifty-odd years. His dark hair was only touched with gray and he was perhaps a shade too portly, but he carried it well. In all, he was a good-looking man, with a commanding expression enlivened by intense blue eyes. His daughter, his only child, had those eyes from him, as well as most of her looks. Her mother was short, plump, and nondescript. Their marriage had been arranged, as was their parents', and the only regret her mother had about it was that she'd produced just one child. One beautiful daughter she doted on, and lived vicariously through, although lately that daughter's lack of a husband increasingly mortified and distressed her.

She scarcely seemed to notice her husband's absence from her life, but his daughter always had. His regrets about his marriage must have been many, because now in most respects he lived as a single man. And because that had always hurt his daughter, and because she thought it was odd that he cared about her now, she told him so.

His shoulders went up, he looked down at his hands. "No, it's only odd that I didn't say anything before. But I thought you and young Damon Ryder would make a match of it. We all did."

"So did I, Father," she said, raising her head high.

He looked up at her directly. "So he married another. There was no formal agreement, and you never kept company with him once you were of age to do so. It was just that we were near neighbors, and you got along as children, so we parents thought you two would suit. He grew up and surprised us. It wasn't the end of the world, Annabelle."

It had seemed so to her. She looked away, swallowing hard. No one would see her cry about it. She hadn't for years, and she would not now.

"As for his friends," he father went on heavily, "that soldier Raphael Dalton, and the Earl of Drummond . . . Fine men to be sure, but I never believed either of them was right for you, whatever your mama said."

"Then why didn't you tell me?"

He gave her a level glance. "Would that have done anything but anger you? I believed you wanted them because it was the only way you could continue to see Damon. And perhaps make him regret not choosing you?"

Now she turned her gaze from his.

"It wouldn't have been good for you in the long run," he went on. "But my telling you that would have been worse, I think. No parent with one wit in his head would tell his daughter he believed her and her love didn't suit. If I had, and you had married one of them, I'd have been forever an enemy. If you had not, I would have been blamed for poisoning your mind. My dear Annabelle, had you said you were in love with a Gypsy I would have held my tongue. Though in that case, I could at least have tried to bribe him out of your sight. How could I discourage men of Drummond and Dalton's stripe? They were—are—good, honorable men. But you were lucky, I think."

"Though of course you couldn't tell me so," she said bitterly.

He shrugged. "I haven't been an attentive father, perhaps, but neither have I been a domineering one. I am a caring one, whatever you think. I never ordered you to marry, though I could have done. Your mother started nagging at me years ago because I did nothing when you were still unmarried. She hounds me now, telling me every lady your age in London is wed. She worries about what people are saying. I thought you'd remedy the situation in your own time. That time hasn't come. Now I do worry about what your future will hold. I believe Pelham to be a good man who could make you happy if you gave him the chance. I'm here to tell you that he offers you his hand."

"Why didn't he come to me? Why apply to you? We are not so old-fashioned."

"Neither is he. But he cared for your feelings. He didn't want to cause more gossip. He felt he might have stirred up more if he took up your time, only to find out your heart was otherwise engaged, or you were utterly uninterested in his offer."

"Very kind of him I'm sure," she said through clenched teeth. "But again, why should such a paragon offer for a woman he doesn't know? A woman he's surely heard gossip about? And not charming gossip at that." Her mouth twisted as if she tasted those bitter words. "I know what they say. Doesn't he care that he's seeking a marriage with an incurable flirt, a selfish, vain female who can't see beyond her own looking glass?"

"That could be merely jealous tattle said about any beautiful woman. There's no talk about your reputation, which is unassailable. He doesn't believe gossip anyway. He's lived with it too long. After his father died, his mother married unwisely; she wed a dirty dish, a very bad man. He left scandal in his wake, bankrupted her, and ruined her name before he too died. Miles Croft made his own fortune and has just inherited another, along with a title that makes him Viscount Pelham. Now he wants a wife to add luster to his name and family. His sister is of marriageable age. He loves her, his brother, and his mother, and believes that if he marries well it would go a long way to clearing the way for their advancement in society, redeeming what his mother did to their name."

"And he wants nothing for himself?" This time she couldn't keep the scorn from her voice.

"Don't speak foolishly. You're beautiful, Annabelle. He's seen you. He's heard the gossip too, and likes the way you comport yourself in spite of it. 'Like a deposed princess who knows her throne still exists,' he said."

Annabelle fell still. She did hold her head high. It was that, or hide it. She had no choice, she wore a smile and faced the world. And the world accepted her whatever they said about her in private. Gossip hurt, but she was sure that cowardice would kill her. She was her father's daughter in more than looks. When she'd been a child he had only to enter the house to make her drop whatever she was doing and race to him. They fished, they went riding . . . but as soon as her childhood was over, their friendship was too. What father passed his time with his adult daughter, after all?

He was admired by everyone who knew him; even her mother didn't speak ill of him. Annabelle herself had always wanted his respect. Now a stranger that he recommended wanted to marry her for her name and her looks. All her life she'd used her appearance to win her way, yet now she was loath to do so. She'd hoped to marry for love. She remembered why she had not.

"And you will be seven-and-twenty in the spring," her father added, "and Pelham does not mind."

Her eyes flew wide. She went a trifle pale.

He winced, and turned his head so he couldn't see her face. "I too thought you and Damon would make a match of it. When you didn't, I thought you should be given time to find love, even though that's a modern notion. I didn't marry for love, nor did your mama, but these are different times and I believed you should at least be able to heal your heart, given time. You have not.

"And . . ." He rose, paced away, and said without looking at her, "There comes a time when a man wants to lead his own life. Your mother doesn't mind my absences. You do. But how long

must a man live for his child?" He stopped and
faced her. "You're not a child anymore, Annabelle.
I want . . . whatever I want is the least of it. If
you stay on here, you'll dwindle to being your
mother's companion. I think you deserve more."

"And you think I can't get a husband on my
own?"

"I think you'd be hard put to find a better one
than Pelham. If you can't find love, Annabelle, I
believe it is time to find accommodation. Before
it's too late."

"Well, then," she'd snapped, anger, hurt, and
shame making her want to strike out, if only at
herself, "why not?"

"Good!" he'd said before she could correct
herself.

And then it was too late. Pride, guilt, and
shame stayed her tongue. Viscount Pelham
turned out to be as her father had described:
charming, if lightweight in his conversation, hu-
morous, harmless enough. He looked at her with
admiration, looked well himself, and often made
her laugh. He didn't paw her or embarrass her. He
seemed to have chosen her for the same reasons
he did the expensive and fashionable clothing he
always wore.

He was well read, well schooled, well man-
nered, and maybe best of all, not very well known.
He'd been away from England for ten years, most
of his adult life. No one knew ill of him, or much

of him either. He'd never been accepted or rejected by any other woman, and if he'd had mistresses they were unknown too. She'd begin her
new life with a clean slate with a man who had no
history her enemies could gossip about.

His family was no trouble either. In fact, their
awe of her was flattering. His mother was shy, his
sister obviously impressed by her brother's beautiful fiancée, his younger brother openly admir-
ing. Though Annabelle looked carefully, there
was no impediment: except, of course, that her
heart wasn't involved.

She agreed to give him her hand, though she
was sure her father would change his mind, or the
man himself would say or do something to end it,
or let her do so.

That had not happened. Time flew by. Their engagement was as short as their acquaintance. She
couldn't back out, so she found reasons to go on.
At least she'd no longer be an object of pity or
scorn. She'd been spoiled since birth, but as a married woman she'd have more freedom than she'd
ever known. That wasn't what she'd wanted, but
if love wasn't possible, freedom would do. It was
certainly better than the ignominy of dwindling
into spinsterhood, her mother ashamed, her father disappointed.

Now Annabelle slid an appraising glance at her
new husband. He passed scrutiny, as always. A

man of average height, well formed, fit and trim. She could have wished he were taller, but she found no fault with the rest of his appearance.

Viscount Pelham was always clean and well dressed. He was not unhandsome. His looks were masculine rather than classic, saved from severity by the slight curl in his brown hair, which even cropping couldn't prevent. He had clear skin, if a bit too bronzed for fashion, but he'd been a sailor, and she supposed that accounted for it. His features were even, the most attractive being his remarkably fine eyes, the color of rain washed with blue. Sometimes when he was bored they looked glacial, but when he gazed at her they were a twilight hue. A scar, from some childhood incident, she supposed, sliced from the bottom of his wellshaped lower lip down to his square chin. Annabelle reminded herself to ask him sometime how he had acquired the wound. She'd been too disconcerted by their sudden engagement to discuss personal matters. For his part, she supposed he'd been disinterested in her reaction to his looks, much less his history.

Theirs was not, after all, a love match.

A shadow fell over her, and she remembered her role. The bride looked up to see a giant blond man looking down at her, a smile on his lips, sadness in his gaze. She responded by raising her chin. Lieutenant Eric Ford had once been interested in her, but she believed that had only been to divert her interest from his friend Raphael Dalton. Still, she might have tested that interest. But he had no title, and she had no heart anymore. Besides, it would have required guile and patience, and she had no more resources.

So she agreed with her mother and obliged her father. If she had to wed, it might as well be to better herself. Her new husband had looks too, if less spectacular ones. And he was a viscount.

"Lady Pelham," the blond giant said softly, "I wish you great happiness and a long life together."

"Lieutenant Ford," she answered, "I thank you."

"And you, Miles," he said with more energy as he spoke to her groom, his smile becoming real and warm, "you lucky rogue. Trust you to snare the prize, wherever you go."

The groom sketched a bow. "Thank you, Eric. I'm honored you could come today to share my bliss."

"Share? Ho!" Eric laughed. " 'Envy' and 'begrudge' is a much better reading of my emotions."

"As ever," Miles said lightly, with a wave of one hand.

Then the two men laughed together.

The bride raised an eyebrow. Obviously these two were friends. It was Eric who answered her silent question. "Miles and I met at school. Then again at . . . our various occupations for His Majesty during the late wars. Though your husband went off to sea and I was in the army, there were times when our paths overlapped."

Miles sighed. "And one would think my vision should have been good enough to have seen him coming a mile off."

The huge blond man laughed and gave him a buffet on the shoulder. The blow looked powerful enough to budge a boulder, but it didn't so much as sway the groom.

Miles smiled. "Saw that coming, though. So it's a date, then? Gentleman Jackson's, when I return from my honeymoon. We'll see who can rock whom, shall we?"

Eric put up both hands in surrender. "Hardly. I don't want to widow your bride so soon."

Annabelle tried to keep smiling. She owed her new husband no allegiance, but seeing him belittled shamed them both.

"Because," Eric went on, "titled or not, you'd be hauled off for murder, then topped at Marble Arch for killing me. A silken noose works just as well as the hemp they use for us commoners. And then where would your poor widow be?" Annabelle looked confused. "Oh, I've the reach and the power," Eric assured her. "But your husband's like a terrier—fierce, light on his feet, and devious as the devil, you know."

"She doesn't," Miles said gently. "Now get you gone, Eric. My lady and I have hordes to greet. We'll see this fractious fellow again later," he told

Annabelle. "For now we must do the pretty here, and then at our wedding party. We will see you there?" he asked his friend.

Eric clapped his hand to his chest. "Without fail," he said, and strode away.

"Don't look so surprised. I've been away, but I know a great many people here," Miles told his bride quietly before he gave his attention to the next guest.

Except me, she thought with wry resignation before she put her smile back on and turned to accept more congratulations on this, her wedding day.

"That was superb!" Annabelle's mother said with immense satisfaction as she eyed the wreckage of her ballroom later that night after the last guests had left. "The best wedding party London has seen in years, if I say so myself! Unusual to host both a wedding breakfast and a ball, but I shouldn't be surprised to see it done everywhere from now on."

The banks of flowers that had lined the ballroom were wilted and sagging, their petals strewn everywhere. The floors were littered with the detritus of a successful party: grains of snuff and remnants of feathers were ground underfoot. Bits of fallen food and smears from squashed cakes, liquid spills and scuff marks from hundreds of slippers and boots marred the polished wood. It would take the staff days to buff it out, almost as

long as it would take to scrape off the drippings
from the myriad candles in chandeliers and
sconces that now flickered fitfully as they burned
down to their sockets.

"Well done," her husband agreed.

"Thank you," their new son-in-law said, bowing. "It was everything and more than I expected.
Your festivities certainly showed the world this
was a welcome match. My mother was delighted.
She left early only because she was unaccustomed
to the lateness of the hour and the noise. My sister
and brother were forced to leave with her or
they'd be here still. You've done us proud, and I
thank you."

"It was everything I could have wished,"
Annabelle said, and looked toward the doorway.
She hesitated. It felt odd to say good night and
leave this house. That was why she was still there.
Most couples raced off to their honeymoons; she
and her new husband had lingered until the last
guests left. She'd told Miles she wanted to enjoy
every moment of her wedding party. He'd honored her wishes. She ought to be content, but still
it felt odd, if only because she'd had to ask someone else permission for something she wanted to
do. That hadn't happened in years.

But now he was still talking to her father, and so
Annabelle didn't have to leave yet.

"I am so pleased," her mother told her in a conspiratorial whisper. "His mama, for all her past,

acts the lady now, and is immensely grateful to us. The brother and sister will do. I'll take the chit in hand, see if I don't get her married off wonderfully too. What a splendid idea. It will give me something to do."

"Oh? So I'm in retirement now?" Annabelle asked, with a smile to show she was joking.

"Why, of course," her mother said. "You're married."

"I'm married, not dead, Mama," Annabelle said with a touch of asperity.

"I only meant that you can go to parties by yourself now if you wish, but as you'll likely be increasing any time now, that will stop soon." Her mother looked up to see her husband and son-in-law patiently waiting for them. "Oh dear, is it really time to say good night?"

"Unless you want to offer me more lobster," Miles said, and before she could call to one of the weary waiters who were cleaning up, added, "I'm joking. I've no room for another bite."

Miles and Annabelle walked out to the hall, and then to the door.

"Good night, good-bye," Lord and Lady Wylde called after the newlywed couple as their coach pulled away.

"Good-bye," Annabelle whispered, looking back at them and the brightly lit house. Then she turned to look resolutely ahead, into the dark.

Chapter 2

Annabelle sat back in the darkened carriage. She'd really gone and done it. She was on her way to a new life. It hardly seemed possible.

"We'll stay at my town house tonight," Miles mused as the coach moved through the darkened streets. "Then we'll pass a few weeks at a lodge in Devon that came with the estate. It's a charming place, with a lake, a waterfall, gardens, and most of all, blessed solitude. A perfect spot to get to know each other better."

He waited for her reaction. She gave him none. A trip to the Continent would have suited her better. They did need to get to know each other better, but the place sounded like a dead bore.

"Then," he went on, "I thought we'd go on to

Hollyfields, my uncle's estate, now my family seat. It's very grand. You'll like it there, I think."

He told her about his new home, Annabelle listening with half an ear. For a certainty, she'd visit it. She didn't intend to spend the rest of her life there, though. She'd loved living at her family estate when she was young, but then she'd had her parents, her pets, and her friends. That was a long time ago. She'd die of loneliness in the countryside now. London was her home.

His town house was near the park, only streets from her parents' home, so they arrived there in no time. She was very glad of it. It wasn't that she was weary—she was used to social gatherings and even later nights—but there was so much to think about. She wanted to be alone.

His house was spacious and well appointed. She'd visited it before. Odd though, Annabelle thought, as a servant helped her off with her cloak in the front hall, that she didn't know which room she'd call her own. Her whole situation was odd, she supposed. Her life had been aimed at getting married, yet now that she was, she realized she'd never contemplated life beyond her wedding. Not with this man, at least.

Well, she guessed they'd rub on well enough. He was amiable. And he'd wanted her. It diminished him a bit in her eyes, since a chase was always more interesting than capturing a man with a bat of an eyelash. But there were worse things than having a comfortable husband. And who knew what fascinating flirtations lay in her future? Her spirits rose. It would only be coquetry, of course. She did have morals. But a few interesting flirts would spice up what looked to be an increasingly tepid life.

"I expect you're weary," her new husband said. "Unless, of course, you'd care for anything? Most of my staff have been given the evening off, but I know my way around the kitchens."

"No, thank you, I need nothing now."

He nodded, offered her his arm, and led her up the stair. When they reached the top, he paused in the corridor in front of a door. "The bathing room," he said with a smile. "I'm very proud of our plumbing. We get hot water on the second floor. I detest going to bed in all my dirt, although tonight it would only be stray grains of rice and a petal or two. I've arranged for a bath to be waiting for me elsewhere, and so invite you to use my sumptuous one. If there's anything else you need, send to me," he said, bowed, and left her.

She was vastly relieved. Glib as she was, she wasn't in the mood for conversation, and a hot bath sounded wonderful.

It was. Her own maid had come with her as part of her dowry, and if it weren't for the luxury and novelty of the well-appointed bathing room, Annabelle could have imagined she was still at home.

Her mood improved even more when she saw her room—a big airy chamber with long windows covered by soft draperies. The furniture looked new, in the latest Egyptian style, delicate, gilded, made of light wood. The lamplight showed fine Turkey carpets, a wardrobe, a desk, and an enormous bed piled with coverlets. A half-opened door led to a well-furnished dressing room. Everything was in shades of gold, blue, and rose.

Annabelle dismissed her maid, shed her robe, and slipped a night shift over her head. She stepped up into the high bed and sighed as she sank into the plump feather mattress. Not so bad, after all, this marriage business. She had a grand new house, freedom, and peace of mind.

She'd forgotten to blow out all the lamps, as one still burned. But she was too comfortable to move. She closed her eyes—and opened them when she heard the door open.

Her new husband ambled into the room and closed the door behind him. His hair was dewed with droplets of water, and he wore a long dressing gown. As he approached the bed he began to draw the sash and shrug the dressing gown off.

Annabelle sat bolt upright. "What are you doing?"

"Going to bed. With my wife," he added blandly.

"I had not thought . . . I didn't think . . . You surprise me, sir," she managed, because, after all, of course he had the right, but she hadn't imagined he'd want intimacy so soon.

"Now, why should you be surprised?" he asked, pausing by the bedside.

"You don't know me! That is to say, we don't know each other."

"Indeed?" he said, looking at her with interest. "But we are married, are we not?"

"Yes, but we're scarcely well acquainted, even so."

He put his head to one side. "Time to remedy that, I'd think."

He was so mild, so logical, so peaceful that she relaxed. This wasn't a man in the throes of any kind of lust. He simply didn't understand. "But we are, in many respects, strangers," she explained.

"Yes. And so, soon we won't be," he said gently.

Her hand flew to her neck to cover her chest where her shift didn't. "I'd think there'd be plenty of time to . . . start that."

She knew about lovemaking, of course, had been aware she'd have to submit sooner or later. But this man had been so quiet and disarming, she'd believed that intimate relations with him, like her eventual death, would take place in some unspecified future she didn't have to worry about yet.

"You are ill?" he asked.

She shook her head.

"Frightened?" he persisted.

"Definitely not!" she said.

"Revolted by the thought of my touch?"

"Don't be ridiculous!"

"But not longing for it," he said on a sigh. "Well, then, we'll see what we can do about that." He plucked up the coverlet.

"You want me to long for you?" she gasped. "You mean to treat me like a . . . prostitute?"

He blinked. "Of course not. My dear Annabelle, you're quite mistaken. One doesn't care what prostitutes think. That's why they're so popular. I do care about how you react to my lovemaking, though. Look," he said, with a smile that held true amusement, "if we put this off you'll become so anxious you'll startle at every sound. Just think, every time I make a move toward you, you'll bolt, wondering, Is this the moment, does he mean to begin now? Come, we're husband and wife. You're very lovely, you can't be that surprised . . ." He hesitated, one hand on the sash of his dressing gown.

His eyes grew thoughtful. "Or is it that you thought I wouldn't be interested? Have I been that mannerly? I'd have thought you'd have seen it in my eyes—but you weren't looking, were you? A convenient marriage isn't necessarily a barren one, and I'm not just speaking of getting children. Sharing pleasure can be part of the arrangement. Even if it weren't, I won't have an unwilling bed partner. I thought at your age . . ." He saw her expression and changed what he was going to say. "But if reluctance to bed your husband is why you haven't married before this, you really ought to have told me."

"That isn't why I haven't married!" she said quickly.

"But you aren't willing?"

"I thought to know you better before we proceeded."

"Given the progress we've made toward that end so far, that isn't likely in the near future. Unless we proceed, of course. I'm quite looking forward to it."

She bit her lower lip.

He paused. "I'm not unreasonable. It may be that this was a mistake, after all. If so, something may yet be done to end this marriage—if it's done before we begin it, in a physical sense."

She gasped. Was he threatening her? Annulment or divorce proceedings were rare and scandalous, beyond any vile thing the gossips had ever said about her. "No! I'm willing," she said breathlessly. "It's just that I hadn't expected—I don't know what I had expected. But I'm ready. What is it you want me to do?"

He sighed again. He perched on the edge of the bed and touched her face with his fingertips. "This," he said, almost to himself, "is going to be a long night."

Annabelle's eyes flew wide.

She was beautiful when she was horrified, Miles thought with wry appreciation of his bride's expression. His sense of humor was aroused, along with another vastly interested part. She sat rigidly in bed, her rapid breathing making her lovely breasts rise and fall, her eyes so wide he could see their blue gleam even in the dimmed light. She really was a spectacular-looking woman, he thought again.

He was tempted to bend to her, terrifying her even more, and then shock her by merely kissing the tip of her delightful little nose before leaving her alone for the night.

Three things made him hesitate. The first was that he was fairly sure that it would be a disastrous way to begin this marriage.

His bride wasn't an innocent miss. She was a grown woman, who, if rumor could be believed—or even only half believed—had been head over her pretty heels in love with another man, or three. So she couldn't be ignorant of what he intended. If anything, he'd counted on her being eager, frustrated after years of abortive lovemaking, because he doubted she'd ever completed the act. He was almost certain she was still a virgin. After all, she knew how the rules of society were played, and even more to the point, the men with whom her name had been linked were men of honor. If one of them had dallied with her, he'd have married her, and that would have been the end of that.

Undoubtedly, if there'd been any extensive love-making, and she'd been as eager to wed as gossip had it, she'd have used that for a reason to have been legally married long before this.

Virgin or no, she had to be sophisticated after so many years on the town. So she'd think a hesitant groom a poor specimen, and that impression would last long into their marriage.

The second reason was that it was his bed, and this was his bedchamber.

The third was that she was so damned beautiful.

He liked dark ladies; he'd been dazzled when he'd first seen this one. That was nothing to how he felt when he'd walked into his room just now. He'd seen her dressed in magnificent gowns of gold cloth, azure silks, blue satins, and gossamer gauze. She was even more alluring to him tonight, sitting in his bed, clad as she was in a plain white nightrail. Because now he knew she was his.

He knew her body well. Women's fashions made sure of that. She was petite, but perfect in her dimensions. Her breasts were high and shapely. Whenever she'd danced with him, it had taken all his resolve not to stare at the curved valley between them and wonder if her skin would taste as cool and sweet as it looked. She was lean, but had rounded hips. He'd always noted her trim little derriere and found it enchanting. Her face was famous, but it was that delicious mouth that never stopped tempting him. He was fascinated by it, the way the short upper lip over the fuller lower one seemed to make her mouth beg for long, involved kisses.

He hadn't pressed her for them during their brief courtship. It wasn't a love match, after all. Openly lusting for her would have made their arrangement look as if he'd wanted her only for his sexual convenience, and not a marriage for their mutual benefit. But there was no question that convenience had mattered to him.

He'd needed a wife, and quickly, but he had other needs as well. Being married to a woman he desired was an important reason it was Annabelle and not another well-born lady there tonight. It was true he'd married because he'd had to, but he didn't want to keep mistresses for the rest of his life.

She was clever and witty, very up to snuff. She must know what being a wife entailed. He'd been content to wait until she could have no objections to his physical attentions. That was now.

He bent closer—and heard her gasp. He pulled back, struck by several terrible notions. He'd thought her coolness toward him part of her general affect. What if it was specific? Could she have mistaken the reason for his politeness and thought him less than masculine? Or had he been wrong on several counts? Had she been forced to marry him? By her father—or her own anatomy—

or, rather, the consequences of being too free with that anatomy?

Neither thought appealed. Nor did the sudden unsettling notion that it might simply be that she didn't like to be touched. Had that been the reason she'd never married; was she the sort of woman who preferred to be worshipped, and to worship, from afar?

"Annabelle," he said slowly, "is there anything I should know?"

"Like what?' she asked, looking genuinely puzzled.

"Is it me? The idea of making love to me? Or the idea of making love to anyone? Damme," he muttered when she just stared at him, "are you a virgin, my dear?"

She nodded.

He relaxed. Unless there was some impending miraculous birth, he was spared at least one dire possibility. It wasn't that he especially looked forward to bedding a virgin; in fact he'd heard initiating a female was more trouble than it was worth. But at least his wife had played fair and wasn't carrying anyone else's child. He resolved to go on. He had to know where the difficulty lay. Besides, everything had to have a beginning, and he definitely wanted lovemaking to be a part of this marriage.

"Do you dislike the thought of physical intimacy?"

"No, or I wouldn't have married, would I?" she snapped, looking edgy and defiant.

"Do I repel you?"

"I said you did not," she said with some of her old asperity.

"Is there someone else?" he asked more gently.

She looked down at the bedcovers. "No. Nothing like that. It's only that you startled me. You were disinterested in the past. Or so it seemed. I mean, I didn't think it would be a priority with you. And so I wasn't quite ready."

"Oh well," he said with relief as he shucked off his dressing gown, "that's something I can do something about."

She closed her eyes.

Chapter 3

~~~~~~~~~~~~~∾⟁∾~~~~~~~~~~~~~

Miles climbed into the bed beside his bride. She still hadn't opened her eyes.

"Very proper," he said, close to her ear. "My mistake. I suppose I ought to have crawled into bed, pulled the covers up over my ears, and *then* wriggled out of my dressing gown. But I thought that might be even more alarming."

She giggled. He cocked his head to the side. It was a strange sound coming from her. A giggle? From this worldly lady? There was, he realized, much he didn't know about his bride.

What he did know, he liked. Apart from her looks, he appreciated her wit, and she had the social skill and standing he needed in a wife. All surfaces, he knew. He'd never asked for more. Nor had she. They didn't need to know more, strictly

31

speaking. Not for marriage, and certainly not for what they were about to do. But it made things a bit difficult for him, this, their first time.

He wasn't a cold man, as his sister, Camille, accused him of being. Or heartless, as she'd insisted. He was practical, or at least he'd been harried to practicality by his little family. He returned to England with his pockets full, only to find he had his hands full as well. He needed someone to manage Camille and find her a place in society before she ruined herself as his mother had done. He needed someone to help his mother regain her place in society, and someone for his brother, Bernard, that wretch, to aspire to, so he'd get on with becoming civilized.

But it was true that he'd only thought himself in love twice. The first time he'd been at university and became lost in love for a local barmaid that he'd some vague dramatic plans for saving. Until she told him with no nonsense that he hadn't the funds for the kind of savings she was after. The second time had been Clarissa, and she'd been forced to marry someone her father wanted. Still, since he'd got the himself drunk for only a few weeks after her defection, he couldn't have been that far gone. He might remember her now and again, but that didn't mean he pined for her. He was, as he'd told Camille, a practical man.

He might not always have been so practical, but

there was no way to know. Mama had gone and married Peter Proctor. Now all his notions of love had been sacrificed to duty, and at two and thirty, he doubted he was susceptible anymore. But, luckily, a fellow didn't need to lose his heart to find pleasure. And Lady Annabelle filled all his requirements for a wife, not the least being that her looks pleased him mightily.

There was nothing wrong in taking some comfort for himself while he set his family to rights, was there? He'd been on his own too long anyway, and looked forward to sharing his life. If he had to marry, he decided to make it as pleasant as possible for himself. And he had no patience with young misses. He shuddered to think of making love to some giddy girl. The worldly widows he'd met since he'd started looking for a wife hadn't been his style either.

He'd been hunting for a wife since autumn, when he'd returned to England and discovered the mess his family was in. The females whose minds meshed with his didn't have bodies that could; either they were too old or they were already married. He didn't have the luxury of waiting much longer for true love to come to him—if it even could. Camille was bent for hell in a handbasket, if not on purpose, then because she was far too open and friendly; she practically begged for someone as evil as their stepfather had been to lure her into an equally disastrous marriage. Her come-out in London had already been delayed, he couldn't let her wait another year.

And if his mama wept any more she'd float away. It was even worse when she tried to be stoic. She was too alone. If he married someone who could settle her back in society, she might smile again.

And his brother, Bernard, would be done with school one of these days, if he could only apply himself to it, and he needed a name he could be proud of.

Miles needed a wife, and quickly. He'd taken an exquisite one, sophisticated, awake on all suits— except one, it seemed. Now he had to teach her how to give and receive pleasure, because sharing pleasure made it even better. He thought he could accomplish that.

He knew his physical assets as well as his financial ones, and used both to his best advantage. He wasn't extravagantly athletic, like one of the Corinthian set. Nor was he remotely a dandy, or in the current style of willowy, brooding, demon-ridden poets either. There wasn't anything wrong with him, but he was, he thought, rather spectacularly ordinary.

Still, he'd built a fortune out of nothing, and had always been able to win the women he wanted by using the same tactics. A man with few assets had to compensate. And, as far as he knew, he'd never made love to a woman who regretted it. He was determined that his bride wouldn't regret him either. The sooner he showed her that, the better.

He turned on his side, elbow on a pillow, head propped on a hand. He smiled at her. "Do you usually sleep sitting up?"

He heard a surprised chuckle. "Are we going to sleep?"

"Eventually," he said softly.

She went still. Then silently, obedient but stiff, she lay down on her back, until she looked exactly like the figure of a woman carved on her own tomb.

He sighed. Then he reached over and toyed with an inky curl, slowly pulled the ribbon from her hair. Her freed tresses spilled out, black as the surrounding night. They tumbled through his fingers as he ran a hand through them.

"Annabelle?" he asked. And didn't give her time to answer. Instead, he raised himself over her and brushed his mouth across hers. It took all his resolve to resist the urge to discover whether that slight tingle of electricity he'd felt would grow to fire. He drew back. And waited.

Did he expect her to speak? Annabelle wondered.

How could she? This was a kind of agony. She was a woman who always knew what to say, what to do. She knew, of course, what he meant to do.

She'd grown up in the countryside and had noticed animal behavior. She'd spied humans coupling in the shadows in unsavory parts of London her carriage had passed through too. Once, at a masquerade, she'd come upon a couple who weren't as hidden as they thought they'd been. A person couldn't live to her age and not know what men and women did together.

Her mother had offered marital advice only days before, a labored duty for her, talking about what she herself obviously detested. Embarrassed, Annabelle made a joke to turn her attention. They were close, but never in the way of friends. Annabelle hadn't had an intimate girlfriend since she herself had been a girl. Her mother said that was due to jealousy on other girls' parts, because she was too beautiful. It didn't matter. She knew enough.

It seemed an awkward, undignified business at best. But she was a woman of honor; she paid her debts. This was part of the bargain. It was a social embarrassment she couldn't talk her way around.

He brushed his lips against hers again, and she realized he was waiting for a different kind of response.

She lay resigned, and let him do as he would.

But he wouldn't.

"Has my wife fainted, I wonder?" he mused, moving his mouth from hers.

"I was just trying to be accommodating," she snapped, because she couldn't bear being made fun of. But then she shivered because he moved his mouth to her ear, and the sensation of his light breath there diverted her.

She'd let men kiss her before, so she could see what it was like and how she'd respond. No man's kiss had ever been as she'd imagined Damon's would have been, so she stopped experimenting. Still, there'd been times when it was expected, and she allowed it. Miles had also kissed her, but his had been infrequent, undemanding kisses, more ceremonial than ardent. They were different tonight. His mouth was questioning hers, and it moved her as never before. She closed her eyes, and was diverted even more.

It must be the lateness of the hour, she thought, the deepness of the night, the proximity of this man and what she knew he had every right to do. He was warm, his scent clean: soap, red wine, and some newer, sweeter spices. She was curious, Annabelle admitted to herself, which was natural enough after all these years.

She shivered. He hadn't grabbed or grasped her, merely letting his lips brush against her, here and there, and what seemed like everywhere.

"Accommodating is nice," he breathed against her neck. "I'm not complaining about accommodation," he whispered as his mouth touched the inner curl of her ear. "But cooperation would be much better," he said as his lips airily grazed hers again.

Her eyes flew open. "Cooperation? What do you want me to do?" She really didn't know. As she understood it, this was a thing a man did, and a woman let have done. She was letting him, wasn't she?

He drew back, watching her with a slight frown.

She'd been promised to Damon Ryder, kept company with the Earl of Drummond and Rafe Dalton, among many other men of the world. And she didn't know what he wanted of her? If she were lying, he'd soon find out, so what would be the point? He was fascinated anew.

There were men who considered only the act itself worthwhile, and that act a hasty matter of minutes. Such men prided themselves on their speed of completion. Their own Prince was said to be one such. Miles believed that lovemaking, like enjoyment of wine or food, was an Epicurean matter, something to be lingered over. Or so he felt, and he doubted other men Annabelle kept company with felt differently. There were, after all, things a woman could do and keep her virginity intact. Hadn't she experienced anything of lovemaking at all? There were a dozen questions he couldn't ask her, not here, not now, not yet.

Or she could be shamming. Words wouldn't

tell him what he most wanted to know. But damme, he thought, this was awkward.

"Well, you're here. And you're complacent enough . . ." He hesitated. If she was lying, he didn't want to say anything she'd find amusing. If she wasn't, he didn't want to alarm her. Inspiration struck. "Doubtless some men would be vastly content with complacency. But I've always felt that lovemaking is like the dance. If one person is stepping to the music, turning, keeping time, and so on, and his partner is merely letting herself be moved by him, it isn't much fun for either, is it?"

She looked puzzled.

"For example," he persisted, "even in the dance a lady holds on to her partner. So to begin, if you could think of this as sort of a horizontal waltz?" He fought the urge to smile at his simile, a warped version of what prudes said about the waltz. Laughter could ease the way in most instances, but it wasn't appropriate now—if she was being sincere.

He thought he saw her skin take on a ruddy hue, but it could have been a flare of lamplight. She put one hand on his shoulder, the other on his upper arm. Just lightly, tentatively, but it made him shiver.

"Yes," he breathed. "Now, if you could try to . . ." "Respond" was the word he was looking for, but it wasn't a thing he'd ever had to ask a woman to do. In fact, at this point, or rather, in this position, a bargain had always been struck or an understanding reached, and eagerness had never been a problem. He struggled for control and inspiration. "Let your emotions free," he told her. "It is like dancing, my dear. It's also like swimming," he said a little desperately, when she simply lay there staring at him. "Do you know how to swim?"

"My father taught me," she said in a small voice, looking at him as though he'd grown another head.

"Excellent. So if you could just let go . . . I mean let go of your guard on your feelings, not of me; that felt very good," he said on a huff of a laugh as she dropped her hands as though his skin were boiling hot. "Yes, thank you, that's better," he said when her hands came back to where they'd been. "Holding me is good, touching me would be too." He felt the tension in her body. "But only if you wish to," he added quickly.

"For now," he said, "I only meant that you should trust that I won't let you sink or fall. Just feel what we're doing. Like listening to the music when you dance," he said, as he put his lips to her cheek. "Like floating free," he said as his mouth sipped at her neck, and his hand moved to her breast. "Like being free," he murmured as he pushed her shift aside and brought his lips to the suddenly peaked nipple his palm had discovered.

She caught her breath. The sensation was exquisite. She'd been touched before too, briefly. But this! This was beyond words. She was shocked at her reaction and pleased by his. Because he seemed as thrilled as she was. But surely he didn't mean she should do to him as he was doing?

It was hard to think of what he meant or what she should be feeling, because as his lips and hands moved on, feeling was definitely overwhelming her thinking. That seemed to please him so much, because he was murmuring, "Yes, so sweet, yes, precisely, this is so good, isn't it, Annabelle?"

It was. His body was strong, his touch featherlight, yet searing. He had wide shoulders, a hard chest, and lean muscles in his arms. The feel of him against her skin was strange, yet thrilling. Her eyes were closed tight so she wouldn't see what she was doing or having done to her, which might embarrass her enough to ruin it. It also kept her pleasure focused where she could concentrate on it. She couldn't feel guilt because they were married and this was permitted, but it went beyond her imaginings.

Her night shift was gently pushed aside; she felt soft curly hair under her hand and realized she was stroking his head as it moved to her other breast. His lips on her nipple felt marvelous, his tongue made her senses leap. It was shocking; it was delightful. She squirmed to help him get her shift further off her shoulders, then wriggled, trying to move it down from where it had rolled up in a coil at her midriff. Finally, in frustration, she raised up her bottom so they could just get the night shift off and gone because it was the only thing between them. He'd said this would be like swimming, like dancing. But it wasn't. It was like nothing she'd ever known.

When his hand went lower, her eyes flew open. He was watching her, his eyes heavy-lidded, his voice soft but strained.

"I won't hurt you," he said. "This is not perverse. Try it, trust me, just wait, you'll see."

She slammed her eyes shut.

He tried not to smile. It took a few more minutes of caresses that she hadn't minded before his hand returned to where it had startled her. Then, after a brief moment's tension, he felt her relax again. She caught her breath, but not in fear. He did calculations and permutations in his head. How long to linger, how far to go before he took a more active part, and how far he could go before he couldn't stop even if she wanted him to.

She was so smooth and rounded, her heated skin smelled of peonies, and she moved in his arms without knowing she did. They slid against each other, restless, warm, damp. He was relieved, incredibly moved. After all her hesitancy she was pure fire, responsive, accepting everything he did with only soft murmurs of surprise now and then. Too soon, he realized that there was only so much further he could go without stopping—so he didn't. Every sign told him she was ready for him.

She didn't know she was ready, much less that he was.

When his breathing changed and he rose up over her, she opened her eyes, and realized she was sprawled like a doxy beneath him, spread like the sheet beneath her. So when he came to her at last she'd tensed because of embarrassment and shame for her wanton behavior. And when he entered her, it stung, and when he pressed on, it hurt. She lay shocked and confused by the sudden change in sensations as he moved on and on, caught up in the dynamic rapture of a moment he couldn't share, or know she didn't share.

There was disappointment as well as anger in her gaze as she watched him, for both herself and her new husband. Because he was hurting her and because she'd followed his lead until she'd lost the rhythm of it and couldn't follow anymore. She no longer knew if she could or should, and that pained her more than what was happening, because she was the sort of woman who had to know the right thing to do.

He finally finished with a few last deep surges and a groan of repletion. Then he lay still. He raised himself on his elbows as soon as his wits returned, and looked down at her. Her head was turned to the side, her eyes were closed. He stifled another groan, this one having nothing to do with ecstasy. He fell beside her and gathered her in his arms.

"I'm sorry," he murmured. "It's never easy the first time."

"It had to be done," she said.

He frowned. "It wasn't a surgical necessity, though it probably felt like one. If it's any comfort, it doesn't hurt like that ever again."

"Yes, of course, so I've been told."

"Annabelle," he said quietly, "I am sorry."

"Yes," she answered.

He stroked her hair, but it was like molesting her because she lay rigid and unbending in his arms. So he loosed his hold, and she finally moved. "Well," she said briskly, sitting up, pulling the bedcovers up to her breasts, "I think I'd better clean up."

He didn't know what to say, so he stayed silent as she slid from bed.

She bent to retrieve her night shift and held it against her body as she made her way to the dressing room and the washbasin and pitcher she'd seen there. She closed the door quietly behind her.

By the time she'd cleaned herself, put her shift back on, and returned to the bed, she could see he was motionless, breathing quietly, blessedly asleep. She didn't know what she could have said anyway, and so she gratefully climbed back into bed and settled herself a careful distance from him.

Well, she thought. Done. After all her successes
and all her defeats, her goal had been attained.
Wedded, bedded, it was all over and done, even if
it hadn't been done as she might have wished.

There was no sense crying, no use for it either. If
she couldn't get any man she'd wanted, she'd settled for an amiable husband. That hadn't
changed. Miles wasn't a bad man; he was neither
cruel nor inconsiderate. He was just a man. She
didn't love him, and this thing they'd done didn't
bring her the comfort it brought him. But he was
obviously pleased. If she felt let down and
cheated, it wasn't his fault or hers, it was just the
way things were.

So. She took a deep, painful breath. There
wasn't as much freedom in marriage as she'd
thought there'd be. This sexual thing was uncomfortable and embarrassing, and moreover, she
was at his disposal now, for more of this or anything else he might demand. Still, she'd try to be a
good wife to him because that was only fair, and
whatever else she was, she tried to be fair. He'd really done her no harm she hadn't allowed. She
certainly could bear this now that she knew what
it involved.

Her head ached, her throat felt heavy, she
couldn't swallow the lump lodged there. She refused to disgrace herself; she would not weep. She
ought to have expected it, but such intimacy without real intimacy hurt her heart as much as her

body. It wasn't his fault. She supposed he'd done the best he could. But she felt as though a cold wind was blowing through her soul. She ardently prayed that being amiable also meant he'd be fashionable, and so would be an absent husband to her.

She turned on her side, away from him, and finally slept.

Miles waited until he heard her breathing even before he opened his eyes. He hadn't wanted to risk her knowing he was awake because he hadn't known what to say to her. He'd done the best he could. It hadn't been the way he'd wanted it for her, but at least she should have few complaints; he had, at least, tried.

He stared at the ceiling. He ought to be more than content. He had a beautiful wife, an obliging one who'd given him exquisite pleasure. He'd just had an amazing interlude with her that should have made him the envy of most men in London. With any luck, he could expect to have many more during their lives together.

Why then did he feel guilty, cheated, and empty?

He was moderately depressed and felt let down, far more than the "little death" experienced after release. He should be feeling exhausted and triumphant, instead of weary and uneasy. But he'd never made love to his wife before, and he supposed that even though he'd considered all sides of such a marriage, he'd still had some adolescent dreams of romance stuck in his head and heart.

It had been folly to think a virtuous highly bred woman could enjoy bedwork the way professional or experienced females did. But she might come to enjoy it more. At least he had something beautiful to look at while he made love, and his children would be well favored and clever. There was that.

He reminded himself he was a practical man. He turned on his side, closed his eyes, and resolutely shut off his thoughts. It was time to sleep. This feeling, he told himself as he'd told Annabelle about the pain involved in losing her virginity, was doubtless a thing that would change in time as he grew accustomed to it.

But it was a while before he slept.

Chapter 4

Her head ached when she woke, and her limbs felt as heavy as her heart. Annabelle found herself alone in the bed and was so immensely grateful for it that she forgot her physical discomfort. She didn't know what she could have said to her new husband if she'd woken and had to look into his eyes. If he'd been hearty, she'd have hated him. If he'd been apologetic, she'd have hated herself. Seeing him looking smug, the light of conquest in his eyes, would have infuriated her, but if he said nothing she supposed she would have been insulted. And if he'd made further advances to her . . . she shuddered.

She didn't know how she'd have reacted even to a pleasant inquiry as to how she'd slept. She'd never slept in the same bed with another person, and the novelty of that was something she'd have to get used to. Or would she? She sat up sharply and considered it. Would he expect her to? Could she say no? Or would that be considered poor-spirited? Was a wife supposed to share her bed as well as her body? She had no married friends but she knew her parents hadn't shared so much as a joke in years.

This required some thinking. The astonishing thing, she realized, was how much she'd deluded herself in her rush to marry. Because she obviously hadn't allowed herself to think of such things before. At least now she had some time to ponder such questions before she met her husband again, time in which she hoped she could form a good plan of behavior.

As for what had happened between them last night? She supposed the best thing to do would be to ignore it and hope he'd do the same. How else did couples deal with matters of such intimacy? At least, couples who'd married for convenience. Probably real lovers would have no problem. In fact, it must be exquisite joy to sleep next to your love and wake and see his face before you saw your own . . . She refused to think about that further.

Annabelle remembered her physical discomfort when she stepped out of bed. She had to pause, because she felt so dizzy. Then she discovered she had to move slowly because she was as creaky as an old arthritic woman. She made her way slowly to the window and pulled back a curtain. She recoiled, the light hurt her eyes. Still, by squinting she could see that the morning couldn't be that advanced, because there was no one on the street. Miles must have gotten up and gone early. In fact, she'd gotten up earlier than usual herself, because her maid wasn't there to help her dress.

Just as well, Annabelle thought, letting the curtain fall back. She wanted to show him she was unaffected by what had happened last night, even if her body wasn't. Her head throbbed, and she felt as if she were moving through slow syrup, and every joint ached. Turning her head made her vision swim, making her even dizzier. She knew why the muscles in her inner thighs felt sore, but the rest didn't make sense until she realized she must have drunk more toasts than she'd known at her wedding dinner. She was probably suffering the aftereffects.

There was nothing she wanted more than to crawl right back into bed. But she also wanted to show her new husband she was ready for whatever else marriage would bring, so she forced herself to get on with it.

"Oh, my lady!" her maid cried when she cracked open the door and saw her mistress seated at a dressing table, brushing her hair. "I'm that sorry I didn't come in earlier! I thought you'd be sleeping after . . . I mean, Lord Pelham, he said as to how I should let you sleep."

"Very kind of him," Annabelle said. "But as you see, I'm up. I never sleep well in new places."

She handed the hairbrush to her maid and sighed with relief. Her arms ached too, making the simple matter of arranging her hair a trial. But it was important that she look well this morning. She stared into the glass as her maid arranged her hair. It, at least, looked fine; her curls were shining and bouncy. She studied her face. Not as bad as it felt. A trifle pale, perhaps. But there was a light blush on her cheeks. Her eyes seemed particularly bright. All she had to do was put on a pretty gown and she'd do.

"Bring me the new rose-colored lace," she instructed her maid. "I'm tired of being in blue."

The footman led Annabelle to breakfast. Miles was already seated at the table, but he rose when she entered the morning room. She could see nothing objectionable in his expression, just a simple welcome. She was grateful for that.

"Did you sleep well?" he asked.

It would have been awkward if it weren't such a commonplace question, something any host would ask of any guest. She'd been asked the same at dozens of country houses where she'd stayed.

"Yes, thank you," she said. "And you?"

"Tolerably well," he said, as any gentleman would. "I'm surprised to see you up and about so early. I thought ladies of fashion slept until noon."

"I didn't know your plans for the day or when I should rise," she said simply. "We never discussed them yesterday."

"An oversight, to be sure. Won't you have some breakfast? We can talk about plans while we eat."

She looked at the array of chafing dishes on the sideboard. "Yes, thank you," she said.

She moved along the sideboard, investigating the various dishes, and in the end chose shirred eggs, baked tomatoes, bacon, toast, and ham.

But after she sat and the footman brought her plate, she found the sight of the food took away her appetite. She didn't want to eat anymore than she wanted to dance right now. Her face grew warm remembering how Miles had compared lovemaking to dancing. Her eyes widened, and she put down her fork. She'd heard that some women felt the effects of pregnancy immediately, but had thought it an old wives' tale. But she was definitely feeling unwell. Could that one embarrassing, painful episode have caused her to start breeding already? She didn't know whether to be pleased or dismayed.

"The food isn't to your taste?" he asked.

"No, there's nothing wrong with it. My appetite and the hour don't seem to agree. I usually do rise later, and I suspect my stomach knows that, even if I don't. Just some coffee for now, please," she told the footman.

Miles looked at her, noting how the rose-colored gown reflected the charming flush on her face and pointed up her sparkling eyes. Now he knew firsthand that fashion didn't lie; she had a form to match the delicate loveliness of that face. He saw the way her breasts rose and fell with her breathing and remembered the way they'd looked in the candlelight. He'd never forget how they'd felt in his hands and against his lips.

He'd gotten himself a lovely bride, all right. He idly wondered how many years it would be before he could get her into bed in the daytime, if ever. About a century, he thought. They couldn't even speak easily now. They'd been more informal with each other before they'd married—before last night, at least.

He couldn't regret making love to her because he suspected conditions would have been the same, or worse, between them if he hadn't. But he did regret how awkward it made things. He sighed. There went any idle, ridiculously wistful hopes he'd entertained about them spending several days together alone, lingering, learning each other. That kind of behavior was only for lovers. And he supposed he'd disappointed her last night. He'd certainly disappointed himself.

The thought of passing the rest of the day treating each other to more artificial smiles and clumsy conversation made him shudder.

"Well," he said, laying aside his fork, "since you're up and about now, what do you think of us getting an early start on our honeymoon instead of staying on here? My family's already on the way back to Hollyfields. Yours certainly doesn't expect to see you here in London. We really have little to do here now. So, why not just be off on our honeymoon? The weather's so fair today, and who knows how long before it changes? The road awaits. Unless you had other plans?"

"My plans?" She hesitated, then smiled. There was such a world of sorrow in that smile that he was taken aback. He wished he could say something to cheer her, but wasn't sure what had made her so unhappy. "I had no plans," she said with that same wry smile. "None at all."

It wasn't difficult for them to leave at a moment's notice. Her luggage hadn't been unpacked and his valet had already prepared his for a journey, so it was a simple matter to load the bags into another carriage and be on their way. They took one coach for her maid, his valet, and the baggage, another for themselves. But Miles didn't sit with his bride. It was a warm spring day, he loved to ride, and most of all, he didn't want to spend the day in a closed carriage pretending to enjoy his new wife's company. He had the feeling she was just as pleased to be away from him.

Damn, damn, damn! Miles thought as he rode along beside her coach after they left the traffic of London behind. It was a rare day, there was a soft breeze. The sun was pale but warm, the scenery was spectacular; crimson poppies and bright yellow rape blossoms blew in the fields he rode past. He had a beautiful wife, he'd been married for just one day, the rest of their lives lay ahead . . . Damnation! he thought.

Because he didn't look forward to talking with her any more than he did bedding her again. And now they had years of life to face together. It went beyond their disappointing wedding night. That might have been his fault, he admitted, but he knew any future sexual splendor could only come if a woman was in love either with the man or with the act itself. He hadn't given her any good opinion of lovemaking, and theirs wasn't a love match. But he'd thought they'd match so well in other things that love might come. At least, he corrected himself, that *like* might come.

He felt very sorry for himself.

But what other choice had he? He'd come home to face a sea of troubles, and like Hamlet, had decided to take arms against them. If things went on as they were, he could see his mother dwindling into a deeper melancholy, and maybe dwindling away altogether. There were other ways to suicide than by gun or potion. He'd worried that she might discover that by continuing to lose interest in life, she could end it. She'd grown thin and listless, and there wasn't a doctor who could help her. Then too, there was a real chance that his sister could run away with the next man who smiled at her, and his brother could keep getting into trouble at school.

His lectures, orders, dictates, and threats had done nothing. Reasonable speeches and polite requests had done no good either. He'd done the next best thing he could. He'd married a woman who would bring fresh air and life into his house. She'd open his home to society and let his family in too. He'd done the best he could, so too bad for him if it wasn't better.

But it was spring, and riding in the countryside on such a glorious day made a man feel ashamed for being ungrateful. All he had to do to be happy was ruthlessly root out all foolish romantic dreams once and for all. He'd done it before, how else could he have married? He could do it again. What did he know of marriage, after all? Maybe something still could be made of his.

After his father died, his mother had married a man so unendurable that Miles had gone to sea as soon as he was old enough. No more running for him now. He was weary of it. This time he had to shoulder his burdens and get on with life.

Annabelle might never be a loving wife or comfortable bedmate. That had been a gamble. But the certainty he was betting his life on was that she'd see his mother safely established in society again; be an example to his sister and introduce her to decent men; and be someone for Bernard to aspire to, so that he might try to grow up and find a similar wife for himself.

Poor Bernard, he thought before he could stop himself.

So Miles put his heels to his horse and rode off down the road in front of the coach, to shake out his fidgets, to test his resolve. What he really yearned to do was to gallop off the road, ride far away, and never look back.

They stopped for luncheon at an inn by the side of the road.

"Well, it's snug, at least," Miles said in rallying tone as he surveyed the small private dining room. The inn was ancient but clean, its very decrepitude lending it a certain charm. The front windows were of thick, old, warped glass that made it hard to see out. But they let in enough light for him to see that his new wife didn't look well.

She looked wan and distracted.

"Are you feeling well?" he asked, feeling like a fool, because it was clear that she wasn't.

"In truth, I seem a bit off color." She smiled at him, a ghost of her usual charming smile. "I think it's a reaction to everything that happened yesterday."

His expression went blank.

"I mean," she said, realizing just what he thought she'd meant, "the wedding, and the preparations for it. You have no idea of how many fittings I had to stand for to get my trousseau done in time. Nor how many arrangements my mother and I had to make, or rather, argue about. Just thinking about the negotiations we went through deciding which relatives and friends would be invited to what party tires me even now. After all, we had a wedding, a reception, a wedding breakfast, and a ball to follow. It was novel, it set a precedent and is sure to be copied in future—or so we'd hoped. But I'm not as young as I used to be, I suppose," she added with a deprecating grin that almost lit her face.

"You'll have all the time in the world to relax when we get to the lodge," he said. "I mean that," he added, surprising himself by what he had to say. "I think it would be best if we postponed getting on with the more intimate side of our marriage, at least for a while."

Her head shot up and she stared at him, eyes wide.

Was that delight or shock? he wondered as he met her azure gaze. A man could indeed drown in the blue of those eyes, he thought in baffled frustration, as he continued, "It's nothing you did, or I did. But that part of our marriage is a thing that needs our getting to know each other better, I think. At least, if it's to be done to better effect. And you're tired, anyone can see that. Let's go to the lodge and take our time before we go on to Hollyfields and the rest of our lives. We'll take our time with other things as well. A honeymoon is supposed to be to get to know each other. We'll do that . . . if you agree?"

She nodded. "But please believe I didn't mean you caused my weariness today."

"Never fear, I do believe you. I am, after all, a monster of arrogance. Now," he said, still smiling, "this collation looks fine, doesn't it? The shepherd's pie especially; it's full of gravy. Or would you prefer the kidneys?"

"Neither," she said with a shudder. "I think it's best that I eat lightly today after my overindulgence yesterday."

"As you will," he said, taking a slice of mutton.

As he helped himself to a portion of meat pie, he didn't see the look of dismay that crossed her face when she saw the food he was about to eat.

She rose to her feet. "If you'll excuse me? I must find the ladies' convenience."

He leaped to his feet. "Is it the traveling? Is that what's unsettled you? We can stop here for the night. We have another five or six hours more to go. If you're prone to road sickness, we can easily stay on here and take the rest of the trip in smaller stages."

She shook her head. "Travel doesn't bother me. I really do think it's something I ate—or drank—yesterday. Please go on with your luncheon. I'll be better once I'm out of sight of it. I'll be ready to leave whenever you are."

"I'll speak for a few bottles of water and lemonade for you to take when we leave. Even some sugar water will do," he said. "You need something to drink on the trip. Many a sailor regrets his first voyage and doesn't even want to drink because he worries that it will come right back up. But you'll only feel worse if you let yourself dry out. I'll stop the coach every so often to be sure you do drink. It will help, you'll see."

She nodded and left the room quickly, before he could help himself to the kidneys.

She did sip some lemonade. Miles insisted at the next stop they made. But Annabelle felt worse as the day wore on, and could drink less as the hours went by, and so he stopped insisting. She refused to have him stop their journey. And so he was vastly relieved when sunset came and they finally turned off the main road and up the long drive to the lodge.

He welcomed the dappled shadows as he rode under the towering trees lining the winding drive. He heard the rushing chuckle of water in the stream at the side of the road and relaxed. He felt better now that he was there, and he was sure she would too. The lodge was a place to heal body and soul. Steeped in solitude, filled with natural beauty, the house and its grounds offered simple pleasures like fishing, walking, and simply sitting in the gardens at the edge of the pond. When he'd been far from England he'd dreamed of this place, the only piece of his inheritance his stepfather couldn't get his hands on to sell out from under him.

If he and Lady Annabelle had any future, they'd find it here. And if they didn't have a future together, then at least this place would salve his soul and prepare him for the years ahead.

They rode past purple walls of towering rhododendrons, went around a shadowy curve walled in by huge ferns; when they came out into the sunlight again, cows in a nearby meadow raised their heads to watch the little caravan take yet another turn in the drive. The lodge appeared around the next bend. It had two stories and twenty rooms, but didn't look overwhelming. Built of mellowed stone, it fit into its surroundings as naturally as if it had grown out of the earth like the trees around it.

When they stopped in front of the lodge, Miles swung off his horse and strode to the first coach. He waited impatiently as the driver let down the stair. His fine lady might be used to stately homes and palaces, but he honestly felt few places in England could match his country retreat for beauty and tranquillity.

The coach door opened, and Annabelle peered out. She bent so she could step out the door and down the stair. She took the steps carefully, touched the ground, took Miles's arm, and looked around.

Then she stared at him with great surprise, swayed, gasped, closed her eyes, and collapsed in a heap at his feet.

Chapter 5

Miles carried his bride over the threshold, but there was no joy in it for him. "My wife has taken ill," he told the shocked staff as they stood in the hall staring at him. "Get a doctor. Get her maid in here. I'm taking her up. Is the blue bedroom prepared?" he called over his shoulder as he went up the stair.

"Aye, it is, my lord!" the housekeeper said.

Miles moved quickly, but kept glancing down at the woman in his arms. She looked drowned. She was white and cold, utterly insensible. He saw her breast rise and fall so he knew she at least lived. He was calm because he'd learned to be calm in emergencies, but he was alarmed. He'd swear this wasn't any simple malaise. He'd seen stricken men in battles, land and sea, and so knew grave illness when he saw it. This wasn't motion sickness or a result of something she'd eaten—unless it was poison. Because his new wife was that desperately ill.

She was light but felt curiously heavy in his arms. All the spirit that animated her was gone. She was still lovely; even inert and lifeless as she seemed, she was tragically beautiful, a drowned Ophelia newly plucked from the waters where she'd submerged herself. Ridiculous to feel guilt, he told himself. His lovemaking hadn't caused this; this was something else. But he remembered how stricken she'd been after they'd made love yesterday. She'd tried to hide it, but he'd known. And so he felt more than guilt as he laid her down upon the bed.

He touched her face. It was hot, but when he ran his hands down her arms they felt cold. He held her small icy hands between his own and chafed them. Where was the damned maid? The blasted doctor? Miles turned to leave to summon more help, but spun round again when he heard her moan.

She was struggling to sit up.

"Hush," he said, sitting on the bed and holding her. "You fainted. Lie back now. If you sit up too soon, you'll swoon again."

"I do not faint," she said weakly.

That sounded more like her. He managed a

smile. "Maybe not. But you did this time. Wait, let your head clear."

She lay back on his shoulder and looked up at him. Her eyes were a brilliant blue—too bright, he realized. He felt the shivers that coursed through her. She frowned. "Miles. I feel terrible. Really dreadful. It's more than my stomach now. My throat hurts almost as much as my head does, and my head throbs so much I can hardly think. But now I don't think it's because I'm . . . with child. Do you? I mean, do you think it's possible?"

"Oh Lord," he said, holding her closer. "No, Annabelle, I sincerely do not."

"Well, that's a relief," she said.

"Yes," he agreed, hoping what he said was true, because the thought of her conceiving after her first experience with him, and such an inadequate experience at that, chilled him as much as it obviously did her. But then she shivered again, and he realized it wasn't fear that was making her shudder. That worried him even more.

"I'm her husband. There's no need to make me wait outside," Miles said stubbornly, positioning himself with his shoulders against the wall as he watched the doctor examine Annabelle.

"Whatever you wish," the doctor muttered. A fattish man, obviously summoned from his dinner table, the physician didn't seem as impressed by

Miles's rank as he was by Annabelle's illness. "And you say this feeling started this morning?" he asked Annabelle after inspecting her tongue again.

She nodded, then grimaced at the pain nodding caused.

"Any cough?"

Miles began to shake his head, but she spoke. "Yes," she said, "it began this afternoon, in the coach."

Miles went still. He hadn't known. He hadn't ridden with her.

"No spots," the doctor murmured as he pulled aside the dressing gown Annabelle's maid had gotten her into and inspected her white breast. "No rash. Just a sudden onset of nausea, stomach pain, then fever, chills, head and muscle aches?"

"Yes, is that good or bad?" Annabelle asked, too worried to be embarrassed at her state of undress.

He muttered something indistinct, pulled her gown closed, and laid his head to her chest to listen again.

"Just come from London, have you?" he asked her when he straightened.

"We have," Miles said. "Does that matter?"

The doctor scowled. He stood up. "I've gotten letters from a colleague in London. There's a virulent infection going round there. This seems very like it. We hadn't got it here yet. Now, of course, we have."

"What can we do for her?" Miles asked.

"I'll leave medicines. See she takes them as prescribed." He went to the dressing table and took vials and powders from his bag. He mixed two potions, poured a powder into a slip of paper, and wrote instructions.

But when he said good-bye to Miles at the door, he added, "Her maid can tend to her. Keep away from her if you want to avoid infection, and keep her away from the rest of the staff if you can, because the infection spreads like wildfire, and I'd hate to see it get a hold here."

"When will she recover?"

"She's young and healthy; she could shake it off in a week. But she may not. I think it's a form of a contagious distemper from France. They always send us their finest," he added sourly. "This may be an influenza. It was epidemic there; God save us from such here. We had a bad course of it in '03. It can be virulent, it can be milder. Let's hope this is the lesser version. See she drinks a glass of lemon water every hour and takes the medications. And pray. I'll be back tomorrow. Send to me if spots appear or if she becomes worse, of course. Good night, my lord."

But it was to be a bad night, followed by too many others.

A week after he arrived at the lodge, Miles felt as ragged as he looked. He rose from the chair by Annabelle's bedside where he'd once again spent the night. After a quick look to reassure himself that she still slept, he went to the window and pulled back a corner of the curtain so he could see outside.

It was raining again.

What a strange honeymoon, he thought as he gazed at the drenched landscape. He hadn't had time to feel sorry for himself and didn't now, because all his sorrow was for his wife. There was, he now believed, a very real chance that he might be a widower before this honeymoon was over.

She was sinking into deeper illness with each day. Her cough was rough and incessant, and her fever ran high. Getting her to take her medicines was enough of a battle, they couldn't begin to make her eat. Miles stayed with her from the first; that comforted him more than it did her because she was too caught up in the sickness to notice much else. He wondered when he'd admit it was time to send word to her parents. But he didn't want to terrify them for no good reason, and it was all so unbelievable. Or was it just that he refused to believe it? He'd married a beautiful, vibrant young woman. She might now be dying. All in a week. All since the night he'd laid passionate, uncaring hands on her.

Miles rested his forehead against the windowpane. He knew his lovemaking hadn't caused this, but it pained him to think that it hadn't really been making love. After all, he couldn't claim to have loved her, or even liked her more than many other women he'd bedded. Was this terrible guilt he bore just another consequence of the folly of marrying without love?

He'd seen death in battle, seen healthy young men bleed their lives away. Watching beauty dwindle was another thing altogether. She was so vulnerable, and there was nothing he could do against her invisible enemy.

He felt pity as well as helplessness as he watched her fading away. But it was all for a stranger, and surely she should have someone who loved her beside her now, someone who would regret her illness for more than pity's sake. Still, to summon her family now? He'd been a sailor and had learned superstition. Sending for her parents would be like admitting defeat: speak his name and you let in the Angel of Death.

But she wasn't getting better, and nothing they did for her made any difference, except for the worse. Blistering and cupping to reduce the fever hadn't done her any good that he could see, only disfiguring her fragile white skin. The fever parched her soft rosy lips, cracking them, turning them white, making them peel. The powders the doctor gave her made her retch; she couldn't keep them down any more than she could retain any food. She became thinner, frailer every day.

They'd cropped her hair the fourth day. Miles had protested, but the doctor insisted. It drained her strength, he'd said. Perhaps. But Miles's own knees had felt weak as he'd seen her beautiful inky tresses seized, clipped to the scalp, and burned in the fireplace. She'd been too sick to protest, perhaps too sick to notice. But it had near killed him.

The bloodletting the fifth day had almost finished Miles and the doctor. Miles had come into the room after washing up that morning to see the doctor holding her limp wrist, watching her rich, dark blood flowing and the color in her face ebbing as he drained her life away. Miles had lost his temper and maybe his mind, because he'd shouted, ordering the doctor to stop and get out, threatening mayhem if he didn't obey.

And so now it was just he and her maid and the housekeeper attending to her, because the doctor refused to return. Just as well. Miles didn't trust him anymore, or himself with the man. Instead, he'd sent for a surgeon in London, an excellent man. Harry Selfridge had served with him, and owed him, and would come.

But would he be too late?

"Yarrow and elderflower?" Miles said on a tired laugh. "Lungwort and cinquefoil? And then I suppose you chant, 'Round around the cauldron go, in the poisoned entrails throw?' I think not, Mrs. Farrow. Thank you, Mrs. Kent," he told his housekeeper, ignoring the plump little woman he'd just spoken to. "But I don't believe in witchcraft."

"Nor do I!" the plump woman spoke up. "The yarrow, elderflower, and peppermint is a time-honored specific for the influenza. The lungwort and cinquefoil is for the cough. Speedwell and agrimony might help as well. These remedies have been noted as far back as Culpepper and haven't yet been repudiated by modern physicians."

Miles rubbed a hand over his aching eyes. His housekeeper had come to his study and told him that a healer everyone in the district respected had come to see him. He'd invited Mrs. Farrow in, if only to have someone else to talk to about Annabelle's illness. The middle-aged, neatly if not fashionably dressed woman had impressed him. He'd been expecting an ignorant crone, but Mrs. Farrow spoke in accents befitting a duchess.

"My father was a landholder here in the district," she'd told him proudly, "but his mother and her grandmother before her were herbalists, and they taught me their lore. I've researched even more. I may not be able to cure your good lady but I will not harm her. I may well be able to settle some of her symptoms, my lord; at the least I can make her rest more easily."

"But herbs and such brews . . ." he said unhappily.

"May do her some good; I promise no more. When Mrs. Kent sent to me and told me of your lady's plight, I came at once. I know her symptoms. Dr. Morrison should have sent for me. We're old adversaries, but even he can't and won't gainsay me. Mind, he won't recommend me. I suppose it galls him that I have as large a practice as he does. And as many satisfied patients, I might add. Nevertheless, if you refuse, I'll go. I came out of duty, not for personal gain. I have patients aplenty."

Miles rubbed his chin and was startled by the scratching sound. It had been a long time since he'd shaved. It had been even longer since he'd cared. He honestly didn't know what to do. Yet another day had passed and Annabelle was no better, perhaps worse. She slept most of the time now, the fever baking her. He bathed her with cold cloths when her skin seemed afire and packed blankets around her when she shivered. But to dose her with magic?

He stood, irresolute. He'd been in his study composing a letter to Annabelle's parents when this woman appeared. Now he realized his thoughts were as disorderly as his appearance. He hadn't slept or eaten properly in a while.

He wasn't grieving for Annabelle now, it was too soon. Now he was grieving for her bad judgment in having wed as senselessly as he had. But how could she have imagined sickness? She should have, and so should he, because now he realized how cruel it was for her to be at death's door while she was among strangers, and that, after all, was really what they were. Of all the things they'd discussed as they'd courted, gossip, fashion, theater, they'd never actually talked about the nub of it. Why marry someone you didn't burn for, or at least care for? They hadn't spoken about it because they'd both known why and had accepted it.

They'd married for convenience. But they'd both been idiots, he saw it now. The nearness of death had brought it home to him. In the long hours as he sat at her bedside and watched her sinking, his heart had sunk too. Now, too late, he realized his folly and hers. It was more than a pity that she should die without having known love, it was damnable. But what if he made another idiotic decision now either by permitting this woman to dose Annabelle, or by sending her away?

"I have a physician from London coming," he said.

"He isn't here," she said. "Have you time to wait?"

"I? I have all the time in the world, but my wife . . ." He hesitated. He'd sailed a good part of that world and had seen the strange things men thought would cure them of everything from syphilis to simple colds: charms of all varieties from dried monkey feet to bags of herbs worn around their necks—and sometimes he'd been almost convinced those things had worked. He'd seen those same sufferers drink odd potions and feel better in an hour too.

What other course did he have? His friend from London would be here, or so he hoped. But in how long? And would that be too long? And so, Miles thought wearily, the only question now was: What would he want if he were the one lying in that bed?

"Mrs. Farrow," he said courteously, "would you care to come with me and see my lady before you promise more?"

She nodded. She walked into Annabelle's room with him and looked at the woman lying in the center of the great bed. She caught her breath. "Ah, the poor child," she said, low.

"Do you still think you can help?" Miles asked.

"I must."

"Then do," he said.

He sat and lowered his head to his hands and didn't look up until he heard the woman ask him to help raise Annabelle's head, so they could try to give her a sip of the first potion she'd brewed for her.

Miles's friend, the surgeon from London, arrived at sunset. Harry Selfridge was a tall, lean man whose spectacles covered soft brown eyes.

"I came as soon as I received your letter, Miles,"

he said as he stripped off his gloves. "Called for my coach, and left my consultation room filled with patients."

"I'm devilish sorry for having rousted you—"

"Don't apologize! It was no imposition. I owe you much more than this for your aid on the *Forthright* as well as when I had that unfortunate incident in Spain. I only hope this in some small way can help repay you. How is she?"

"You don't owe me anything, but do whatever you can, Harry. She's in great need. I dismissed her other doctor. I needed someone I can trust."

"That would be me. Where is she?"

Miles led him to the stair. His step faltered, he hesitated, then turned to his old friend. "I—have a woman from the village tending to her now, or at least until you came. She seemed competent, and I needed help. And . . ." He lowered his gaze and added, his cheekbones growing ruddy, "I'm taking her advice even though I have doubts, but her cures don't seem too vile. In fact, I helped her give my wife a potion of peppermint, elderflower, and yarrow today. I'm not an utter fool," he said when his friend looked at him sharply. "The woman seemed to have good credentials, and damn it, Harry, what else could I do? I dismissed the curst doctor on the spot, tossed him out of the house because it seemed to me he was killing her faster than the influenza could. Herbs, at least, I thought would be benign."

"Herbs? Benign? Like hemlock, henbane, and belladonna, eh?" Harry then patted Miles's shoulder. "Never mind. Yarrow and elderflower are specifics for some infections. If that's what it is there'd be no harm in it and possibly much good."

Mrs. Farrow looked up when they entered the bedroom. "She's still sleeping," she told Miles, "but her breathing seems easier. That could be only my wishful thinking, though. What do you think, Harry? And how have you been?"

"By all that's holy," the surgeon said with a smile. "Gloriana! You found yourself a worthy ministering angel," he told Miles. "We're old friends, Mrs. Farrow and I. Her essays are well regarded at the Academy and her research has been of great interest to us. How have you and your good husband been keeping, Gloriana?"

"Well enough. Had His Lordship told me you were the surgeon he sent for I'd have been easier in my mind. The lady is not in good case, Harry. Not at all."

"Well, let's have a look," Harry said, approaching the bed. He stared at his new patient, felt her forehead, and bent his head to her heart to listen close. Then he gently lifted one of Annabelle's arms and winced at what he saw. "Cupping?" he asked sadly, pushing back the sleeve of her dressing gown to look at the array of dark red circles that disfigured her slender arm. "Of course, unless she was attacked by an octopus," he answered himself bitterly. "On the breast as well, I suppose?"

Mrs. Farrow parted Annabelle's dressing gown, and the surgeon winced. "Oh Lord. The devil was thorough with his remedies, wasn't he? And these horrors here, along her ribs? Blisters, I suppose? Raise a blister, lower a fever, but that was in the last century. It won't go out of style until the next, I'm afraid."

He continued his inventory. "This gash here at the wrist, of course, was for the bleeding. Certainly efficacious for fevers due to infection caused by shot. But for this?"

He turned to Miles. "He was lucky you only threw him out, I would have killed him. Now," he said, looking at his patient again, "let me see what I can do."

Chapter 6

M iles felt a touch on his arm and he woke instantly, looking up in confusion. He'd only meant to rest, but when he'd closed his eyes it wasn't yet dawn, and now the room was filled with light.

"How long have I been sleeping?" he asked, starting from his chair, his eyes wild. "How is she?"

"Shh, she's doing well. At least her condition hasn't changed, and that is well," Mrs. Farrow said. "Harry went to bed. I had the night watch, remember? But I must get warm water and need someone to sit with her while I do. I hesitated to leave if you were asleep. I know it's foolish of me because she doesn't know the difference, but I hate to leave her alone for a moment."

"Not foolish, kind and considerate," Miles said,

his heart slowing to a normal pace again. "Go and get some rest yourself. I'm refreshed."

She gave him a quizzical look.

He looked down at himself, and added, " 'Refreshed' admittedly, is perhaps not the right word. I look like I've slept in my clothes, because I have. But I do feel better for it."

"My lord, closing your eyes for five minutes is not refreshing. Nor is not eating or exercising. You've been glued to this room since she fell ill. I wouldn't have woken you unless I had to. I suppose I didn't have to, but . . ."

"I know," he said gently. "She's very alone and her condition unpredictable. Go now. I'll watch."

But watch for what? he wondered as he sat by his bride's bedside again. Could she slip away in her sleep? And if so, what difference did it make if he stayed? For that matter, what difference would it make to her if she woke to find him there? How could he give her any comfort? He hardly knew her. He sat sprawled in a chair, watching her and bedeviling himself.

She dreamed on. He kept watching to make sure she was still breathing. Her face was so pale, her lips so white; thank God Mrs. Farrow had thought to put a pretty lacy little nightcap on her, because though Miles had seen much and endured more without flinching, the sight of Annabelle's poor cropped head did strange things to his stomach.

If the worst came to pass, he thought with a

surge of self-loathing, he'd never marry for convenience again. He'd never compromise on something as important as marriage even if it meant never remarrying at all. Now he saw what he hadn't thought of before. Fools rush in, they said. He'd indeed been that. He'd agreed to a life of loneliness with a woman he didn't know. And if things had gone on as they'd planned? What hope would there have been for children conceived and raised with no loving parents? What hope for himself?

And if she lived? How could they make a go of it now that he realized what a huge mistake they'd made?

When the door opened, Miles looked up to see his friend Harry peering in. "No change that I can see," Miles said. "Go back to sleep."

"Can't," Harry said on a yawn as he came into the room. "It's the same thing at home. I can't rest if there's even a small chance I can help. I know that a successful London physician should see the supposedly ill and quack them to their heart's content, then go home to sleep the sleep of the very rich. But most nights I'm at St. Guy's tending to those who can't afford to see me by day. I don't know how my Mary Anne puts up with me."

"I never thought to ask. How is she?"

"As always, more than I deserve. She's sorry she couldn't attend your wedding, as was I. I was detained by a stricken patient, of course. They tend to go into crisis whenever I have something merry planned. My Mary Anne was too busy keeping our newest babe close company to travel so far as out the door. Due next month, if all goes well. But once that's done, she looks forward to meeting your wife." He paused, cleared his throat, adjusted his spectacles, and scrutinized Annabelle. "You know?" he said softly, after studying her for a moment. "Your wife just may be able to be introduced to mine someday, after all."

Miles rose to his feet. "What is it?"

"It's what it isn't. She's holding her own. And days have passed without her worsening. Her color's no worse, her breathing isn't labored. I don't say it's time to celebrate, but here's the dawn and here she is. That's good, that's very good. The tides of life run lowest at dawn and dusk. That's when the weak slip away. She's holding on. That's something."

"What's happened?" Mrs. Farrow asked. She stood stock-still in the doorway holding a basin of steaming water, staring at the two men standing over the patient's bed.

"Nothing," Harry assured her. "We were only just commenting on that. She's still with us, Gloriana, and that's good."

"Well," she said with heartfelt relief. "Then you two might want to leave for a bit. They say conversation can penetrate the sleeping mind, and I know pain and discomfort do. So it only makes sense that comfort can too. I thought I'd wash the lady's face and hands for her, freshen her for the morning."

"Excellent idea," Harry said. "Let us know when you're done. Come along, Miles, we'll swallow some strong coffee, put some heart back in you too."

They sat alone in the morning room, eating a hastily assembled breakfast they'd foraged from the kitchens.

Harry cast a shrewd eye over his old friend. He sipped his coffee and murmured, "If you were my patient I'd give you two days, at most. You look dreadful." His voice softened. "You must love her very much."

Mile's lean face was shadowed by a new growth of beard, and his eyes had dark circles under them. But the stark sorrow in them made him look even more haggard. "No," he said quietly, "there's the damnedest part of it, Harry. I don't. How could I? I scarcely know her."

Harry winced. "Ah! An arranged marriage."

"No, I'm free to do as I please. The despicable thing is that I arranged it."

The surgeon's eyebrows rose.

Miles sighed. "Well, perhaps not. Family is the reason I married. Mine. I came home to find them in chaos, Harry. That filthy beggar Proctor left my mother penniless. I sent her money but I couldn't send her backbone, nor could I buy her acceptance in the polite world. His lying and cheating had put an end to that. She wasn't good *ton* anymore. And my sister?" He gave a hollow laugh. "She bloomed into womanhood and yet still acts like a hurly-burly girl, spends more time in the stables than on the dance floor. The bizarre thing is that men like it. I'm afraid they'll misunderstand it too. And that's not just because of the possible scandal, but for her own future's sake. The less said about my brother, the better, because if I get any angrier at him I'll thump him before I greet him next time he gets sent down from school—which could be any moment, if his past record holds.

"In short, I needed a wife. Someone to literally help set my house in order. Someone who could give us entrée into society, as well as being a woman my mother would approve of and follow. She's very biddable, you know. Otherwise she'd never have married that cad."

"Your mother's not so malleable as you think," his friend said with a frown. "Proctor was a wretched man and that marriage a mistake, but as I recall, for all her submissiveness, your mother was a strong-minded woman, in her own way."

"You haven't seen her in years," Miles said dismissively. "My father was a strong man who set her standards."

"He was a very good man."

"No, he was better than that," Miles said roughly. "I didn't expect my mother to remain a widow, because she isn't the sort who can get on by herself. She could have done well with a different second husband. Now she's a shadow of her former self. Trying to cope with Proctor broke her spirit; seeing what had become of her nearly broke my heart. What my siblings were doing snapped my temper. So what was I to do?

"It was driving me mad, Harry. The idea of marrying occurred to me and wouldn't leave my mind. It seemed the answer to all my problems, not only for reestablishing my mother in society. A stylish and strong-minded wife could set an example for my sister. A fashionable wife could help present her in London, show her the right way to go on. And whatever else he is, Bernard's still young and impressionable. If I married a beauty it would get his attention, and she might be able to sway him too."

"And for yourself?" Harry asked shrewdly.

"Me? I couldn't find love, so I settled for a wife I could admire."

"And why did she marry you?"

Miles shifted in his chair. He looked down at his cup. "Circumstance, unhappy endings to a few associations she'd hopes of that left her looking for a husband to stop the whispering about her lack of success on the marriage mart." He looked up, his eyes sleet stark. "I'm not telling tales out of school.

You know it; who in London doesn't? That's exactly why she married me. And just like me, there are worse bargains she could have made. In fact, as marriages of convenience go, our was better than most. At least we both knew what we were doing and had free choice." His voice became low, hoarse. "Or so I thought. But damn it all, Harry, now I see what a mistake it was."

"Oh, I see," Harry said lightly. "So dying at her age would be better if she loved you?"

Miles's head shot up.

"I think," Harry said slowly, "that she may live. But I also think that if she does, you have an even bigger problem than guilt to deal with."

"You really think she can recover?"

"Yes. If she passes this crisis, and it looks more and more like she may. The influenza is sweeping London. It takes some people very badly; the old, and especially the poor, are dying like flies. But the young and the rich, those who have good constitutions and the wherewithal to eat properly, are surviving nicely. How are you feeling, by the way?"

"I'm fine," Miles said impatiently.

"Indeed? And have been so since you came to London?"

There was something in his friend's tone of voice that made Miles stop to think. "You know, I did have a minor indisposition before the wedding. I put it down to last-minute anxiety. A cramp, a lack of appetite . . ."

"A little more time in the water closet? As I thought." Harry nodded. "Doubtless you had the same thing, but lightly, and you survived it nicely. It happens that way, sometimes."

Miles's lips became tight. "I gave it to her, you think?"

"You and half the population of London. But that's what makes me more optimistic. It's not the influenza itself which kills, it's the debilitating effects and what that leaves the body open to. A sound foundation doesn't crumble as rapidly as a poor one." He rose. "Let's go up and have another look. But I begin to believe she'll do."

"God, I hope you're right," Miles breathed as they walked to the stair. "If she does rally, how long before she fully recovers, do you think?"

"That's anyone's guess. She took it hard, it may be a while. If you're thinking of resuming marital relations, I must caution you—"

Miles stopped to stare at his friend. "That's the furthest thing from my mind! I was thinking about her recuperation, and how long we should stay on here if she does well. We'd planned to be here only a matter of weeks, then go on to Hollyfields and join the family. But as it is . . . How long before she recovers her looks, do you think?"

He saw the look Harry gave him, half shock, half distaste. "What a friend you are!" Miles said, shaking his head. "You should know me better. I'm not asking for my sake. I only want her to recover, but I promise you that if she does, the first thing she'll worry about is her appearance. She's very proud of her looks, you know. She's very proud altogether," he added. "That's what attracted me to her. They gossiped about her in London, but she bore it like a queen who knew her subjects were always going to chatter about their betters.

"The first time I saw her," he said reflectively as he paused before the stair, remembering, "she was going to a ball. She didn't know me or even see me. I was standing in an alcove. She was waiting to be announced. She caught my eye; she's very beautiful, and I've always preferred dark women. She was wearing something blue, the color of her eyes. She has magnificent eyes."

He smiled as he went on. "There she stood watching the company, unobserved. Except, of course, by me. And the strangest thing was that apart from being so incredibly lovely, she looked tentative, sad, somehow fragile. It called to me. This magnificently beautiful woman, afraid? She stood there looking into the ballroom, assessing the lay of the land like a captain surveying enemy ships before raising the colors. It seemed that important to her, and she seemed that daunted. And then, damned if she didn't draw in a deep breath like she was going to jump off a cliff. So deep it moved her breast—and you know I was watching that," he added to make his friend smile too.

"Then," he went on with a hint of wonder in his voice, "she smiled and walked right in as though she didn't have a worry in the world. She looked amused, blasé, confident. It was as if all the doubt and fear I'd just seen had been a mirage. She had beauty, sophistication—and courage. And that, I thought right then, was exactly what I was looking for in a wife.

"So she's brave, Harry," Miles went on, his face grave again. "She'll have to be. All I want is for her to live. You gave me a crumb of hope, and now I see the dangers even in that miracle. Because I just realized that if she recovers she has a harder road ahead than most women. How is a great beauty like Lady Annabelle going to deal with how she looks, at least now?"

"The Lady Annabelle?" Harry exclaimed, blinking. "*She*'s the lady . . . ? I'd forgotten! Of course, that's who you married, now I remember, though I got no hint by looking at her . . ." He paused, his expression troubled. "That *will* be a problem, won't it?" He sighed. "I can't say. I honestly don't know when her looks will return or if they'll be as they were. Her hair will grow in, of course. But it may not be the same texture, at least not at first. In fact, it may fall out."

Miles winced.

"Before it grows back in again," Harry added quickly. "A fever sometimes causes that. Her complexion will return, as will her figure, in time.

A nourishing diet and plenty of rest will help that. The scars from the cupping and blisters will fade too. She'll recover health and looks, in time. Time is the key. It's not exactly like rebuilding a ruined cathedral . . . but it may seem almost that long to her."

He squared his narrow shoulders. "For now, Miles, let's see her wake, be coherent, and remember. Then let's see her walk and talk again. Then . . . well, time will tell."

Miles put a hand on his friend's shoulder. "Just heal her, Harry. I'll leave the rest to fate."

"I'll try," Harry said earnestly. "I can't do more. It is, as you say, not in my hands anymore."

The sunset was pale, twilight coming soft and slow. It had been a beautiful day, mild and clear. Now birds were cooing their evening songs, a mild breeze stirred the trees. The scent of flowers was heady on the evening air. Miles paced a garden path and consulted his watch again. He'd only have to stay there a few minutes more. However pleasant it was, he'd taken this walk alone outside only to stop Harry's nagging and Mrs. Farrow's complaining that he never left the room upstairs. She said she didn't need another invalid to watch over. Harry had been more precise. "Get out," he'd said.

Miles took in a deep breath. The air was piercingly sweet. He looked up and saw the first shards of stars peeping out of a deepening purple sky. It was like balm, he could feel his muscles unknotting, his spirits rising. God, how he'd missed this.

The navy hadn't been his first choice of career. He liked the sea, but loved the land. But it had promised him what he'd needed: a chance for rapid advancement and an opportunity to make money. And a life in the open air. What his career had in fact netted him was too many hours in cramped and stifling cabins, too much time away from the open air just outside, just beyond his reach. Being an officer wasn't like being a gentleman on a cruise. He didn't often have time to enjoy the sea air.

He touched the long indentation on his chin, and smiled, remembering that when he did have outside duties, they were often dangerous and occasionally painful, giving him interesting scars for his change of routine. But his work had also gotten him the advancement and the money, and that was what he'd needed most.

It seemed to him that his life since his father died and his mother so hastily remarried had been a relentless search for what was needed. When would it be his turn to get what he wanted? Or were they the same?

Harry and Mrs. Farrow were right, he thought, as he drank in the slow sweet twilight, he'd needed this. They dared not open a window in

Annabelle's room. A draft, however soft and redolent of flowers, could be her enemy now. But the fresh air was his friend. It lifted his spirits, reminding him there was a world outside his problems, a world filled with sweetness. He could feel the knots in his back unwinding, the peace of the settling dusk calming his nerves.

This lodge was a small place compared to Hollyfields, but he liked it better. It hadn't been built to impress but rather to express the beauty of its surroundings. He gazed around the garden. Someone had kept it up well. There were early roses and late primroses; an arch covered with purple wisteria was already fading into deeper purple shadows; a bright yellow laburnum just beyond fought the dimming of the light.

Here a man could walk his fidgets off, roam green fields, or stroll down country lanes. He could ride through verdant meadows and pause along the banks of clear streams, take a rod and try his luck at catching a fine fat trout for his dinner. He could rise at dawn and sit at the pond side watching water lilies open, or go to the lake just down the road, take a small skiff, lie back, listen to the water lap, and watch the day slide away. He could . . .

The day *was* sliding away. This was the most dangerous time, Harry had said, when a life could slip away too.

Miles turned and strode back into the house.

Chapter 7

Miles had just finished his hastily eaten dinner, and now he sat in a comfortable chair by his wife's bedside. He was reading. He hadn't had the peace of mind to concentrate on a line before his talk with Harry, but now that he felt he didn't have to sit poised, listening for his wife's last breath, he could at last actually read again. It was luxury. But his senses remained alert.

He looked up at a sound, his muscles tensing, then relaxed and smiled at the maid who had tiptoed in to light the lamps. The long twilight was over. The maid glanced at Annabelle's bed, and then gave Miles a sweet sad smile in return to his. She left as quietly as she'd come in. He picked up his book again with a soft sigh of pleasure.

He didn't recognize the difference at first. He

knew only that he was distracted and couldn't concentrate on the words he was reading. He looked up. Nothing had changed. The lamps were lit, the room had a rosy glow, a small fire in the hearth kept off the evening's chill. But there was something new in the atmosphere. There was definitely a different feeling to the room.

Miles put down his book, rose, and though he suddenly didn't want to, went to look at Annabelle.

She looked back at him.

He tried to speak, his voice caught, he tried again. "Annabelle?" he asked softly.

"I have been ill," she said.

He nodded. "Very ill." He touched her forehead. It felt cool.

"I remember some of it. How long has it been?"

"Too long," he said.

"Am I better now?"

"I think so. What do you think?"

She tried to wet parched and peeling lips. "I'm thirsty."

"Of course," he said. "Just a moment." He went to the pitcher and basin near the bedside, and marveling at how steady his hands were in comparison to how fast his pulses raced, he moistened a facecloth. Then he returned to her and dabbed her lips with it.

She gave him a curious look. "That was nice. But I'm thirsty. May I have a glass of water?"

"I don't know," he said, "I have to ask," he added before he strode to the door and shouted, "She's awake! She's talking!"

"I was that ill?" she asked when he came back. Her eyes were wide.

They were the same, at least, he thought on a surge of rising joy. Blue, intense, looking larger than ever. He took her hand, hiding a grimace at how frail it felt in his. "You were very ill," he said.

"But I can't have water?"

"Buckets, if the doctor agrees."

She tried to sit up, sank back, and frowned. "I feel so dizzy."

He put his arm around her, trying not to shudder at how fragile she felt in his arms, how pointed her shoulders had become. "Don't worry, it's natural. You've been in bed a long time."

She touched her head, and frowned. "A nightcap? I don't wear nightcaps."

"You do now," he said, and looked toward the door, wondering if he'd have to shout again. There were things she had to know, but not now, and not from him. Maybe not even from a doctor. Where was Mrs. Farrow?

He saw Annabelle lick her lips and put the wet cloth to them again.

"A drink soon then?" she asked.

"Soon," he said.

She looked up at his face and frowned again at

what she saw there. One of her hands went to her face, "May I have a looking glass?"

He didn't answer.

"May I?" she asked again.

"Ah! Here is Mrs. Farrow," he said with boundless relief. "Annabelle, Mrs. Farrow is the good woman who's been nursing you. She's a neighbor and an herbalist, a hard combination to find. Lucky us. Mrs. Farrow, I can finally properly present my wife, Lady Pelham. And here, on Mrs. Farrow's heels, is Dr. Selfridge, a famous surgeon and an old friend, come all the way from London Town—and from his interrupted dinner too, unless I miss my guess. Harry, meet my lady. Now. Mrs. Farrow, Harry: my wife would like a glass of water."

Neither of them budged. They stood looking at Annabelle, wreathed in foolish smiles.

"A glass of water," Annabelle agreed. "And a looking glass," she added.

Their smiles faded.

"First things first," Mrs. Farrow said briskly, recovering herself. "With your permission, Dr. Selfridge, I think a lady who has woken after such a long beauty sleep needs a good wash, don't you? You'll feel so much better then, my lady."

"So she will," Harry said heartily, "but first, my lady, if I may just have a look at you, and a brief listen to your heart first? Then Mrs. Farrow can set you to rights, and then we'll talk."

"How long have I been sleeping?" Annabelle asked after Harry had listened to her heart, looked at her tongue and into her eyes.

"Ten days, all told," Harry said, stepping back.

Annabelle sat up sharply, her gaze flying to Miles. "Were my parents informed?"

"No," he said, "I didn't want to alarm them. Do you mind?"

"I'm very grateful," she said, sinking back on her pillows again.

"Now shoo, gentlemen," Mrs. Farrow said. "I'll call you when my lady feels fit to be presented to company again."

But when Mrs. Farrow finally did leave Annabelle, she closed the door behind her. She went into the hall where Miles and Harry were standing, chatting, and shook her head.

Miles grew pale.

"No, no," she said at once, "she's well. But so exhausted, poor lady. She fell asleep when I was done washing her. She thanked me sweetly and said she'd never felt better, and just slipped off to sleep again. A healthful sleep," she told Miles. "Don't worry, I made sure before I left her."

Miles turned to Harry. "Is the crisis over?"

"I believe so. She suffered from your previous doctor's ministrations as much as from the influenza, but didn't have any complications. Her lungs sound clear, her heart is strong."

Miles nodded. "How long before she's entirely well? I mean, as she was before she fell ill."

"I think she'll follow the usual pattern," Harry said. "Don't you agree?" he asked Mrs. Farrow.

She nodded. "I think so. If you'll excuse me, gentlemen? I believe I can safely leave her tonight, and I haven't been home in days!"

"Mrs. Farrow," Miles said, "I hope you know how much I appreciate your contributions. I'll have the carriage waiting."

She smiled. "Thank you."

"Now, tell me about my lady," Miles said, staring at Harry. "How long until she's recovered?"

"She'll need two or three days to regain enough strength to be less sweet than Mrs. Farrow said she was just now. Your lady may be an angel for all I know, Miles, but I promise you she'll be tetchy and cross when she feels good enough to move around but still too weak to actually do it. That's natural. After that, if you two are still speaking—because that's a critical stage of illness, at least for the patient's family—let me see . . . With proper care I think it will only be a matter of weeks until she's herself again."

Miles face was solemn. "I see. And how long before we give her a looking glass?"

"That's for you to decide, Miles," Harry said.

Miles grimaced. "Given my way, I'd say not until those weeks were up. I'd hide every mirror in the house until then, if I could."

"Rather like Sleeping Beauty's family hiding every spindle," Harry said. "That didn't work either, did it?"

Miles laughed. "Exactly. What I'm actually asking is if the shock of seeing herself too soon will set her back."

"Worrying about it will set her back more, I'd think," Harry said. "But if you prefer, leave the matter alone for now unless she absolutely insists, because fretting will distress her. She can't get out of bed yet. I'd suggest waiting until she feels more the thing. When she feels better, her mood will be more optimistic."

Harry paused and took off his glasses. He huffed on a lens, withdrew a handkerchief, and polished it up, never looking up at Miles. When he put on his glasses again, his voice was cool and correct, and he didn't meet his friend's eye. "I know she was a great beauty, Miles. But I think you're making too much of it. Unless, of course, the way she now looks bothers you that much. That's a very different story. If that's the case, I suggest you find a reason to travel until she *is* herself again. Surely you can find business in London to attend to? Because in her present fragile state negative opinions will influence her, to her detriment. Far better that she believes you to be called away on business than knowing you find her repulsive."

Miles hands closed to fists. "You're a complete ass if you think that of me," he said, with obvious difficulty.

Harry took a step back. Mrs. Farrow looked startled.

"I won't defend myself again," Miles went on in a clipped voice. "If you're a friend I won't have to. And it's only because you are a friend that you don't have to defend yourself against me. Hear me out. I know the lady's habits, if not her mind. What I worry about is that she'll be the one who'll want to leave because of how she looks. And it's difficult to run away from oneself."

"Surely she's not that shallow?" Harry exclaimed.

"I don't know the lady," Mrs. Farrow interrupted, "but I do know women. Even a farm wife would grieve if she lost her looks. It's not because we women are so foolish or shallow. Rather, I think it's because we're led to believe we have little value outside of how we appear." She smiled to take the sting from her words and went on, "I think we'll continue to feel that way until you gentlemen start flocking to ugly women, paying them compliments on their stringy hair and big noses, poor figures and drab looks, praising their minds and not their appearances."

"Nonsense," Harry said. "How are we to know their minds until we know them?"

"Precisely," Mrs. Farrow said smugly. "And how often do men ask an ugly duckling to dance? Or an ugly old hen, for that matter? Much less sit down to chat with one so as to get to know her beautiful mind?"

Harry opened his mouth to retort, but Miles spoke first. He obviously hadn't been paying attention to them. "I think," he said bemusedly, "I'd better stay close to her for the next few days. She needs the bed to herself of course. I'll sleep in the dressing room so I can be near, in case . . . of anything. I want to be on the spot."

Miles woke and lay still. The cot in the dressing room wasn't comfortable, but he'd slept in many worse places. Early morning sunlight streamed into the room. He hadn't pulled the draperies closed last night because he'd instructed the maid not to come in to draw them open in the morning. Now that he was assured of a good night's uninterrupted sleep, he didn't want to forgo one of his life's great indulgences anymore. He flung back the covers and stretched, feeling the sunlight on his bare body, and almost purred with content. After so many years of sleeping in the close company of so many men aboard ship, he deemed sleeping naked a great luxury.

He squinted at the light and judged it to be just

past dawn, at least six bells. He listened, hearing only the morning songs of birds. He rose, padded over to the window, and threw it open. Another reason to sleep in here, he thought as he breathed in deeply. He could have all the fresh air he wanted without worrying about it harming Annabelle.

Annabelle. He had to see how she was, assure himself that last night hadn't been a dream. He ran a hand over his chin. Should he wait, shave first, make himself presentable? He couldn't wait. He dashed some water on his face, rinsed his mouth, then threw a dressing gown around his naked body, and went to the door that adjoined Annabelle's bedchamber. He cracked it open.

It was dimmer in the blue bedroom, but a drape had been pulled back from a corner of one long window so he could see in. But he couldn't make out Annabelle's slight form amid the heaped coverlets on the great bed. He went quietly into the room.

And almost fell over her.

She lay in a huddle on the floor in front of the dressing table. His breath caught; he dropped to kneel beside her. She was curled up on her knees, facedown, arms around her head, her body drawn into a knot.

"Annabelle?" he whispered, "Annabelle?"

She turned her face away.

"Annabelle?" he asked, touching her shoulder.

She shuddered.

He gathered her insubstantial weight in his arms, lifted her, and strode to the bed. She refused to unclench her body, so he sat, holding her tightly in his arms. He'd been too aghast to look at her before, but now he peered down. And felt his heart clench as tightly as her body.

Her nightcap was off. She saw him looking at her and buried her face in his chest. He looked down at a pale pink scalp covered with a faint regrowth of black hair, stubbled as his own unshaven chin. Something was poking into his chest. He moved a hand down to discover that she held the handle of a silver-backed mirror. He tried to gently pry it from her white-knuckled grip.

"Please let it go," he said softly. "It's digging into my chest, you see," he added, knowing that it hurt her more.

She loosed her grip and he tossed the looking glass on the bed.

"Ah, Annabelle," he said. "I'm so sorry. It will change, you know. It will go away, or rather, your looks will come back. It's only for now. You'll see."

He wanted to stroke her, but when he ran his hand along her back he could feel every vertebrae even through the material of her nightgown. So he merely let his hand rest on her back. He tried to see her expression.

"It isn't that important," he insisted. "It's only here and now. You were so sick we thought we might lose you. All you lost were your looks, for now."

Her head shot up. "What else did I have to lose?" she cried.

He sought words but couldn't find them. He didn't know her well enough to know what else she did possess. Was she proud of her singing? Her skill at the piano or harp? Was she a fine needlewoman? Did she like to grow roses or orchids? What did she excel in, apart from being lovely and moving so gracefully in society?

"Your life," he finally said. "You could have lost your life."

"I am no one, nothing now," she grieved.

"You are Annabelle," he said firmly, "Annabelle, Lady Pelham. A clever woman with wit and style. So much so that I don't doubt you can make baldness a virtue. Why, I fully expect to find every lady in London shaving her head within a week!" He hoped to hear that unexpected giggle of hers again. She remained still. "Except," he quickly added, "by the time we go back to London you'll just have a new shorter hairstyle for them to copy."

She raised her head, and looked into his eyes. "It's not just my hair," she said bleakly. "Look at me, Miles, if you can bear to."

"You're pale," he said, scrutinizing her, "which will pass too."

"I'm changed," she said dully. "I'm white as a

fish belly. If that were all, I could deal with it. But look at me," she insisted, her voice rising. "Have you really seen me? I have black circles under my eyes, my lips are ragged and gray. My arms are covered with black and blue marks and red round puckered scars, and there are slashes on my wrists and bruises on the insides of my elbows too." She rocked with grief as she added, "And my breast and stomach are covered with so many dark red circles!"

He held her tighter to stop her rocking, but added lightly, "My dear, please listen to yourself. First you complain you're too white, now you say you're black and blue and red. Sounds amazing colorful to me."

She didn't smile. Her eyes, those lovely blue eyes, the only things to escape the ravages of illness, turned to his. "And my body . . . it's wasted."

"A fine thing to say about having married me," he said.

She stared at him.

"I see you've lost your sense of humor too," he said sadly. "Annabelle. I looked. I saw. I see. But believe me, I'm so glad you're here to complain that what you look like hardly matters. If you don't believe me when I say that you'll regain your looks, at least believe that. You live. That's foremost with me."

"That's guilt and duty speaking," she said

softly. "Because there's no other reason for you to want me alive, at least as I am now. Why should you? You hardly know me."

That last was so true he couldn't speak for a moment. She'd said what he'd been thinking, and ruing, for all these past days. But he'd commanded men in worse situations; he knew how to deal with shock. His own shock couldn't be allowed to rule the day. "Thank you. But I am not quite a fool," he said. "I wouldn't have married a woman who was one. You're clever, and you have—or did have—a sense of humor. You have a well-informed mind. That, I know."

His hand went to caress her hair until he realized he couldn't. He held her shoulders instead. She didn't answer, but he felt her body grow less taut. She lowered her head to his chest again. "I am ashamed that you should see me so," she whispered.

He chose to misunderstand her. "Don't be. Why, even the best, bravest men can falter under fire or when they think their ship is sinking. So don't worry. I'll forget that I saw you losing your faith in me, if only for a moment."

Now he heard it. Faintly, but definitely. He heard her giggle. And he, at last, could breathe again.

Chapter 8

~~~~~~~~~

"**I**'d like to sit in the sun, please," Annabelle said.

Miles stopped in his tracks. He'd been about to put her down in a chair in the shade of an old linden tree, where she'd sat for the past several clement days. "Harry would have my head for it," he finally said, looking at her where she lay in his arms. "You can't risk a draft, and it's breezy today."

"The breeze is warm," she said. "I'd like to feel the sun on my face."

"You'll get freckles," he said, because he couldn't tell her what he was really worrying about, which was what might happen to her poor exposed scalp if she sat in the full sunlight. She couldn't wear a wig, not any from the local shops, or even one of the fine ones they'd found up in the attic that had been left by previous occupants. Wigs had only been out of fashion for a quarter century. Before that, almost every occupant of the lodge, gentleman and lady, had worn one. Miles had searched the attics and come down dusty and triumphant to present a selection of them.

Annabelle had looked at the outmoded styles with horror.

But Mrs. Farrow had been as pleased at Miles when she saw them. "The good thing about human hair," she'd assured Annabelle, "is that all they need is a good wash to be renewed."

"I can style them whichever way you want, my lady," Annabelle's maid had promised.

There was a fantastic choice, the colors and textures of hair as varied as the people who had worn them. Annabelle selected three whose color almost exactly matched her own. When her maid had finished with them, and shown the wonders she'd done with scissors and brush, Annabelle's eyes had lit up, the look of delight on her thin face momentarily reminding Miles of the woman she'd been.

But wearing them proved impossible. The pressure and weight of even the lightest of them hurt Annabelle's head. When she tried again after a few more days when her headaches began to subside, the prickling of the newborn hair on her tender scalp made wearing a heavy wig more than burdensome; it made the itching exquisite, she said. So she decided to wear lacy caps as she waited for her hair to grow back, and pretended that nothing would suit her better.

She looked quaint in her frilly caps, nothing like the beautiful Lady Annabelle, but rather like a starved little Pilgrim. It hardly mattered to Miles. He'd gotten used to this pale stranger. Her terrible sorrow was hard for him to bear, especially since he was sure she never complained about what really hurt her. She grumbled about the hardness of chairs and the coldness of rooms, but seldom about important things, and never about her appearance. He didn't have to hide all the looking glasses in the house. After that first incident, she avoided them entirely now.

"Freckles?" she said crossly now. "Wouldn't that be better than pallor? I won't stay long in any case." Her voice grew softer. "It's just that I so want to feel the sunlight on my skin. Odd, isn't it? The sun is a fashionable lady's worst enemy, but now I yearn for it . . . I suppose because I'm not fashionable anymore. Oh! Enough of my self-pity, put me down before your arms start aching. And in the sunshine, please!"

He almost smiled at her comment about him getting tired of holding her, but it was too sad. He carried her out each day because he couldn't bear to give the task to a footman. It was as physically easy for him as it was emotionally difficult to hold his fragile wife in his arms. Her weight was so insignificant now he could bear her all day with the ease of carrying a handkerchief. She reminded him of a little spider monkey, and felt like one in his arms, making him think of the one his onetime mistress in Spain used to carry on her shoulder. In fact, when he picked Annabelle up the similarity of the sensations that came to him was immediate, striking, uncomfortable, and impossible to forget.

Annabelle had been a tiny woman made larger by her personality and those incredible good looks. Now she was merely a small woman. Her hair was the least of what had changed. Her bones were prominent—he'd never realized how small-boned she was, he'd been too busy noting her breasts and hips and rump, he supposed. That embarrassed him now.

She'd said that she'd had nothing to lose but her looks. He'd been appalled for both of them when she'd said it. One thing was sure: little of her beauty remained. She'd had fine features but now the gauntness of her face overwhelmed them. Her figure had vanished. So what did she have left?

She'd been so bitter and morose those first days of her convalescence he'd thought she'd lost her personality too. Now she was mending and grew less irritable every day. So it well might be that she'd recover everything illness had taken from her. Even if that were so, Miles wondered about their future together. If she regained her looks it might be enough for her, but would it ever be enough for him again? Her illness had more than transformed her, it had made him think about the meaning of marriage.

Now he looked around the garden for a place to set her down, a place sunny enough to suit her whim, shady enough to ease his qualms. Being in England, sun was at a premium even in the summer so the gardens were all in full sunlight. This was a country lodge, but also a gentleman's home, so the lawns all around it were closely cropped by sheep or neatly scythed by gardeners. There was forest, but it was a long walk away. Brooks and streams ran everywhere, and a clever former owner had even diverted one to run near the lodge. He'd constructed a concrete channel, lined by flowers that led to a pretty ornamental pool filled with water lilies and golden fish. But that was in full sunlight too.

Miles supposed he could set up an umbrella for his invalid wife, and should have done. But for now?

He compromised. There was a small bench set beneath a huge elm, and he put her down there in the dappled sunlight at the edge of the canopy of leaves. He tucked her wrap around her shoulders and then sat beside her, watching as she closed her eyes and lifted her face to the sky.

It was very quiet, nearing noon. The birds had

finished saluting the morning, and the only sound was the soft flutter of the leaves above them. Miles stretched out his legs and gave himself to the silence.

"You must be bored to bits," Annabelle said suddenly. She didn't open her eyes, and spoke as though to the sky. "Fine honeymoon for you this is, carrying an invalid from chair to bed and back again. You can go riding, you know." She paused, swallowed, then added in that same cool voice, "You can even go away for a while if you wish. Back to London—or wherever."

"Can I?" he said, carefully.

"Of course. It is, after all, only guilt and duty that keep you by my side, isn't it?"

She still didn't look at him. But he watched her. Her face seemed to have taken on a bit of color, and he wondered how much was the effect of the sun on that fragile skin, and how much the effect of whatever emotions she kept so strongly in check. It was no little thing for her to send her husband away on her honeymoon. He had few illusions about their relationship and knew it wasn't as though she couldn't bear to be without him. But she had no family or friends there, only servants. So it was noble as well as kind of her to offer, and he was touched and shocked by it. Whatever else he expected of her, it wasn't that.

Duty and guilt? How could he deny it? He

couldn't claim love or even friendship kept him there by her side. She'd never believe him. To say he stayed because of worry for her health was true, but too cold and even cruel.

"I'd look very fine leaving my wife on our honeymoon just because she was indisposed, wouldn't I?" he said lightly. "And how many people would believe me if I said that?"

She seemed to relax. That, she seemed willing to believe.

"I'm not entirely a town creature," he went on. "I do love this place. I can ride, as you say, or go walking. And I really enjoy fishing; the trout here are amazing."

Her eyes snapped open, she turned her head to look at him. "Trout? Really?" she asked excitedly. "But you were a sailor. I thought you seafaring fellows only caught whales and dolphins and such."

He laughed. "Few whales. But mackerel and many another fine dinner. Not much sport in that; ocean fishing is a matter of tides, luck, and strength. But trout! Now, they need a man with stealth, cunning, and skill. One who's willing to practice to find the perfect cast, and research in order to pick the best lure. It's a lot of bother for just trying to prove I'm smarter than a fish. But when—if—I do, it's as delicious as any fine dinner—even if the fish gets away."

"Yes," she sighed, "I know. I wish I could join you. But I can scarcely walk, much less go wading if I had to. As you say, it doesn't take muscles. Still, I haven't the strength to pull in a minnow." Her spirits lifted again. "But tell me about them, please. How big do they run here? Where's your favorite place to cast: deep pool or running stream? At dawn or dusk? And do you use flies that you make yourself, or do you buy them?"

He laughed. "You, a fisherwoman? You amaze me. Tell me, who designs your fishing gowns?"

"Not a fisherwoman, an *angler*, if you please," she said, and then added wistfully, "I wear boys' clothes—that is, I used to. I fished with my father when I was a girl. We'd leave at dawn and stay until dusk, or until we got something for our efforts. He had special boots made for me, and when we saw how my clothes looked after a dunking when I went too enthusiastically after a fish on the line, he let me wear breeches."

Miles couldn't imagine this woman ever wearing boys' clothing, wading in icy water, casting a line, pulling a fish from a hook. Not as she had been before her illness, or as she was now.

"I was very good at it too," she said, raising her chin as though she'd heard his thoughts. "I used a blue elver fly, my favorite lure. It took me a while to learn to cast; in fact, I almost didn't get beyond that point. A bad cast made me the recipient of a hook in my arm. It had to be cut out, and left a scar. See?" she asked, pushing up a tight-fitting sleeve to prove it to him.

She pointed to the thin white line on her fore-arm, looked up, and saw his expression. There was more than pity, there was shock and sorrow. Then she realized that the scar was hardly dis-cernible among all the purple and yellow bruises and cuts on her thin blue-white arm. She hastily pushed her sleeve back down and raised her head higher. "I suppose it's not so bad now, but then I thought Mama would have a fit," she said briskly. "My father said it would be a badge of honor. Well," she admitted, "he had to say something to stop both our tears."

"Call that a scar?" Miles said quickly, schooling his expression to one of mock scorn. "See this?" He tapped his chin. "From a cannon. I got it in battle."

"Oh my!" she said, diverted. "Were you in much danger?"

"From myself," he said with a laugh. "Because, you see, I got the wound quite literally from a can-non. Some fool hadn't tied it down, and it went rolling during a groundswell. I tried to be a hero and secure it myself. It almost secured me, to the deck, and forever. Now, if you want to see a battle scar, there's one on my leg, and another on my hip . . ." He paused, and using a mock spinsterish air, added, "But only if you ask me nicely, and when we know each other better."

Annabelle went still. He realized it was perhaps not the best thing for him to have said to his wife, a woman who should have known where all his scars were by now. "So," he said too brightly. "As to your wound, I suppose that put an end to your fishing lessons?"

"Oh no," she said. "We went out again, though we both were more careful after that. I got quite good, actually, although I never caught the grandfather of all trout my father told me about. I'm glad of it. I think I caught sight of him once, sleeping in the shallows, the sunlight shining on his scales. He was huge. Wily and strong, my father said. We named him Uncle George and my father insisted we say good morning to him before we started fishing, then bid him good night before we left, even though we couldn't see him. If we didn't, he said, we'd never catch a fish again because he was the king of the stream."

She smiled in reminiscence, "I don't think my father wanted to catch him. In fact, if he ever did I'm convinced he threw him back, because Uncle George made that pool, and without him it would have just been fishing."

"I tell you what," Miles said on a sudden inspiration. "Would you like to watch me fish? We can take a chair for you, maybe in a few days when you're feeling stronger and it's a little warmer. My favorite spot is under some overhanging branches, so it's cool there even on mild days. It's in a deep part of the pool, near the rocks, just before the streambed takes a dip and the water starts rushing away. It won't be as much fun as fishing for you but I'm sure you'll enjoy criticizing my cast and my lures."

He smiled as he said it and saw her beginning to smile in return. "You know, I think I'll take you there now just to see it—if you'd like."

"I would."

"Then let me get a warmer wrap for you," he said, rising. "While I'm at it, I think I'll send a lad to the village to see if we can get you an invalid chair. We won't have to use it for long," he added, seeing her suddenly stricken expression. "If you really needed one I'm sure Harry would have said so. He wrote out a long list of instructions before he left and didn't so much as mention one." Harry had also cautioned that they shouldn't be deceived by her continuing recovery. He'd confided that she wasn't out of danger and would be in jeopardy until she got her strength back. So they had to be careful with her. Surely, Miles thought, diversion would speed that recovery.

"Now that I think of it, it's an excellent idea; I can wheel you everywhere. I'll even get you a knobby walking stick," Miles added, seeing her distaste for the idea. "You can wave it and grumble, and smack me smartly if I take a wrong turn. If you're going to play the invalid for a while you might as well give a complete performance, right?"

She grinned. It was no longer the provocative expression it had been, but it brightened her white, tired face.

"I'll just be a moment," he said. He waved his arm to catch the attention of a gardener working near the house, signaling him over. "I won't leave you alone," he told Annabelle as the old man began shambling toward them. "Here's a fellow to keep you company while I'm gone and see to any need that might arise, and he can entertain you with talk of turnips and thistles."

"I'd be delighted," she said. "I used to garden too."

"You amaze me," he said, bowed, and went to talk to the gardener.

And you astonish me, Annabelle thought, watching him stride away. How kind he'd been to her. When she'd woken from her sickness and saw his worried face, she'd been aware of a deep feeling of content to find him there. When she'd seen her own face the next terrible morning, she'd thought he would be repulsed by the sight of her and she wouldn't see him again. But he'd remained at her side, showing her nothing but patience and charm.

Now she watched him walk away and appreciated the sight of him. He moved with easy grace, the sunlight turning his brown hair the color of ripened wheat. He was a very handsome man, she realized. It was surprising that she hadn't particularly noted it before. He'd been only one in a crowd among the fashionable gents in London, but here she could see her new husband was indeed a very good-looking man.

He was dressed casually, but he wasn't a man who confused relaxation with slovenliness. He didn't wear baggy, dirty clothes the way some rusticating gentlemen and country squires did. His boots were kept polished, he wore a neckcloth tied in a relaxed style, but it was clean and white. He wore subdued colors, today a brown jacket, with dove gray breeches. Everything was fashionably fitted, but not extremely so; he had room to move in them.

He'd have looked well dressed walking in Regent's Park, but she wouldn't have noticed him there, where all the fops and dandies in their high neckcloths, tight jackets, brightly hued pantaloons and glistening boots caught the eye. They would look absurd here, she thought. And then, for the first time, she wondered if they didn't look absurd where they were.

Odd, she mused, watching Miles. She'd thought a sailor would have a rolling gait, like the old salts one saw near the docks in London. But Miles walked like a man used to covering distances on foot. Fashionable breeches showed every line of a fellow's legs, and so some gentlemen padded out their calves. Miles didn't have to, she could scarcely forget that.

She remembered those muscular legs, the furze of hair that covered them, and how strange that had felt against her own—and then, between her own. Sitting there in the mild and pleasant air, drowsy and warm, she allowed herself to remember that night without the anxiety she'd felt then. In fact, as she recollected those moments, she began to feel weak and languorous again, but not sick in the least.

Now she remembered that light hair covered all his limbs like the nap on a peach's firm skin. He had soft hair on his chest too; she recalled how odd, yet thrilling, it had felt against her breasts. He had hair *there* too; she'd felt it. Now she wished she'd seen it and more. But everything had been done beneath the covers, and she'd been too occupied with how startling it was to notice more. Now too she remembered his kisses, and what he'd done before disappointment ended the stirring of pleasure she'd felt. She remembered too the look in his eyes, and what he'd said . . .

"*Milady*, you feelin' up to snuff?" a strange man's voice asked. "Pardon my sayin' it, but you looked like you come over queer all on a sudden."

"Oh no, I'm fine," she said, looking up to see the old gardener standing beside her, a worried look on his seamed face. "I was only resting my eyes."

"Well, you looked suddenly red-like. Do you want me to get someone from the house to carry

you out of the sun? Or would you let me? I'm
stronger than I look. Have to be, what with
bendin' and plantin' and pullin' roots."

"I'm sure you are," she said quickly. "But the
sunlight doesn't bother me. I'm enjoying it. So
rare these days. An English spring is lovely, but
usually damp."

"Well, you have the right of that, milady," he
said enthusiastically. "I disremember such a long
fine string of spring days . . . no, I lie. The spring
of '07 was just such a spring, would you believe
that the daffodils poked up in January and then
wasn't it a shame when the cold came back and
froze them?" He went on to talk about spring-
times he remembered. He was a very old man, so
he recalled many of them.

Annabelle let her mind roll on, following the
trail of something indescribably sweet. What was
it that had so fascinated her a moment ago? Ah,
yes. She'd been remembering when she'd made
love to Miles, or rather, when he'd made love to
her. Because all she'd done was submit, and feel.
But there'd been so much to feel. And so much to
hear; she wouldn't forget the gratified sigh that
came from deep in his chest as he drew her close
to his own warm body. And what he'd said to
her . . .

She stopped. She sat, half hearing the gardener
now talking about the terrible hailstorm of '03,
and felt cold as that day must have been. Because

now she remembered Miles hadn't said a thing to her as he'd made love to her. He'd taken her gladly and had very generously tried to give her some of the pleasure he'd obviously felt. But he hadn't said a word.

What could he have said, after all? Never "I love you." That was a fiction they didn't even try to maintain. Not "How I want you," or even "How much pleasure you give me," or anything sexual, because she supposed that was the sort of thing a man said to his mistress. Sudden bitter laughter rose in her throat like bile.

What could he have said, after all? "I married you because it was expedient, as you married me, but isn't this pleasant?"

What would it have been like if he'd loved her? If she'd loved him? Would she ever have the chance to know, or would he shun her in the future except when he needed an heir? And if he did only use her for breeding, should she seek out a lover? But if a husband had been hard to choose, how much harder to find someone handsome, kind, generous, and discreet, someone she was attracted to, someone like . . . Miles?

Annabelle's eyes widened. Could a woman find pleasure without love? A man certainly could. As for that, when the inevitable day came, would she really feel nothing but relief when he went off to his mistress, as her mother had said would be the case?

"Well, here comes His Lordship," the gardener said, cutting into her thoughts. "Been good chattin' with you, milady, and I hope you feel more the thing soon as may be."

"Thank you," she said absently, looking up at Miles.

He carried a heavy tartan shawl. "Thank you for taking such good care of my lady," he told the gardener. "Now," he said, looking down at her, his eyes alight, "This is how we do it. I arrange this shawl in my arms, pick you up, wrap you like some kind of Scots sausage, and carry you off. Then we take this worthy shawl, spread it on the ground, and voila! It becomes a blanket for you to sit on while you admire my choice of fishing spots. We'll see if we can find a grandfather trout to rival your Uncle George. Shall we?"

She didn't answer at once. She'd been charmed, but suddenly realized that he was talking to her as if she were a child. Was that just the way people always spoke to invalids? Or had her sickness changed his attitude toward her?

She couldn't bear to look at herself now, but she didn't have to. He did. Now that he'd seen her this way, there was the chance he might never again look and speak to her as a man speaks to a desirable woman—or find her desirable again. Surely, when she regained her strength and her looks, they'd go back to the way they'd been . . .

The way they'd been? They'd been married

strangers, having conversation merely to fill the time. Making love without love. It was acceptable then. But now to face a lifetime of it seemed unendurable. She shivered though no cloud passed over the sun.

"Are you well? Would you like to go back?"

"No! Never that!" she blurted.

He looked at her curiously.

She realized what he'd really been asking. "No, please," she said, "I don't want to go back to the house yet. I feel fine, really. I'll feel better after meeting your grandfather trout."

"Your wish is my command." He arranged the shawl over his arms, picked her up, wrapped her well, then smiled down at her. "Ready?"

"Lead on," she said. "I have no choice but to follow."

Chapter 9

~~~◯◯~~~

The servants at the lodge stared at the elegant carriage with four outriders as it came clattering up the drive. They hurried to tell their master when the door to the carriage opened and a very irate-looking gentleman quickly stepped down and marched toward the house without even waiting to see the lady behind him alight.

But Miles was already coming down the stair. The sound of the coach's arrival had been heard upstairs in the bedroom where he'd been keeping his wife company.

A footman swung the front door open. Earl Wylde stood on the step, slapping his gloves against his hand. That was the only thing to show his agitation, because his expression was stiff and cold.

"Your note said my daughter was ill," he immediately said when he saw Miles. "You wouldn't have written to tell me if it was a slight indisposition. Naturally I came at once. Newlyweds or not, it's hardly a thing I could ignore."

"Nor should you," Miles said. "I'm happy to tell you she's recovering. But she was quite ill for a time."

"For how much time?" the earl demanded.

"Ten very bad days, and nights. It was the influenza, which can take some people very badly. She's out of the woods now."

"Oh, what a relief!" Annabelle's mother breathed from behind her husband. "Thank God! And what a pother! We threw our belongings into bags the moment we got your message, and scrambled to get here. My husband wouldn't even stop on the road to refresh . . ."

"Ten days," the earl said coldly, cutting his wife off. "Then why weren't we informed sooner?"

"Forgive me," Miles said. "That was wrong. I didn't want to send word until I'd lost hope, and I refused to do that. I wrote when she was on the mend."

"Laudable sentiment," the earl said through gritted teeth, "but you're here in the middle of nowhere. I could have brought first-rate physicians from London."

"She had one," Miles assured him. "Dr. Selfridge, from London, a consultant to the Prince himself. He only left yesterday. And she was tended by an excellent local herbwoman whom he has utmost confidence in. In fact, Mrs. Farrow is with her right now. They're reading together; Annabelle's eyes grow tired quickly, so we've been doing it for her."

"May we see her?" the earl asked tightly.

"Certainly. At once, if you like," Miles said, gesturing to the staircase. "Or would you prefer refreshments first?"

"Thank you, but we couldn't eat a thing until we see her," her mother said, as they headed for the stair.

But it was Miles who went into the bedroom first. He moved to block the earl and his countess. "I don't think it would be kind to shock her," he said. "Let me tell her, please."

The earl reluctantly agreed. Miles slipped into the room. "I've a surprise for you," he told Annabelle, closing the door behind him. "That noise was your parents arriving. They're just outside, eager to see you. And they're angry with me for not telling them about your illness sooner."

"Why did you have to tell them at all?" she asked.

"Because it will be some time before you're fully restored to health, and because they are your parents."

She wet her lips. Her hand went to her cap. "Do I look all right?" she asked nervously.

"You look fine to me," he said, and then striving for honesty, added, "Much better than you did a week ago, wouldn't you say, Mrs. Farrow?"

"Very much so," Mrs. Farrow agreed. "You've color returning to your cheeks, you've eaten more each day and have lost that gaunt look. No question, you're much improved."

It was true, Miles thought, but he and Mrs. Farrow had only been looking for the improvement in her. Now he allowed himself to see Annabelle as her parents would: pitifully thin, hollow-cheeked, pale as whey, wearing a huge white lace cap to cover her bald head. Her parents would be expecting the beautiful bride they'd last seen. He tried not to wince. Still, he hadn't lied. She looked much better than she had a week ago.

"Shall I let them in?" he asked.

"Yes, of course," she said, sitting up straighter. She turned to the door, and smiled.

Her smile faded, she grew even paler, and tears began to roll down her cheeks. Not from the joy at seeing her parents. But because she saw their expressions when they saw her.

It took a day to calm her. Yet even after they'd stopped her from constantly wringing her hands, Annabelle's mama finally fled Annabelle's room in tears. "I don't know what to do!" she cried to her new son-in-law. "If I say she's looking better and promise her she'll regain her looks, she says I only care about her looks. If I don't mention her looks, she asks me why not? I can't please her, what shall I do?"

"Wait a bit," Miles said. "She's naturally upset at her condition. It makes her prickly with you, and herself too, believe me. Give her some time. She'll recover in her own time."

"He's right," the earl said.

Miles noted that it was the first time the earl had directly addressed his wife since they'd arrived. The two weren't angry with each other, at least not that he could tell. They just seemed to lead adjacent lives. Their daughter's illness brought them together in mutual concern, but not much else.

"We can do nothing but upset her now," the earl went on. "She's mending. That's enough for now. She's getting good care, and we can't help with that, so we should go back to London." He looked at Miles. "I'd like to visit her again after you get to Hollyfields. You've said you won't go until she's ready to travel. So I'd assume she'll be more herself by then."

"Yes, and we'd like that," Miles said. "This is a momentary reaction; illness has made her cranky, and who can blame her? By the time we get to Hollyfields I'll wager she'll be in better spirits, and will gladly welcome you."

"I'd like a word with her before I go, though," the earl said.

"Yes, do that. She won't fly up at you," the countess said on a watery sniffle, dabbing at her eyes. "Tell her I do love her . . . in spite of how despicably she treats me."

The earl sighed, exchanged a quirked smile with Miles, nodded, and went to say good-bye to his daughter.

Annabelle sat in a chair by the window, wrapped in a blanket, a shawl over her shoulders.

"So," her father said when she didn't look up at him, rocking back on his heels as he watched her. "We're leaving. It seems the best thing to do. You'll get better, perhaps faster without us to plague you. You're getting good care, that's all I was concerned about. I haven't changed my mind," he said when she didn't react. "Miles still seems like a good man to me. He gives you utmost care. But that's all I can see. Tell me, do you agree?"

"I have no complaint of him," she murmured, still not looking at him.

He nodded. "I haven't changed my mind about him, as I said. Have you changed yours?"

Now she looked straight at him.

"I'll be honest with you, I always have been," her father said bluntly. "You took him because you couldn't find anyone better. I also believed you didn't care much for him one way or the other. I'd like to know if that at least has changed?"

She shrugged. She was so dejected, so much a shadow of herself, that it was hard for him to read any other emotion. But then her bright blue gaze met his and he recognized a glimmer of the woman he knew.

"He's been better than I expected," she said. "Better than I deserved, I think. It was madness to marry a stranger, I know that now, too late, of course. But yes, he's a good man. You were right. Does that make you happy?"

"Only if it makes you happy," he said, frowning. "I wish it did. I wish many things . . . He said we must give you time to recover. I think you have to give yourself time to see if other things mend as well." He hesitated, then added, "And I see that I must give you time to understand that I've always and ever only wanted your happiness. I wish you'd see that as well." He bent and kissed her forehead. "Your mama sends her love and claims you don't understand her."

They exchanged bright looks.

His voice softened. "She does love you too, you know."

"I do." She sighed.

"I'll tell her you said so. Now I can leave. Be well, my Belle."

He saw tears start in her eyes. "You used to say that when I was a child."

"You're still my child," he said, putting his hand over hers. "Remember that. Now, take care of yourself. And remember too that nature can only do so much. You must do the rest. You have to fight, refuse to give in—to your own doubts as well."

She bit her lip to keep her composure. "Why couldn't you have been like this before, Father?" she asked, raising her chin. "This concerned, this caring, this warm? You were when I was a girl. You haven't been since then."

He glanced away from her and looked down at their hands. "You didn't need me before . . . or so I thought." He drew himself up and stepped away. "Forgive me for that. And remember, if ever you need me again, for anything, you've only to let me know. I don't make the same mistake twice, you know. I make new ones," he added to make her laugh.

But she didn't.

Annabelle felt as lighthearted as she did light-headed. She came downstairs all by herself. Mrs. Farrow watched her, proud as a hen with one chick. Annabelle refused help, held on to the stair rail like grim death, and made her slow way downstairs. Servants standing hidden in alcoves held their breath, Mrs. Farrow never left her side, and even though Annabelle knew she was moving like syrup, she exulted.

Here she was, she had done it, she came down on her own!

"First you must be healthy. When your body's mended, your appearance will be too," Mrs. Farrow had told her. "Fresh air when the weather permits and exercise when you can. You also must take other remedies along with the excellent medicines Dr. Selfridge left for you. Don't worry, I told him my plans for your recovery and he approved."

"Remedies apart from his medicine?" Miles asked.

"Of course. Some of our medicines are the same, but mine will heal the body and nourish it at the same time. Cod's liver oil for your bones, my lady," Mrs. Farrow told Annabelle, "will also improve the sheen on your hair."

Annabelle sniffed. "What hair?"

"The hair that will come in lustrous and shiny," Mrs. Farrow answered calmly. "A drop of golden maidenhair can do wonders too. We'll give you wild thyme for the headache, which will also improve your appetite. Rue may be useful for that too. Poultices of Solomon's seal for the bruises remaining from cupping and leeching will soften and clarify your skin, as will marigold, costmary and chamomile. In fact, a tonic with chamomile when you feel sad is also good for the complexion—there are a host of goodly herbs that serve dual purpose. Those, a diet with eggs, milk and berries, and you'll be surprised at the results."

" 'Round about the cauldron go' indeed," Miles

commented. "Mrs. Farrow, if you weren't too pretty to be a witch, I'd worry about you."

"Pretty, indeed, my lord. I might be a crone, how do you know I haven't taken a concoction to change that? Please don't tell my husband I said that or I'll never hear the end of it!" Miles laughed, and the older woman added, "Just be sure your lady takes her medicine, and whether I'm a witch or not, you won't have a thing to worry about."

"I won't worry," he'd said.

But Annabelle had, and still did. Still, here she was, ten days later, standing in the front hall, determined to make it all the way to the salon on her own so that when Miles left the library he'd see her there.

He saw her sooner than that. He strolled out of the library and stopped when he saw her standing in the hall. She was gray-faced and wavering. She wore one of her enormous lacy caps that made her head look larger than her body, and that body was clad in a long-sleeved high-necked blue gown that hung and floated in folds around her. She looked so small, thin, and insubstantial that his first impulse was to catch her up in his arms before she fell down. He took a step forward. Then he saw Mrs. Farrow behind Annabelle, frowning at him. She gave him a palm down signal with one hand.

Let it be.

He looked at Annabelle again and noticed her eyes: bright, filled with life and joyous expectation.

"My lady," he said as understanding dawned. "Did you have a footman carry you down? You should have called me."

"I came down by myself," she said.

She raised her head high because the words suddenly sounded childish to her own ears. What a fool she must seem! Only a pathetic invalid would take pride in such an infantile accomplishment. She was Lady Annabelle Wylde—Pelham, she remembered. The belle of London society. And here she was pleading for applause for coming down a stair?

"Did you?" he said with every evidence of real surprise and delight. "Wonderful! By yourself? Soon we'll be running foot races. I'd better get in practice. Now come, sit down and tell me about it. Or would you rather go out dancing?"

"I was going to the salon."

"What a coincidence, so was I." He offered her his arm.

Gratefully, she took it, trying not to lean as hard as she wanted to. But his arm was rock solid. She gave in and leaned on him as he escorted her to the salon, one of her favorite retreats since she'd been able to leave her bedchamber. The room was cozy, rustic, yet elegant, with rich carpets and comfortable old furniture. Furnished in tones of brown, red, and gold, it looked warm and welcoming in spite of the sudden chill that had set summer back another day. Sunlight poured through long lettered windows, and the glow from the fire that spat and sang in the great stone hearth added to the easeful atmosphere.

He settled her into a chair and smiled down at her. "This is very good," he told her. "I wasn't joking, it won't be long until you're fit again. Don't you think?" he asked Mrs. Farrow. But when he looked up, she wasn't there. "Wanted to give us some time alone, I suspect," he told Annabelle. "The woman is the soul of discretion as well as a ministering angel. I don't know how we'll repay her. She won't take money. Harry said her husband is warm in the pocket so she doesn't need any. Just donating to her favorite charity as she asks doesn't seem enough. She's been our salvation, but I'm told she does her healing out of a sense of duty as well as adventure."

"She told me it's a family tradition," Annabelle said. "If the world were different, she'd be a doctor, or so she said."

"Aha! Have we taken a bluestocking into our midst?"

"I don't think so," Annabelle said thoughtfully. "She doesn't bury her nose in a book all day. But she's as learned as any man and more than most. She doesn't dislike men either; she adores her husband and sons. But she says men treat women like children—until they get sick, and they turn into children themselves. I've never met anyone like her before . . . but then, I haven't spent much time with women."

"Why is that?" Miles asked, taking a chair opposite, leaning forward to listen.

Annabelle hesitated. The subject was one that had often puzzled her, even made her feel slightly shamed—for no good reason, her mother always assured her. But he had asked.

She cocked her head to the side as she thought about her answer. "I had friends when I was a child, of course," she said. "But they fell away as I grew older." She looked down at her hands and then up, fixing Miles with her great blue eyes, defiance and entreaty in her gaze. "Girls—women—begin to compete rather than cooperate when they come to the age when they start looking for husbands, you see. That age is very young. Why, I went to my first ball, in the countryside, when I was sixteen. But the other girls started to react differently to me then."

"Because the men flocked to you?" he asked mildly.

She nodded, looking down again. "Mama said I shouldn't take it personally, but I did. I was hurt. Then—I suppose I tried to repay them by attracting the men and boys even more. And I did! I gathered offers like flowers in springtime. Especially from those gentlemen I knew the other girls were consid— But why am I running on like this?" she asked gaily, trying to cover her sudden embarrassment. "How foolish I must sound, how pathetic, when all I can attract now are physicians."

She bent her head to hide her tears, fumbled in her sleeve and pulled out a handkerchief. "Drat!" she said on a watery sniff. "I hate this! But these easy tears are part of recuperation, or so Mrs. Farrow says."

He waited until she recovered herself, and needed the time to recover himself as well. This was more unwelcome news. Not the tears, he understood that. Her lack of friends. Most women, even the great beauties, had women friends. Another blow to his ambitions, more proof of his folly in marrying so fast. He'd done it to help his mother and sister, and had chosen a bride who didn't get on with other females. Wonderful, he silently congratulated himself. He was well served. His beautiful bride had lost her looks and really didn't seem to have anything else to offer.

But that wasn't fair or right, and he knew it. She had a vaunting spirit, determination, and courage. She'd never whined once, even when she was really sick. In fact, when she was at her worst all she'd done was blame herself. She was bright and perceptive, she had a lively, unquenchable sense of humor, she liked fishing; who knew what else he would discover? And he'd better get on with discovering it, he thought ruefully, because he had to salvage something from this marriage, for her sake as well as his own. They might have made one capital mistake, but that didn't mean they couldn't yet find some good in it.

He didn't know her any better than she knew him. At least he could try to do something about that. The best way would be to tell her about himself, and hope it would stimulate her own reminiscences. Then he'd wait and listen close, and pray that when she spoke about herself, he'd find something they could build on.

Chapter 10

Miles sat and listened to the fire crackling in the hearth, until Annabelle became composed. When she tucked her handkerchief back into her sleeve, he leaned back in his chair, clasped his hands, and said, "You say you didn't have many friends when you were younger? As for me, I had too many."

"Did you?" she asked, diverted.

"Yes, too many friends, or so my mother said. I was brought up in the countryside. Not at Hollyfields, that's my late uncle's manor house, much grander than where I was raised. No, I grew up at a smaller estate in the West Country. I'll take you there one day. I love the place, but I know living at Hollyfields will give my family more prestige and influence in the social world, and that's what they need now. Ours was a neat little holding, a remote gentleman farmer's manor.

"My father let me run wild there," he went on. " 'Wild—with judicious supervision,' as he put it. He said that since I'd be a man who'd go out into a changing world, I should know more of that world than just the estate and my school. So he let me run with all the local children; blacksmiths' sons, farmers' sons, anyone I pleased. It pleased me, all right. I spent my summers and vacations romping with every boy on the estate and in the village, learning from them. I learned more than my father thought—but I think he knew, and that was precisely what he wanted."

He wore a reminiscent smile. "My father took me fishing too, but it was the gatekeeper and his son who really taught me how to do it successfully. Just as it was a farmer's son who first told me the truth about women and men and the mysterious things they could do together, and the smith's two sons who showed me where to see the local smugglers unloading the district's wine. They and the other children in the neighborhood were my close companions and best friends, and they showed me the way of the world, the good and the bad. Fittingly enough, it was a vicar's boy who was my truest friend when—" His expression changed. He cleared his throat and went on, "In times of trouble."

She'd forgotten her tears at his words, and now her attention was riveted. "What trouble?"

He took a deep breath and studied his clasped hands. "Much trouble. When my father died, and then after my mother remarried. She married a cad; you must know that. She married as hastily as Hamlet's mother did, only thank God Peter Proctor was no blood relation to us. Nor did he kill my father, though I don't doubt he would have if he'd known him and knew how he'd profit from marrying his widow.

"And just like that unfortunate young Danish prince," he went on, his voice too bright for the venom underlying his words, "I came home from school to console my mother, only to find she'd married again. I was appalled. But I dared be hopeful. He seemed a good enough fellow, at first."

Miles rose, paced to the window, and looked out as he spoke. "Proctor was a handsome man, if you like big, hearty florid types. He was genial, he was confident, I suppose he looked like someone she could rely on. Mama doesn't do well by herself," he said with a glance at Annabelle. "She'd been a great beauty and was used to men doing everything for her. My father did. The only thing he asked of her was that she sit like a lovely flower in a vase, decorate his life, and be happy with him. She'd been trained to be nothing else by her own father, after all.

"How many men of our class ask more of our daughters or wives?" he asked with a smile that was almost a grimace. "She thought Proctor was the same kind of man as her father and mine were, I think. She made a huge mistake, of course."

Annabelle sat upright in sudden alarm. Did he realize his description of his mother sounded like a comment on herself? And so was he criticizing her? But he seemed lost in his narration.

"Proctor wanted that of her too," he went on, "and he wanted my father's money. Then when he'd gone through it, in staggeringly short order, he found another use for my mother, or rather, her name and standing in society. He used her as an entrée to the best houses, because though he had some family connections he wasn't of any particular rank, and he wanted to move in society so he could swindle more people out of their money.

"I suppose his beggaring us could have been borne. But his shaming us was insupportable, at least for me." He paused. "An inadvertent joke. Insupportable, indeed. Unsupportable, more like. I left the country because he couldn't and wouldn't support me any longer, and it began to look like he couldn't support the family either. His fraudulent investment schemes were being discovered, it was rumored the stable of Thoroughbreds he was so happy to sell at an exorbitant price really belonged to someone else, his cheating at cards and dice was being whispered about.

It was getting harder for him to live in the style to which he'd become accustomed, on our money. And that money was running out as fast as his luck at the gaming tables.

"My mother's parents were long gone, and her father left his fortune to their son, as is customary. My uncle was a skint. So I joined the navy. I hadn't the money to buy my colors in the army, and I'd been told that in the navy a man could move up in the ranks by dint of his efforts. I did. I worked very hard."

He opened his clenched hands and studied his palms. "The calluses have faded, but I had my share. It was well worth it. I worked hard and it eventually made me a man, and a rich one. The years away were a small price to pay," he said softly, then smiled. "Funny little rhyme, but true. I like sailing and the open sky above me, so the job suited me well."

"But the danger!"

"The danger?" He laughed. "I was young, unhappy with my life on land, and patriotic too. The danger was almost the best part of it. No, I didn't mind my service but I could have lived very happily without all those years away from England, those years following the wind, away from home and family—" He stopped.

He saw Annabelle's expression. "Please don't weep for me. I survived and profited, mind, body, and bank account. In fact, my worst problem with

His Majesty's Service was that I couldn't wait to get home to show Proctor how very well I'd done and how little I'd do for him. But when I left the quarterdeck I was sent on other business for His Majesty, and was out of touch with home for a spell. When I finally did get home I found my prize had been snatched from me. Proctor was dead and gone. All I had left was my fortune and my family." His grin was sardonic. "Poor me, eh? I've got more than most men and absolutely no right to complain.

"So," he said, on a sudden laugh. "Look what I've done! I ask about you and spend the time talking about myself. That will never do, but at least I've shown you the way. Now," he said, sitting opposite her again and looking at her expectantly, "tell me more about yourself. What do you like to do? What don't you like to do? We may not be spending our honeymoon in conventional fashion, but surely we can use the time to get to know each other better."

She relaxed. This was conversation. This she could do well. Polite chatter was something she thought she might be able to do on her deathbed . . . She started to speak and paused. The thought about her deathbed stopped the words in her throat, until she saw Miles's startled look and saw him starting to rise to his feet.

"Don't worry, I'm not having any kind of

seizure," she said, waving her hand to get him to sit again. "I just had so many things to say I couldn't think where to start. I was about to make 'conversation,' you see. Then the thought came to me that though I could chatter all day, it wouldn't be what you asked. I know how to make the most enchanting, the very smallest talk. One must if one wants to succeed in society. But none of it would tell you a thing about me except that I can do it. I think the best way to know about me is to spend time with me. Time, I think, will tell you what you want to know."

His expression became quizzical. "Excellent answer. The best obfuscation I've ever heard. No wonder you're so exalted in society. So," he said over her laughter, "you want me to live with you? All right. I think I can do that."

She gave him an arch look that once would have devastated a roomful of men, "You think you can live with me? That's something you really can't know yet, isn't it?"

"Then I look forward to finding out."

She smiled, but her spirits suddenly sank. Because charming as this wordplay was, it was an absurd conversation for a couple to be having on their honeymoon. It was what they should have discussed during their courtship. This was a honeymoon, when a couple were together as they'd longed to be all during that courtship. That was when a couple got to know and to love each other, this was supposed to be the time when their bodies did that.

That reminded her there was something else that needed to be said, something very difficult. She always paid her debts, and now she couldn't. She forced herself to speak up, though she had to cast her eyes down to do it.

"I'm sorry our honeymoon has come to this," she said woodenly. "One day soon I'll be able to be your wife—in all ways—again."

She raised her gaze and saw his slight recoil before he could check it. "Are you apologizing?" he asked, his expression now bland. "But there's nothing to apologize for. I could as easily have been the one to get sick. About your duties as a wife, please believe I'm content to wait until you're well."

His fleeting expression had already told her more than that. He'd been horrified at the mere thought of bedding her.

"Ah! I didn't mean to start you weeping again." He took her hand. "Tell me, are you weary? I wouldn't be surprised. You did too much in too short a time. Shall I take you upstairs again?"

She nodded.

He scooped her up and carried her to the stair. She held on tight, her arms around his neck. Not because she thought he might drop her, but because she didn't want to weigh too heavily on him . . . and because, she realized, it felt so good to hold on to him.

He was so careful of her it brought those damnable easy tears to her eyes again. She hid her face against his chest. She felt the hair at the base of his neck under her fingers, soft and clean. She breathed in the scent of him too: lemon soap and his own indescribable, fascinating essence.

He was so carefully watching his step as they went up the stair that she found she could look at him unobserved. His eyelashes were dark and short, but very thick. She hadn't noticed that before. She'd never gazed at him this closely or directly before either, maybe because she'd gone through their engagement numbly, waiting for it to be ended, never allowing herself to imagine she'd actually marry him. Maybe too, she admitted now, she'd been uncomfortable meeting his bright, knowing blue-gray gaze.

He was a very attractive man, she thought again, before she caught herself, marveling at her folly. Of course she found him attractive! There were no other men around. But he was, and more than that, he was a good man and she'd never fully realized it. How lucky she was . . . or was she?

"What, weeping again?" he asked huskily. "There, there. Mrs. Farrow will brew you up one of her marvelous elixirs, and you'll feel fine again in no time. You've come so far so fast, it's only a little setback. Hush," he crooned to her, "don't weep or you'll wash us both downstairs."

She obliged him with a chuckle. But it was false. He spoke to her as though she were a child. How long, she wondered, before he looked at her as a woman again? If ever?

"I like dancing as well as fishing," she said.

He paused mid-step, looked down at her, and raised an eyebrow.

"And the theater, as you know, and reading Minerva Press novels, as you don't. And I like marzipan pigs, and speaking of pigs, I make one of myself over Banbury cakes, or any cakes with currants in them. Ask me anything, Mi—"

She was going to say, "Ask me anything, Miles." But she stumbled over the word, realizing she'd never called him that. She never called him anything. She'd wed a stranger and bedded one, and he might forever remain one. He might never bed her again either, although surely duty would one day outweigh his reluctance to make love to an ugly woman.

"What is it?" he asked.

She shook her head violently, not trusting herself to speak, choking back sobs. For all that was true, she was disgusted with herself, shamed at how weepy she was. That made even more tears gather in her eyes.

"That settles it!" he said, striding up the stair

with her again. "Time for bed for you, my lady. Soon you'll be feeling better and soon as you do, we'll go home. This was never meant to be more than a visit anyway. Trust me, you'll feel better once you're at my—our home, with my family."

That stopped her tears.

It frightened them away.

"I repeat, you've color in your cheeks now and your bruises have faded," Mrs. Farrow told Annabelle, "You can look at yourself without flinching. You're doing much better than you seem to think."

Annabelle turned from the mirror and silently held her gown away from her body, showing how loose it was.

"It hardly pays to take it in, as you'll fit all your gowns again soon," Mrs. Farrow said calmly.

Annabelle stared at the older woman, then defiantly whipped off her lacy cap. Her well-shaped skull was covered by a fine dark down that looked more like shadowing than hair.

Mrs. Farrow's expression didn't change. "Yes, it's growing in. And it is even now beginning to curl."

"Yes, very attractive. It looks exactly like the hair I have down there, only not as lush," Annabelle said bitterly, casting her glance down to her abdomen as she pulled the cap over her head again.

"Your hair is growing," Mrs. Farrow said. "You can walk without being winded. You went fishing yesterday—"

"I sat on the bank and watched him fish yesterday," Annabelle corrected her. But she paused, remembering. It hadn't bothered her that she couldn't fish, she'd had too much fun watching.

Miles was an excellent fisherman, casting perfectly, but that wasn't what had pleased her. They couldn't speak, not wanting to frighten the trout away, but they'd communicated. He'd seen to it, even though it meant he couldn't catch a thing. He'd entertained her instead, pantomiming what he was trying to do until she had to stifle giggles. He pretended he was slipping on a rock and about to fall into the water. He'd acted chagrined when he deliberately set his cast wrong, and had feigned outsize joy turning to horror when he supposedly felt a tug on the line—and lost the lure.

He'd caught nothing. She'd enjoyed herself more than she'd thought possible.

Mrs. Farrow saw her preoccupation and added, "You've been here over a month; his family must be wondering why you haven't joined them yet."

"They're certainly not thinking we're having a rapturous honeymoon," Annabelle snapped. "He told them how sick I was. And if you're worried that you have to keep coming here to nurse me, you don't, you know," she added haughtily. "I can do very well by myself now."

"My point exactly," the older woman said, then smiled. "I'd come to care for you for so long as you need me. But my lady, much as it might surprise you, I've come to care for you as a person too. You're a strong-minded young woman, and I admire that. And you're a kind one when you don't have to be. Sickness can make some people monsters, at least I've seen many women who weren't as sick as you were being monstrous to their friends and family. You're always polite, even to servants. And however sardonically you express yourself when you're feeling low, sarcasm isn't the same as throwing things. Believe me, I've had to duck my share of flying chamber pots."

Annabelle grinned in spite of herself as Mrs. Farrow continued. "You're well read, and capable of great humor too. I'm pleased to have met you. I don't suggest you leave here for my sake, but for your own, and his. It's time."

"Dear, dear Mrs. Farrow," Annabelle sighed, her shoulders slumping. "You're right. Please forgive me for snapping your head off. I'm so grateful to you, you couldn't have been nicer to me. You've seen me at my worst and encouraged me to be my best. And so I tell you as I would not, maybe could not, tell anyone else: I'd go tomorrow, but . . . I'm so afraid.

"The thing is that I'm spoiled," Annabelle said, her eyes imploring the other woman to understand. "I used to be so very beautiful. That's not immodesty, I think, at least not now that I'm not beautiful anymore. But now I see how much it mattered to me. It was who I was. I'm not saying it always, or even ever, got me whatever I wanted," she added on a crooked smile. "It did not. But it defined me. I was famous for being beautiful. How can I get on in the world now, looking as I do? And as I will look for some time, if not forever, because I'll be changed by this. I already am. I feel naked. I feel . . . unknown to myself."

"Then I should say it's past time to get to know yourself."

"What is my future to be?" Annabelle whispered to herself.

"No one knows that, my lady, no matter what they look like. But we can't hide from the future, there's no point to it. It will be here even if we do hide. The question is whether we want to live that future in hiding or not."

Annabelle looked up. "Is that a challenge?"

Mrs. Farrow shrugged. "If you take it as such. It's only truth."

"I see. Well, never let it be said that I turned down a challenge, whatever the cost to myself," Annabelle said. She wore a sad smile as she added, almost to herself, "However foolish a challenge it might be. I am, after all, an absolute expert at leaping without looking, am I not?"

Chapter 11

It began, at least by Annabelle's reckoning, three hours and twenty minutes after they left the lodge.

That was when they stopped at a roadside inn to have luncheon. Miles, who'd been riding ahead of the coach, rode into the inn yard and signaled the coach to follow. He dismounted, made inquiries, and then strode over to the carriage.

Annabelle's maid cracked open the window so he could speak to his wife.

"It's clean and the food smells delicious," he told Annabelle. "This is a good place to stop."

"I can ride on longer. I'm not in the least tired. It's scarcely noon," she protested.

"I promised Mrs. Farrow we'd stop frequently,"

he told her. "If you become exhausted there's a chance of a relapse, she said."

"But I've only been riding in a carriage," Annabelle argued. "I'm not exerting myself at all!"

He opened the coach door and held out his hand to help her down the carriage stair. "We have nothing but time," he said. "No one at Holly-fields knows we're coming, so no one's waiting for our arrival. Yes, you're much better now. But it's me I'm worried about. If you have a relapse, Mrs. Farrow will have my head. Now, come, my lady, and join me in a bite of luncheon. Or two bites, if you really want to please me."

She had no choice but to step down.

It was a charming inn, very old, Tudor from the half-timbered look of it, freshly painted and neat. Wisteria and laburnum clambered over one wall and across a trellis, spreading glowing yellow and purple shadows over a small courtyard. A few trestle tables were set out there. She looked at them wistfully. Miles saw the direction of her longing gaze and shook his head.

"Charming," he agreed. "But open to sudden breezes, exactly what Mrs. Farrow said you should avoid. And who knows when clouds might cover the sun? No. It's indoors for you until you can beat me to a table in a foot race, my lady. Come along."

She took his arm and walked into the inn.

The day was bright but not hot, and so the interior of the inn wasn't uncomfortable enough for Annabelle to claim it was too hot for her. But she wished she could sit outdoors. She felt fine, and more than that, she realized she was excited. She reveled in this newfound freedom, so even visiting a simple country inn was thrilling after weeks at rest in bed.

She was nervous about having to live with her new husband's relatives at his country estate, especially since she knew she'd have to stay on there until she looked more herself again. But whatever her worries, it was a fine day; she was alive and healthy again. She picked up her head and smiled. Now that she'd decided to leave the lodge, she was ready to face anything.

But not what happened next.

"My lord," the innkeeper said, bowing to Miles, "and lady," he added with a glance at Annabelle. "Welcome," he told Miles. "Your servants are welcome here, sir, but I think you'll find the private dining room more to your taste. This way, if you please."

He led them past a taproom where several local men sat drinking. The men looked up in curiosity at the gentry who had just come in, then turned their attention back to the ale and local gossip they'd been indulging in.

Miles and Annabelle were seated in a cozy room with old bottle-thick bubble-shaped windows that let in light but gave no sight of the outdoors. The innkeeper's wife, all aflutter, hurried in to take their order. Once Miles had placed it, she curtsied and left. Only then did Miles sit back in satisfaction. He looked at Annabelle. His smile faded.

"Are you feeling all right?" he asked, leaning forward and taking her hand. "You've gone very white."

"I'm fine, just fine," she said. But she wasn't. She felt profoundly ill, but it wasn't something she wanted to explain to him.

She'd walked through a room filled with men, unnoticed. For the first time in her life.

The innkeeper had glanced at her, and then back at Miles as though she weren't there at all. The men in the taproom had run their eyes over her, then looked away, not out of fear of being seen staring at a lady, but because they obviously hadn't thought her worth a second look. Even the innkeeper's wife hadn't seemed to see her.

Annabelle had worried about this day, afraid that when she finally did venture into the world again she'd be stared at because she was so ugly. This was far worse. She was now invisible.

Since she could remember, she'd only to enter a room to become its centerpiece. Her presence always caused some reaction from men and women, even children. Women looked at her face, her hair, her clothing; some with envy, some with calculation, wondering how to achieve her "look." And some looked at her with despair of ever competing with her.

Annabelle was more used to men's reactions since she scarcely bothered looking at women. She'd seen naked lust in many men's eyes when they first saw her. More often their expressions showed sudden flaring interest, approval, and desire. That desire might not be lecherous, but men, even happily married ones, enjoyed the company of a beautiful woman. It lit them up, they stood straighter and smiled more in her presence. Even children reacted differently when they saw her. Most became shy around her, then watched her with fascination. A few had asked if she were a fairy princess.

Never had anyone simply not seemed to see her.

Annabelle reviewed her appearance. She knew she didn't look as bad as she had a few weeks ago. She wore a cap, but also a fashionable coal scuttle bonnet that covered it, exposing only her profile from the side. That profile showed a pale, hollow-cheeked face, true. And her gown was still loose. But she didn't look on the brink of death anymore, and there was nothing hideous, nothing extraordinary . . .

Annabelle suddenly realized that it might be worse for a female to be plain than to be ugly, because at least an ugly person was noticed.

"I . . . I suppose I'm not used to looking as I do," she finally told Miles.

"You look fine," he said again, and she realized he didn't understand, or was deliberately misunderstanding her.

They finished their luncheon in silence, because she didn't feel like talking any more than she did eating. But if she didn't eat he'd start fussing at her, so she gave all her attention to her meal. Then they quit the place, and moved on.

When afternoon shadows grew longer, Miles rode up to the coach window to tell Annabelle they'd be making an early stop for the night.

"The Rose and Peach, just ahead, an excellent inn," he assured her when he saw her bleak expression. "Renowned for its cuisine. Historic too, since Charles II stopped here, and our George has been known to drop in from time to time." That information only made her look more unhappy. "You'll see," he promised, and rode away.

Annabelle tried to kindle her courage as they drove into the inn yard of the Rose and Peach. As she'd feared, Miles was right. This was a popular hostelry, with many fashionable carriages in its courtyard. Facing the world as she was had been hard enough, but now she might have to face the world she knew.

"My lady?" her maid asked, "are you well?"

"Yes, fine," she said, because what else could she say? If she refused to stay there, the next inn might be just as crowded, just as fashionable.

They had to stop sometime, and she was growing weary. She might not be able to say anything, but she could do something, she thought with a spurt of hope. She tied her bonnet tightly, and vowed to keep her head down in case she saw anyone she knew.

But even so, as she ducked her head to leave the coach, she hesitated, suddenly realizing that even if she did meet someone from London, they probably wouldn't recognize her. She didn't know whether to be glad of that or not. So it was a very subdued young woman who exited the carriage on her husband's arm.

She was no more confident when she went down the narrow corridor to the private dining room at the Rose and Peach. But Miles didn't seem to notice.

Annabelle watched as he carved her a slice of the roast the waiter brought. Her new husband was all in tones of brown and gold tonight, his jacket and breeches matching his tawny hair. Riding in the sunlight all day had gilded his face with a slight tan as well. She thought he'd never looked better.

"It's a bit early for dinner, but I thought you'd be easier eating straightaway," he said. "It will be crowded later, and I wasn't sure we could get a private room then."

She nodded, relieved and appalled, because then she knew he knew exactly what was bothering her—why she was so upset at lunchtime, and precisely why she was so quiet this evening.

"Thank you," she said softly, and tried to swallow the food he said was so excellent, even though it tasted like dust to her.

Their bedchamber was on the second floor, the uneven floors sloped, the slanted ceiling sagged. That was only due to age, otherwise everything looked well cared for. There was no dust or smell of mildew even though every stick of furniture was generations older than the guests. There was a dressing table with a mottled mirror over it, with a spindly chair beside it. A larger chair stood near the bed. That huge bed took up the rest of the space. Though the bright coverlet on it made the room look cheery, it covered a mattress that looked as uneven as the floor.

Miles saw Annabelle hesitate in the doorway, scrutinizing the room.

"Not what I wanted," he told her. "But all I could get. I asked for two rooms with a connecting door. We're lucky to get this. They're filled to the roof tonight. Literally. My man and your maid have accommodations in the attics with other servants. Don't worry, I won't disturb you, I can as easily sleep in a chair. It's luxury compared to some of the berths I've had to make myself comfortable in."

"Oh no," she said, "that's not a problem, the bed looks big enough for us *and* the servants. You're welcome to use it too. I just was marveling at how tilted the room is."

He laughed. "I hadn't really noticed. The rooms I stayed in at sea were always tilting."

She laughed with him. But the truth was that what he said made her even more sad. She didn't want him sleeping in a chair, not so much for his comfort as for her own. She wasn't used to traveling and was heartsick about her appearance, as well as feeling suddenly weak and weary. And so, childishly, she wanted someone near her tonight. But she couldn't beg him any more than she could blame him for not wanting to share her bed.

He stayed in the doorway. "I'll send your maid to you," he told her. "As for myself, I think I'll go downstairs and see to the horses. Yes," he said with a grin, "a euphemism for going to the tap-room and having a last glass of ale or two. It's too early for me to think of sleep, though past time for you. Mrs. Farrow said you have to go to bed with the birds. It's a different sort of bird for me, I'm used to going to bed with the owls. But I rode all day, so I won't be up late. I'll be quiet when I do come in. So good night, my lady, sleep well."

Sleep was the last thing on Annabelle's mind when she finally dismissed her maid. She sat at the little dressing table and examined herself by lamplight, looking at herself with all the intensity of someone trying to memorize the face of a stranger.

She no longer winced at seeing her bald head. She was too used to it and, besides, her hair was growing in. There was almost an inch of it. She looked like a shorn black sheep now. Few men had hair that short, but it was at last discernibly hair. Her eyes weren't as shadowed. She could almost recognize herself. What was missing?

She glanced down at her body. It was clearly not the same. She'd never known she had so many bones. They bracketed her abdomen. She felt them when she turned in bed, and was shocked by them when she bathed. She had collarbones and sharp elbows, wrist bones and ankle bones, as though her skeleton was aching to be seen. She shuddered at the thought. It almost had been.

Time, Mrs. Farrow had kept insisting. Annabelle turned down the lamp, and stood up. She had nothing but time, yet how did one pass that time? She pulled back the coverlet and climbed into bed. The soft old feathers in the mattress welcomed her, cushioning her weary bones. For the first time in a long time she was able to forget they were there.

But even though the bed was comfortable, Annabelle couldn't sleep. She was too busy wondering about the bed she'd be sleeping in tomorrow night. And so she was still awake worrying a long time later, when Miles quietly opened the door and came in. She almost spoke, then remembered that he'd wanted her to sleep. And there was, after all, little to say.

He undressed quickly. She watched through half-closed eyes as he took off his garments, folded them neatly, and laid them aside. He was neat as a cat. Gentlemen required valets and he had one, of course. But he didn't need one. His time in the navy had obviously made him well able to care for himself.

She watched through her eyelashes as he removed his clothing. The body he revealed was muscled, compact, well proportioned. She'd learned anatomy from antique male statues she'd seen in London's galleries. Obviously that curious part she was looking at now could grow to something formidable, but relaxed as he was, it only looked proportionate as the rest of him. He was very well made, she realized once more, her gaze sweeping over him. The soft low golden glow of the lamp burnished his body, and for the first time in her life, Annabelle beheld something she thought more handsome than her own body had ever been.

Then he hesitated. He padded over to his carpetbag, took out a nightshirt, and slipped it over his head. He hadn't worn one that first and only night he'd slept with her. But perhaps it was because he was in a public inn. Or maybe he didn't want to embarrass her.

He blew out the lamp, went to the window, and threw open a shutter, scant moonlight outlining him as he stared out into the night. He turned and came toward the bed. Annabelle snapped her eyes closed. She heard him pause and knew he was looking at her. Then he climbed into bed, lying down at the extreme edge of it, beside her but not near her. And that wounded her as much as anything else this sad day had done.

She could endure, if only barely, being ignored by strangers. But it was, after all, still her honeymoon. And here she lay with a new husband who didn't want to risk his body touching hers.

"I wondered if you'd taken a bed in the barn," she said into the darkness.

"You're awake!" he answered, turning toward her, raising up on one elbow. "Are you feeling ill?"

"Why must you think I'm sick every time I do something unexpected?" she said crossly. "I'm fine. I just can't sleep."

"I should have had you downstairs with me. Two glasses of our landlord's ale and you'd be asleep before you could climb the stair. No wonder his inn's filled to the limit. The man brews pure lightning."

"Are you bosky?" she asked curiously.

"No, no." He laughed. "Merely merry. It takes more than that to addle my wits. Now, why aren't you sleeping?"

"Worrying," she admitted, the darkness, the

lateness of the hour, and the intimacy of the moment making her candid. "I don't really know your family. I'm going to a new place to assume a new place in life. And I'm not myself; I feel naked and unarmed."

He moved closer and carefully gathered her into his arms. She went to him willingly, and laid her head against his shoulder with a small sigh of relief. His nightshirt was scented with faint lavender, and he'd bathed, she realized. His hair was damp and he smelled of sandalwood soap. She inhaled the scent deeply, it comforted her.

His hand went to her back, then to her hair. He touched it, stopped.

She went rigid.

His fingers opened, he ran his hand through the crisp hair covering her scalp, the springy curls closing over the backs of his fingers as he did. He laughed, low in his throat; she felt it vibrate in his chest. "I do believe you may set a fashion," he whispered. "Let me see. What will you call your new hair style? The gladiator? No. Too masculine. I've got it. À la mouton. It feels very like a spring lamb's. No, à la terrier. That's it! I had an Airedale with exactly the same fur. But don't worry, I loved that bit . . . dog."

It was outrageous, absurd, she couldn't help it; she giggled.

That pleased him. He lay back on his pillow, taking her with him. She stayed quiescent in his arms, secure and oddly at peace. Because he couldn't see her, and she could feel his every breath.

She relaxed as she listened to his steady heartbeat, feeling an overwhelming urge to let him know that she appreciated all he'd done and was sorry for inconveniencing him. It was the hour, it was what she'd been through today; she knew that. But it was also the solid warmth of the man, the way her body suddenly began to tingle wherever it was in contact with his. She was aware of her breasts prickling where they lay against his chest, her legs where they touched his. It shocked and solaced her, and she felt wondrously alive. For the first time in her life she felt real physical longing for a man.

She'd yearned for a man before, but he had chosen another. But this was a very different sort of yearning. She knew what Miles's strong body could do to hers, remembered how he'd touched her on their wedding night. And he was her husband, as close as the hard pulse she now felt beating so thrillingly throughout her body.

She was resting easy now, Miles thought, relaxing. He'd made her laugh, which made him proud. But he wasn't comfortable. She lay in his arms but had grown so thin, her bones were poking into him. He felt a sharp collarbone jutting against his chest, her ribs rubbed against his; she was so tiny, fragile, wasted, that he was afraid of moving lest he inadvertently hurt her. Nor did he want to hurt her feelings. This was the first time she'd sought physical comfort from him. He wasn't comfortable, but he'd been far more uncomfortable in his life. The least he could do was hold her until she fell asleep.

She brushed her cheek against his. And then, softly, shyly, suddenly rose and brushed her lips against his cheek.

He throttled his start of surprise, and lay very still.

She put one hand on his shoulder, and then lightly brushed his lips with hers.

He stayed still, for he couldn't have moved to save his life. But he had to think of hers. He felt an inconvenient urge to laugh. *Now* she tried to tempt him? He could have used this kind of forwardness a few weeks ago when his lust for her had run so high. But now . . . The thought terrified him.

Her lips still felt soft, plush, and sweet, but that was all that was the same. He was sure she'd break in two if he made love to her, and was just as sure he couldn't without feeling any desire to. And he'd not the least desire to. Her body felt as brittle as an old woman's, as delicate as a child's. The thought of having sex with her to comfort her occurred to him, only to wither him.

He brushed her cheek with the back of his hand. "Thank you," he whispered. "But you'd better just say good night to me, lest you give me ideas. If you think Mrs. Farrow would kill me for letting so much as a breeze touch you, I tell you she'd murder me if I did what I most want to do now. We'll have to leave that for another time, another place. The best thing you can do for us both now is to sleep, my dear."

He felt her body stiffen, and she flung away from him. "I only meant to show you my gratitude," she said curtly, thumping her own pillow and laying her head down on it.

"I know," he lied. He'd felt her nipples taut against his skin, and he'd felt the sudden surge of electricity between them, even though his own response had been killed by the mere thought of touching her. "But men are boors. Forgive me for misunderstanding, but we men take gratitude to all sorts of lengths—literally." He chuckled, though he didn't feel like laughing.

She didn't laugh.

Nor did she sleep for a very long time.

He knew; he lay awake for just as long.

Chapter 12

The carriage crossed the bridge over an ornamental pond, rounded the last turn up the long white drive, and then Annabelle saw Hollyfields for the first time. She stared. Her mother would be delighted—her new home was magnificent.

A huge mansion done in the Palladian style, wide, white, and long, it stood on a gentle rise, dominating the surrounding rolling acres, seeming to take up an acre all by itself. A fan-shaped tier of shallow white steps led up to an enormous front portico. The parkland beyond was tamed to look like the background in a painting by an Old Master.

Miles had said Hollyfields was grand. He said she'd like it. She might have once, but after her weeks at the rustic lodge, Hollyfields seemed grandiose. Now too, diminished as she herself was, Annabelle found herself unwilling, unprepared, and anxious about overseeing this great house, as she knew she'd have to do.

He looked fit to command the place; he looked able to command a palace, she thought, watching Miles as he rode on ahead, leading the way, sitting straight and easy on his great roan horse. Her coach stopped when he did. He swung off the horse, tossing the reins to a boy who came running to him. Miles looked up at the house and flashed a smile as the great doors opened. For a moment it seemed he was going to walk straight into the house. But then he turned to the carriage where his new wife waited for him.

"Hollyfields," he said unnecessarily, holding out a hand to help her down.

Annabelle took a great breath and faced her future.

She was as prepared as she could be. She wore one of her best gowns, vibrant speedwell blue with fine yellow stripes, a lovely concoction embellished with tiny embroidered rosebuds. She'd had it made up when she'd been in her prime, but now she thought it suited her even better. The gown's expensive fabric would call attention away from her figure. Long sleeves concealed her thin arms, the high neck covered both prominent collarbones and vanishing bruises, a silken sash under her breasts hinted at the shape she'd lost, and the color matched her eyes, the one thing her illness hadn't taken from her. A blond straw bonnet covered her intricate Venetian lace cap. She'd brushed a faint blush of color on her cheeks. She could do no more.

Annabelle raised her head. She told herself there was nothing to fear. She might not know the house, but she knew who lived in it. They might be surprised at the change in her, but there was nothing to fear from them. Not only would Miles's mother be too well bred to show surprise at how her daughter-in-law now looked, she'd always been meek and deferential toward her. Miles's sister, Camille, clearly respected the London lady his brother had chosen, and his brother, Bernard, regarded her with considerable awe. Annabelle didn't expect entertainment here, but she looked forward to the admiration and acceptance that would help heal her bruised spirit.

She took Miles's arm and didn't have to force a smile when she saw his family standing at the door, waiting. This was her new home, her sanctuary until she recovered enough to leave it.

His mother moved forward, eyes only for her older son. Miles had gotten his eye color from her, but little else. Alyce Proctor was a tall, thin woman. Her fair hair was faded, her personality was muted; now drab and deferential, she looked and acted nothing like Miles or her other children.

Buxom, brown-haired, and brown-eyed Camille was hearty. Bernard, at sixteen, was gruff. He bore a resemblance to his brother, but was shorter and squarer in both face and body.

"Welcome home," Miles's mother said softly before he enfolded her in his arms.

"Miles, Miles, Miles!" his sister caroled, dancing around him until he turned to her so she could hug him hard.

"Capital that you're home again!" his brother said, slapping him on the back.

Then they turned, almost as one, to look at his bride.

Annabelle braced herself. They'd been told how ill she'd been. She'd have to watch their eyes rather than listening to their greetings, because she knew they'd hide their true reactions to her appearance.

"Oh my dear!" his mother exclaimed, one thin hand fluttering to her breast in dismay. "Annabelle? Can this be Annabelle? What happened!"

And then Annabelle knew this was no sanctuary.

"I think one thing must be made perfectly clear," Miles said as he paced his mother's sitting room. He stopped, wheeled around, and stared at his mother and siblings. "She is *not* to be told how bad she looks. And, yes," he went on, staring at his sister, "she'll recover her looks, and no, it's not the sort of thing you should have asked her. And"—he glowered at his brother—"she is never to be told that you wouldn't have known her in a thousand years. My God!" he said, pacing away again, "what could you have been thinking of?"

"They were surprised, my dear, that's all," his mother said gently. "And they'll beg her forgiveness, I promise you."

"I'd rather they didn't," Miles said. "It will only open another can of worms. Let it be. But please, let it not ever be again. Go on now," he told his sister and brother, "I'll see you at dinner."

When they'd made their grateful escapes, Miles turned to his mother. Before he could speak, she did. "My dear," she said earnestly, "please forgive me. I'm the one at fault. My shock and surprise goaded them into whatever they said. I'm entirely at fault, but oh! I couldn't get over the change in her! Poor girl."

Her pale eyes filled with tears. "I'll do my best to make her forget this afternoon. I'll do all I can to make her comfortable here. What she must think of us! I can't think worse of myself. Where were my wits? But you said she'd recovered, and I was expecting the magnificent Lady Annabelle, not that poor sad, sick-looking woman. Tell me what I can do to make amends to her and to you, please."

"No need to make amends to me. I think it's better if you say nothing to her on the subject either. Just please, don't cry."

She nodded, and dabbing at her eyes with a dainty handkerchief, added, "I expect you've had enough of that! Well then, what shall we do for her?"

"Give her time."

"And I think yards of rest!" she agreed. "I sent her to the master's bedchamber, but now I've seen her, I'll have the yellow room made up for her instead. It's always so cheerful and faces south so she can have sunlight on her when she takes to her bed for her afternoon naps."

He frowned. "Her own bedchamber? However she looks, we are married, Mama."

"You want her to share your bed? Surely not. She looks so fragile, my dear," his mother reproved him. "I'm sure she'll be better off on her own, where she can sleep and rest without being disturbed. You cannot expect her to assume her marital . . ." She saw his expression. "Oh! But I never meant to pry into your private affairs. I was only thinking of her and not of your . . . You must do as you think best," she added, biting her lip.

"I think the decision should be hers," he said firmly. "Don't distress yourself. We'll deal with it. Now, I think I'll see how she's settling in. She must be wondering where I am, but I had to speak to you, Camille, and Bernard before another hour passed. Now I need to wash off all my dirt and dust. We've been traveling hard because I didn't want to be on the road one more night. I wanted Annabelle settled in. I'll see you at dinner."

He bowed, then strode away, deep in thought.

He hesitated for a moment when he came to the door of his bedchamber, but then opened it and walked in. It was a huge chamber, easily the size of two rooms, with an adjacent dressing room. His uncle had slept there, and the first thing Miles had done on inheriting the place was to move his uncle's enormous old bed up to the attics and get himself a new one. He didn't know or care much about furnishings, but the bed he'd bought to replace it had pleased his sailor's eye. It was a huge one too, but of lighter wood, and the posts were carved with representations of mermaids and dolphins, tritons and shells. His mother had laughed at it and predicted his future wife would send it to the attic as well.

Now Miles saw his wife standing by the bed. The door to the dressing room was ajar. He got a glimpse of her maid there, unpacking her things, but Annabelle hadn't even taken off her bonnet. Nor had she sat down. She was still dressed for travel, and stood studying a bedpost. She turned when she saw him.

"This bed is most unusual," she said.

He relaxed. She wasn't weeping. That was something. However ashen she'd grown when she'd seen his family's reaction to her, she looked calm now.

"It is that," he agreed, coming to look at the bedpost she was examining. "But it was a bachelor's bed."

"I can see that," she laughed. "Now, this mermaid is almost properly covered by her long hair, but if you look just behind—as you would when you were lying down—as you surely did, you'd see her bottom is bare as the dolphin's she's swimming with. And Neptune! Oh my." She giggled. "That is a formidable trident he bears."

Delighted at her reaction, he peered at the representation of the obviously well-endowed sea god and said, "Well, now you mention it, it is rather intimidating. For me," he added softly. "The comparison, you see."

"Do I?" she murmured. "Don't sell yourself short."

"I don't, I only worried that you might . . . No!" he whispered, pretending shock. "You were peeking the other night, were you?"

She turned her head from him. He couldn't tell if it was to hide her blushes or a smile. But at least her ability to joke was back. It hadn't just been her looks that had entranced him when they'd met, her wit had charmed him too. She hadn't joked like this in a long time. She was healing, even if it wasn't yet obvious to the eye. That reminded him of what he'd come to say.

"I bought the bed in a foreign bazaar," he told her. "It reminded me of my sailing days. But I'm a sober married fellow now so you can choose another, if you like. As to that . . ." He paused and then said too casually, "My mother brought up something I hadn't thought of. You might want your own bed and chamber for a while, at least until you're feeling better. I wouldn't mind if it's what you want. That's something we never discussed. I know many fashionable couples have separate quarters, so if that's what you prefer, another bedchamber can be yours for as long as you like."

He ran a hand along a coiling strand of seaweed on the bedpost as he said, "We have a yellow room just down the hall, which my mother thought you'd prefer because it's sunny. But the red room is historic. I think some princess once slept there; and there's the blue room, that's your favorite color. We have all the colors of the rainbow, in fact. Or we can repaint and paper any room you choose. Would you like to see them and then make a choice? Or would you rather rest first?"

She kept her head turned. "Do you want a separate room?" she asked.

"I want whatever you want."

"Unfair," she said. She lifted her chin. Her

eyes, kingfisher blue, flashed angrily. "That's no decision, and no answer. That's cruel too, to make me choose. Especially now," she murmured almost to herself. "Tell me, Miles, what would you have me do?"

He wondered what to say.

"Really," she added.

He really wanted her happiness. But if he said that she'd only be angrier, and he couldn't blame her, because it wouldn't be a decision. But he was honestly stymied. Again, he wished he knew her better. This was a decision that was more important than he'd realized. It was a decision that would have repercussions, ones they'd have to live with a long time, if not for the rest of their lives together. He thought fast, and then remembered what had struck him as odd about what she'd just said. She'd called him Miles, freely and easily; she'd never done that before.

He had his answer. "Oh then, there's no difficulty. I'd like you with me."

She cast her bonnet aside, and rested her head against his chest.

He felt relief and triumph. His arm went round her waist.

"Well then, good, it's decided," she breathed, relaxing against him. "And, Miles?" she added in a different voice.

He looked down at her, wishing she felt easy

enough in his house to remove her lace cap as well as her bonnet. "Yes?"

She whispered. "All I wanted to ask was . . . please don't banish the bed. I haven't studied half the mermen yet."

"Indeed? Which half?" he asked.

Their laughter was so loud it startled her maid.

"Fishing?" Bernard asked eagerly. He put down his fork and knife. "I can take her fishing, Miles."

"Piffle," his sister said, waving her knife at him. "Your casts wind up in the trees. If she wants to catch apples, then send her with him, Miles. Now, I know where there are some fine fish and I don't just mean sluggards like the millpond carp Bernard nets."

Annabelle tried to look as though she was occupied with cutting the slice of beef on her plate. Miles's brother and sister were fighting for the right to take her fishing, but neither of them was asking her. She supposed their brother must have thrown the fear of God into them after the way they'd greeted her that morning, or rather, the way they'd reacted to the change in her.

But even now, though they squabbled over who could take her anywhere to entertain her— fishing, riding, walking or touring the district— they didn't look directly at her. It was difficult for her to sit and act unaware yet interested at the same time; and hard to eat as well. The way they avoided her eyes kept reminding her how she looked more than words could ever do.

Miles's mama sat and ate her meal, stopping every now and then to hush her brood, often casting sympathetic glances at Annabelle. In some ways that was worse than being avoided, Annabelle thought, because the woman treated her with such outsize concern, it was almost as though she thought her new daughter-in-law was still on the brink of death.

She could have had dinner in her room tonight. In fact, Miles had asked if she'd prefer that after their day of traveling. But she'd nerved herself to come downstairs just because it was a challenge, and she never backed away from them.

"I will take my wife fishing, children," Miles said calmly, immediately diverting the discussion to an outcry about their outrage at his calling them children. "Unless, of course," he said, raising a hand for quiet and looking at Annabelle, "my lady prefers someone else?"

"No, I'd love to *really* go fishing with you," Annabelle said. "I've watched him angling for trout, you see," she told the others, "but wasn't able to try my hand myself. I feel so much better now that I believe I can." She hesitated, then decided to beard the lion, because there was so much they hadn't asked her and she was weary of their unasked questions and assumptions. "I feel better every day," she said, smiling at them. "I know I look very unlike myself, but I promise you I'm mending and hope to be someone you can recognize very soon.

"No!" she went on quickly, as they started to speak, "please don't apologize again. It's very kind of you, but, you see, I know I resemble something to keep crows out of the corn right now. But I'm assured that will change."

Miles looked at her in surprise, then his warm smile sent silent congratulations to her. His brother and sister sat still for once, caught between laughter and embarrassment.

"But, my dear," his mother said, "You must not overdo lest you have a relapse."

"I do *not* overdo," Annabelle said. "Nor will I risk any such thing." She put on a bright smile when she realized she'd said that through her teeth. "Believe me when I say I feel better and anticipate feeling more so every day. Please don't think I need special care."

Before Miles's mother could answer, her daughter spoke up. "Really?" Camille asked eagerly. "Do you think you'll be feeling well enough to go to a party in a few weeks? Sally Hanover, the squire's daughter, is having one for her eighteenth birthday, with dancing, and she's inviting people from everywhere! Well, but she won't be going to London for a come-out because she's already promised to Andrew, a neighbor's son. What with one thing and another, I couldn't go to London for my come-out last year. But this will be the next best thing. Could you go, do you think? Miles said you'd be overseeing my bows in London, making sure I don't make a misstep. That's why he chose you, after all. I mean . . ."

Camille's eyes grew wide and her face red as she realized what she'd said. She hurried on, "This ball won't be as grand as you're used to, I'm sure, but would you like to go? You can give me some hints on how to behave when we do get to London."

Her mother looked up, her faded eyes suddenly glinting. "Do you know," she said slowly, thoughtfully, "that might be a very good idea, Annabelle. The squire isn't as high *ton*, as you're used to, but he knows quite a few good people. Local people, of course. So if you're worried about them noticing the effects of your recent indisposition, you needn't."

"I certainly will go," Annabelle declared before her hostess could go on about her health again. "Even if they have to carry me in on a litter." She grinned. "No, don't worry, because they won't. I'll be there. I may even look a bit less like a sick cat then too."

They laughed because she did. But Annabelle was content. This would give her something to aim for, a goal other than just surviving. Social affairs brought out the best in her as well as all her competitive instincts. She wouldn't compete with Camille, of course. Not only because she couldn't compete with anyone now, but because the poor girl certainly would have enough problems socially without that.

Camille had a pleasant face and outgoing manner, but she was too tall, too wide, and too sturdily robust for real beauty. The girl's face was squared off, as was her figure; her complexion was too fresh, her color too high. She did have lively well-opened brown eyes, her curly brown hair was pretty and her smile infectious, but Annabelle knew gentlemen didn't write poetry to such girls.

Annabelle resolved to be at the dance. She could help Camille, begin to tutor her for her debut in London, and help herself by facing the world again. If anyone there knew her, and the talk about her own altered appearance shocked them enough to comment, she'd bear it. Her only other choice was to hide, and that she refused to do anymore. She'd suffered mockery before, endured shocked whispers too many times. That was why she'd married. Hiding wouldn't end the whispers now. Growing a thicker hide would. If she could escape death, surely she could do that too.

"I long to go to a ball," Annabelle announced into the darkness of the bedchamber. She'd been awake when Miles came to bed. They lay apart on the great bed, but her voice was clear in the silence of the night. "But a country dance will do," she added. "In fact, I'd kill to dance with the kitchen staff at this point. I've been too sick too long. I need to show everyone I'm still here."

"You're here, and here you'll stay," he commented on a yawn. "Now, shh. Go to sleep. The sooner to sleep, the faster you'll mend."

"You talk to me as though I were an infant," she complained. "I'm not a child."

"I know that, too well," he said as reached out to pull her near. She didn't resist. He gathered her in his arms and feathered a kiss on her brow. When her eyes opened in surprise, he lay his lips on hers. He felt the quick response in those warm plush lips as well as the quickening in her body, and the way her nipples rose against his chest. But he felt her ribs prodding him too.

He took his mouth from hers. "Now, sleep," he said. "This too will come later."

She turned away from him abruptly, almost with a flounce. She plopped her head down on her pillow. He chuckled, reached out again and drew her close, tucking her into the curve of his body, covering a small breast with one large hand. She lay stiffly at first, then slowly relaxed, and finally curled into him. He rested his chin against her shoulder. "Shh," he said again, a smile in his voice. "Go to sleep now."

They lay like stored spoons; she fit him neatly,

her bottom snugged into his abdomen. At least that shapely bottom was not bony in the least, he thought with a wry smile. Her growing warmth made the scent of her freesia perfume fill his nostrils. But he didn't worry about an inadvertent arousal disturbing her or himself. He was still too aware of her frailty and how sturdy, oversize, almost brutish it made him feel by comparison. If he was afraid of anything, it was of hurting her physically, or mentally. He had to be careful of how he touched her, and equally vigilant never to show his distaste when he did.

No, he held her close because she needed comforting now. This was all for her. And so he was surprised at how peaceful he felt as he drifted off to sleep with her.

Chapter 13

❝Not red," Annabelle said, "but you know that."

Camille sighed over the fashion plate they were looking at. "Yes, but I was hoping you didn't. Might as well hope for a miracle, right?"

Annabelle raised a brow in mock horror, then laughed as Camille did.

"But I'm not looking for a miracle," Camille said, "just a nice frock or two. Don't look at me like that! I'm serious. I'll do fine whatever I wear, because I'm not looking to find a prince. I just want to have a good time."

"Surely you want to meet some eligible men!" Annabelle said.

"Surely I will. I might even find one I want to marry. But if I don't it won't bother me, because I know I will, in time. I don't have much trouble making friends, you know."

Annabelle didn't know what to say, so she said nothing and turned to a new fashion plate. Camille was one of the nicest people she'd ever met, so she hesitated to say a thing that might hurt her. But her sister-in-law wasn't beautiful or even especially attractive, and Annabelle knew too well how important that was for a single young woman. It wouldn't be easy finding a husband for her, no matter how charming she was. Annabelle could only hope that Camille's cheerful personality would stand up to the inevitable rejection she'd experience. She wouldn't say a thing to question Camille's confidence now. It was perhaps her best asset for the rigors of her coming London Season.

"What about this one?" she asked Camille, showing her a frock that would set off her figure to advantage.

"If you think so," Camille said blithely.

Annabelle cast a fond look at her. In the weeks since she'd come to Hollyfields, she'd found her sister-in-law a delightful companion. The girl was like no one she'd ever known. Forthright as a boy, merry as a child, utterly without pretense, and friendly as no woman ever had been to her. That might have been because she herself was no longer threatening, Annabelle thought. Having no beauty meant no woman could resent her, as her mother had always claimed other women did.

Whatever the reason, though she shared no interests with Camille, since the young woman was a horse-mad, sports-crazed outdoorswoman, still Annabelle couldn't help but enjoy her company. Not only was her sister-in-law as bright as she was friendly, Camille was the only one at Hollyfields who treated Annabelle as an equal.

Miles was attentive, but worried. He treated his wife with the greatest care. That was the problem. He saw to her comfort, made sure she was occupied before he left the house, took her for rides in a carriage and ambles in the gardens, and refused to let her exert herself. He arranged for a local doctor to come see her progress on a regular basis and he made sure she ate and slept properly. All that concern made Annabelle worry about herself more. It also made her wonder if he saw her as a wife or just a responsibility now.

But that was better than how she felt about his mother's treatment.

Alyce Proctor treated her like a dying woman, always sending Annabelle sad smiles, leaping in alarm if she so much as sneezed, fretting aloud if she did anything but sleep, sit, sew, or read. That made Annabelle wonder if all the outsize concern wasn't really wishful thinking. Alyce didn't encourage conversation. In fact, other than concerns for her health, she never exchanged more than the most polite pleasantries with her daughter-in-law.

And now that she'd lost her looks, Bernard, though perfectly pleasant when they met, largely ignored her.

Even the servants tiptoed around her.

Her own mother and father, having consulted with Miles by letter, sent word that they would wait until the end of the summer to visit. Annabelle missed them, but promptly agreed. By then she was sure she'd surprise them with her improvement.

Camille was helping her with that. She'd teased and bullied Annabelle until she consented to go walking with her every morning. Miles thought it was a fine idea, and so Annabelle had done it to preserve the peace. But it quickly became a ritual: Annabelle, Camille and her ten dogs, and their daily tramp through the morning dew.

Annabelle was more used to seeing the moon set than watching the sun rise, but she actually began to enjoy greeting the newborn day and breathing its fresh air. She was also elated when she realized she could walk farther every day. Now she was trying to repay Camille in some small way.

"Not red, no," she told Camille now. "You have to be a married woman or have been on the town a while to get away with that." She neglected to mention that red would be a disastrous color for Camille. She already had too much of it in her face. "Young women wear white."

"Not white!" Camille yelped. "I'd look like a feather bed!"

"No," Annabelle agreed, "Not white. Too insipid, I think," she added, refusing to agree with Camille's accurate appraisal of her figure. "Although that is what's expected of you. Still, I think you have the looks and personality to get away with something different from the run of the mill."

"Pink?" Camille asked hopefully.

Annabelle repressed a shudder. Camille would look like an overblown rose in pink. "No, something cool and elegant," she said, looking at Camille with speculation. "Yes. Pale green. Or a light wash of blue." Colors that would bring down that high color and complement it at the same time, she thought. "Some white fabrics with lovely subtle contrasting vertical stripes, absolutely," she added.

"To make me look willowy? Ho! Even a magician can't do that."

"To make you look fashionable," Annabelle said firmly. "Perhaps even gold, if its not too blatant a shade. It would suit you very well. We'll make you a wardrobe of irresistible materials and attractive colors, not sensational ones. And when you have ten children instead of ten dogs, by all means, you can wear red."

They both giggled at the very idea.

"Telling warm stories again?" Miles asked as he ambled into the salon where the two sat over a table covered with fashion plates.

Camille laughed. "Hardly. Belle's trying to get me to stop telling 'em! She says they may be all right for the gents hereabouts but I'll get my walking papers if I tell stable stories in London Town."

Miles cocked his head to the side. " 'Belle'?"

"Oh, it's what I call her and she doesn't mind," Camille said.

"I don't, truly," Annabelle said, looking up at her husband. What she didn't say was that only one man had ever called her that. It was the first nickname she'd ever had, and as such, it both bemused her and made her sad that no one else had cared enough to give her one.

"I like it. Shall I call you that as well?" he asked Annabelle.

Before she could answer, Camille snorted. "Well, it's a deal easier if you have to call her in a hurry than shouting out a mouthful like Annabelle!"

"I see, as when she's being chased by a bull or in the path of a runaway carriage?" he asked.

"Exactly," Camille said with satisfaction, and looked abashed when both Annabelle and her brother burst into laughter.

"You're not getting Annabelle overexcited are you?" Alyce Proctor asked as she hurried into the room. "I told you it was her naptime, Camille," she scolded. "What are you still doing here?"

"We're looking at fashion plates," Annabelle said. "And I'm not tired in the least."

"What could you have been thinking of?" her mother told Camille angrily, ignoring Annabelle. "It's two in the afternoon, she must have her nap. Now, out and let her go upstairs and rest."

"I don't need a nap anymore," Annabelle said as she rose to her feet. There was color in her cheeks and a militant sparkle in her eyes. There, suddenly, Miles again glimpsed the woman he'd married.

His mother turned to Annabelle. "So you may think, but it's far too soon for you to overdo. I've seen healthier women succumb after an illness when they try too much too soon, and Lord knows you are not a healthy woman, my dear."

Annabelle blinked. "Has the doctor told you something he didn't tell me?"

"He told us to continue to watch over you," Alyce said, "and so I, at least, try to do."

Annabelle's face went blank. She nodded, then turned and quickly left the room. Camille followed, looking dismayed.

Miles stayed very still. "What else did the doctor tell you?" he asked his mother softly, when the other two had gone. "It must be something he didn't tell me. Because last I heard, he was pleased with her progress. Which I also believe you just set back."

His mother's face fell. "Oh my," she said, "I never meant . . . I only wanted to be sure . . . Good heavens, do you think I alarmed her? I'll just go have a word . . ."

He stopped her with a touch on her shoulder. "No, I think you've said enough to her today. Now, again, did the doctor tell you anything I should know?"

"No, no, only what he told you." She looked at her son, and tears filled her eyes. "I see what it is. Yes, of course. She's quite grown up, I ought not to have nagged at her. But I am in the habit of mothering, you see."

Miles remained still. He wouldn't remind her that she was not in the habit of mothering him. His nurses and governesses had done that. She'd been an idol, a beautiful, adored, but distant figure in his early years. When she did pay attention to him he considered himself honored that the exquisite, good-smelling, smiling lady was actually spending time with him.

When he'd grown older she'd been in the habit of being a loving wife to her new husband. That had taken up most of her time. Miles had left her to it, something he still regretted. When he returned to England again he found her changed, all that golden beauty vanished, wasted on a cad who'd used up her money and her personality, as well as her looks. It was more than mere aging—graying hardly showed on a lady who had been so fair, and smiles made charming wrinkles. But her skin had creased like tissue paper and she seldom smiled; her once luminous eyes were washed out and flat. Even now Miles was startled anew whenever he allowed himself to see her as she really was.

What she was at the moment, was weeping. When she did that Miles saw her both as the beautiful lady she'd been and the poor faded creature she was, and felt like a monster either way. "Please don't cry," he said helplessly.

She blew her nose. She raised her head and squared her narrow shoulders. He felt a rush of pity for the display of strength he knew was not there.

"I shall remove to the dower house, as I should have done the moment you returned with your bride," she said resolutely. "No one has lived there for years, it's all cobwebs and mold, owls nesting in the attics. But it can be put to rights in a matter of days, and there I shall go, as I ought. Of course, with Camille and Bernard still here, I'll have to come back and forth a great deal—or shall they move in with me?"

"There are a dozen empty rooms here, Mama," he said wearily. "There's no need for anyone to go anywhere."

"Then I shall avoid Annabelle, and stay out of your business."

"No need for that either. Just don't worry about her so much because it worries her when you do."

"Very well," she said with a coquettish smile that recalled the old days to him. "Then I shall continue to just worry about you."

He laughed, as she'd meant him to, if not precisely for the same reason.

"You look wonderful," Miles said when he saw Annabelle.

She finally let her breath out. He wasn't lying. He could disguise his expression, but over these past weeks she'd learned to read the truth in his eyes. It was an invalid's talent she'd developed in the days when she hadn't trusted words. Now she could see those ice blue eyes were warmed with real admiration. She exulted.

She was only going to a local dance but she'd taken more time dressing now than for her first presentation to society. She twirled before him. "You like my hair?" she asked.

He laughed. "What I can see of it, clever lady."

Her hair was covered by a blue satin toque, a fashionable French wrap of a cap, covered over with artificial blue flowers. Wisps of inky curls showed at her forehead and over her ears. They'd been sewn into the toque, as she'd finally found use for one of the wigs she hadn't been able to wear. The toque matched her gown—blue and embellished by flowers at the long puffed sleeves and hem.

She was excited, elated, delighted. She thought

she looked almost like herself again. It was true she was still too thin and her skin hadn't entirely recovered its creamy purity, but she thought she looked very fine, much better than she'd hoped she would so soon.

"I'll do," she said smugly. "But look at you. You look grand enough for London."

He shrugged away her compliment. "I wear what I must. You'd think a country squire would have a more casual affair, wouldn't you?"

"No," she said, "A country squire is exactly the fellow who wouldn't."

They smiled at each other. But she thought he did look wonderful. Evening dress suited his athletic frame. Buff breeches showed off his muscular thighs, and he didn't need to pad out his white stockings. His broad shoulders were set off by his tightly fitted jacket, his neckcloth was tied in fashionable style. His brown curls were cropped short and brushed forward. He looked very masculine and yet elegant. She felt proud to take his arm and go downstairs to meet the others in the hall.

"But see the evening's star," Annabelle said as Camille joined them.

"Bravo!" Miles said with approval.

Camille's color grew higher. "Well, thanks," she said, and grinned. "I do look a treat, don't I?"

She wore a transparent gold silk overdress over a white gown, sashed at the high waist with tawny silk. It hid the worst points of her figure and gave the rest delineation. Gold flowers woven into her curls lit up her face and brought up bright highlights in her sparkling brown eyes. But she knew she looked well and would have glowed without them.

"She'll do," Bernard said, himself transformed by fashion. He looked down proudly, again appreciating his bright blue jacket, violet waistcoat, yellow pantaloons. Rather, he tried to look down, but his shirt points were so high and his neckcloth so elaborately tied that he could barely turn his head.

"We all look fine as fivepence," their mother agreed. She wore a filmy violet gown and matching violet turban. "But now we must go. Camille and I shall go with Bernard in the coach. Annabelle and Miles can take the smaller carriage. It's warmer."

"It's summertime," Miles said patiently. "We can all ride together."

Annabelle was sorry that they did. Not because of the warmth, but because of what her mother-in-law said as they approached the squire's house.

"You look very well, but this will be a debut," Alyce said as they drove through the squire's gates. "And so I caution you to not take anything you overhear to heart. People can be offhand, even cruel, with strangers."

"I may look better than I ever have, but I've lived here all my life, Mama!" Camille yelped.

"Not you, dear. Our Annabelle," Alyce said, peering out the window at the flaming torches set along the drive. "Oh. We are here."

She was very good at saying things at moments when she couldn't be rebutted, Annabelle thought bitterly as the coach came to a stop. Annabelle was almost sure her looks were returning, and she knew her strength and determination were coming back. Her strength because of the passage of time, proper diet, and exercise. Her determination because she was committed to proving her mother-in-law wrong. She would recover; she would be herself again one day no matter what the woman said.

It wasn't that Alyce said anything overtly wrong, only that all her gentle, concerned inquiries were constant and badly timed. They only served to remind Annabelle, and Miles, of her recent illness, as though it were a shame she had to live down. And no matter how gentle or concerned the inquiries, Annabelle still couldn't tell if Alyce was saying and doing what she said and did with exactly that in mind. No, she corrected herself, she did know. The truth was that for all her obvious solicitude, her new mother-in-law didn't like her. There was no real warmth in her eyes when they met. There was nothing but plati-

tudes and commonplace whenever she spoke to
Annabelle.

But Annabelle didn't know how to change her
mother-in-law's attitude. Her own mother
could . . . No, her own mother would only get
protective and angry and make matters worse.
But it didn't matter, not really, she told herself. She
was almost better, so she'd be back in London
soon, where she'd not only have her own mama,
she'd have all London at her feet again.

The squire's house was decked out for his
daughter's party. Local lads dressed as footmen
augmented the usual staff, the ballroom was
brimming with flowers, musicians had been
hired, a myriad of candles burned everywhere—
and not a one of them tallow, boasted the squire as
he greeted his guests at the door.

"My Lord Pelham! Greetings and welcome,"
the squire said as they entered his house. "And
Alyce, you never looked lovelier," he said as he
took her hand and bowed over it. "Bernard, you
dog!" he caroled as he saw the young man. "Look
at you, dressed to the nines. No!" he gasped, pretending to fall back. "That's not our Camille, is it?
Kissed by the Fairy King, were you? You look
magnificent, that's all there is to it. Magnificent,
ain't she, Sally?" he asked his daughter.

Sally and Camille immediately fell to compli-
menting each other, as Alyce stood watching the

girls fondly. Bernard peered into the ballroom to see who was there. Miles and Annabelle stood where they were.

"Now where's that beauty you married, my lord?" the squire asked as he squinted at the arriving guests. "Don't tell me you didn't bring your bride? Or is she home because she's already increasing? My Martha was always sick whenever she was about to pup, couldn't set toe out the door for the whole nine months. Fast work, my lord. But can't blame you, I heard she was a diamond of the first water, a real stunner."

"And here is my wife, Annabelle, Lady Pelham," Miles said through clenched teeth.

"Oh," the squire said, his broad face turning redder as he looked at Annabelle. "Didn't see you there, my lady. Getting blind as a bat. I need spectacles and that's a fact," he muttered, as his face grew redder. He bowed to her. "Honored to meet you, and welcome to the district. I hope we'll see more of you. The gossip was right, you are lovely. Please, come in and join our party."

Annabelle stepped forward into the hall, glad she had her husband's arm to hold on to, because she couldn't feel her feet. She was numbed. Their host hadn't seen her because he hadn't noticed her, or if he had, hadn't believed she was the woman Miles had married.

But then, Annabelle realized with sorrow, she wasn't, was she?

Chapter 14

The guests danced. First country sets and squares, then minuets, then polkas. The squire's guests kept moving, twirling, prancing, treading stately measures, flinging themselves about with happy abandon. Unlike London soirées, everyone took a turn dancing: old, young, even the aged and lame, chaperones and companions, and poor relatives who acted as servants. All except for the servants themselves and the infirm. And Lady Pelham and her husband.

"Are you feeling well? Do you want to go home?" Miles asked after Annabelle refused to join him in yet another dance.

They sat in chairs at the side of the room and watched the others as they'd done since they arrived.

"I'm fine," she said firmly, "nor should we leave. Your mama's gone off somewhere because she knows we're here and can look after Camille."

"That is odd," Miles murmured, frowning as he scanned the room. "It's not like her to gossip or play cards as so many ladies do at these country affairs. She doesn't fraternize with the locals, just usually watches Camille like a hawk."

"Ah, but she knows she has two eagle-eyed hawks to replace her," Annabelle said, and won his attention back, along with a smile. "Speaking of which," she whispered, "look over there. Your brother hasn't taken his eyes off that pretty girl in yellow. He can't slouch against the wall all night, so surely he'll work up the courage to ask her to dance soon. And just look at Camille! Oh, Miles, why didn't you tell me? She doesn't need my help, or anyone's. She's the most popular girl I've ever seen!"

They both looked to where Camille was romping to a polka in the arms of a gangly youth. Her hair was coming down in tendrils across her flushed face, and that shiny, beaming face was very red. She hadn't stopped dancing since she'd arrived, and there were a cluster of young men waiting for the polka to be over to take their turn partnering her.

"She's popular," he said. "I never said not. That's part of the problem. She's as amiable as she is honest, and Mama is terrified that she'll settle for less than she can get. Mama wants her to find a

better—meaning richer and more highly placed—
husband than she can hereabouts. She may, but I
don't want her spirits ruined by London cats in
the process. My sister needs someone to show her
how to be spirited without running the risk of being called wild or hurly-burly by jealous mamas.
And they will be jealous. Men flock to my sister."

Annabelle nodded. She'd met girls like that before, or rather, seen them, as she'd never gotten to
know any. First, because she hadn't had time for
them. And secondly because they generally were
only on the town one Season before they were
married off. None had been incomparables. In
fact, some had been downright homely. But
they'd all had something indescribable that made
men mad for them. Camille, with her open, easy
ways, was such a female. Perhaps, Annabelle
thought now, that was part of it. She'd never
known a more candid, friendly, kind girl than
Camille. Maybe some men valued that as much as
a woman's appearance.

Miles watched his wife's face, taking more
pleasure in doing so than he had for weeks. She
was coming back. Annabelle was no longer a
great beauty, that was true. She'd been like a magnificent painting before, all sumptuous colors, textures, and shapes that drew the eye. Now she
could be compared to a sketch, a portrait dashed
off by a master that showed only the essentials of
beauty and left the rest to the imagination.

And then there were those eyes. It wasn't just their startling color that made them unique. Now that the rest of her had been toned down, Miles could see the emotions and intelligence that made those azure eyes so fascinating.

He didn't lust for her anymore, but felt fiercely protective instead. Her sharp edges had been blunted by her illness. She'd never been sharp or cruel to him, but she'd been perhaps brittle. He thought she'd grow more mellow in time, but this new Annabelle was tamed. He wasn't pleased about that. Being tamed and being beaten were too closely allied for his taste—he wanted to see the proud woman he'd married. He didn't care if she was as beautiful as she'd been; nothing remained perfect. He could be happy with less than that, but he wanted to see her happy too.

"Belle?" he asked as he rose to his feet. "Will you honor me with this dance?"

She looked up, doubt clear in those remarkable eyes.

"It's time," he said. "Dance or go home. Yes, I'm a tyrant, but they're playing a waltz so you can hold on to me if you get dizzy. I'd like to dance with my wife, if you please." He held out his hand.

She took it.

The dancers made way for the new couple who joined their ranks. Word had gotten out as to who they were. And if there were whispers about the great beauty who'd turned out to be just a small, pale, ordinary-looking woman, the look on her husband's face stilled those whispers, at least those within his range of hearing.

The waltz played on, and Annabelle danced with Miles. She found him a wonderful partner, attuned to the music as well as her needs. She'd danced with him before. But then she'd been too busy craning her neck to see who was watching her, or pretending she didn't notice who was watching her, to take special notice of her partner.

Now he was her anchor and her safe harbor, and she paid no attention to anyone but him. As he paid no attention to anything but his wife. They turned and spun, following the music as he smiled down at her, making her feel real and alive again.

The musicians picked up the beat, and Annabelle flung back her head and laughed aloud as they picked up their pace too. The room whirled around her, she grinned up at her husband . . . and almost missed her step because of the look on his face.

"I think," he said as he began to steer her to the edge of the dance floor, "that we should stop and catch our breath."

"But I'm feeling fine!"

"So you are, and so you should, but I believe you need time to . . . adjust."

She obeyed, for she had little choice, as he was

moving quickly from the dance and out past the ring of spectators. But she was building up to a fine hot anger as he led her to the back of the room. There, far from the bright glow of the chandeliers, she finally looked up at him to give him a piece of her mind. Then she saw his expression clear.

"What?" she said in alarm, her petulance forgotten. "What is it?" She glanced around. "Something wrong with Camille? Your mama? Bernard?"

She'd surprised many expressions on his face before: dismay, worry, and pity. But never a combination of all three. "Belle," he said gently, "your hat . . . or whatever you call it . . . has slipped. Along with your hair."

He hands flew to her head. She felt the slippery fabric of her toque and gasped. It had slipped. Now the fringes of black curls that had been over her forehead were listing toward her right ear; the curls that had been peeping out by that ear were almost resting on her shoulder. She touched the other side of her head and felt her own tightly curled stubble of hair, and knew it could be seen. She hurriedly yanked the satin cap back into place, but it must have been too far because she stopped when she saw Miles face. He seemed to be struggling with laughter and dismay.

"You'll have to be my looking glass," she said tersely. "I can't go to the ladies' retiring room. I will not march through a crowd with my head on backward."

But then she saw his lips quirk, and despite her distress it suddenly all seemed too funny. "Oh Lord!" she said between gusts of laughter she tried to stifle, "It must look like my head's coming off!"

"No. Only like your scalp is moving. Don't worry. Half the people here once shaved their heads so they could wear wigs, so even if they saw you they'd be used to it. Now, instead of using my eyes as mirrors, which I'd enjoy but might not work, would you trust me to do the honors?"

She lowered her head. He raised his hands.

"Oh, there you are," a voice suddenly cried.

Annabelle's head shot up. Her mother-in-law came up to them, trailing a group of people. "Annabelle, guess what?" she trilled. "Here are some of your friends! I thought I saw you leave the dance so I brought them here."

Five well-dressed people stood staring at Annabelle. Five people Annabelle hadn't expected to ever see in the countryside and hadn't seen since her wedding day. Tall, languid, elegant Drum, the Earl of Drummond, and his wife. The blond giant, Eric Ford. And Damon. Incredibly handsome Damon Ryder, and his equally striking wife. All wore matching expressions of shock, which they quickly tried to stifle. The women were having trouble not looking appalled and sympathetic, the gentlemen were trying to school their faces to resemble mere polite welcomes.

Annabelle froze. Since she'd been sick she'd had nightmares in which she appeared in public to find people staring at her, and she'd been overjoyed, until she noticed she had no clothes on. Then the hot rush of shame and humiliation would wake her. She'd thought that was the work of fever. This was worse. She couldn't wake up.

Damon? Her first and perhaps only love? And sardonic, clever Drum? And both their lovely, lovely wives. And handsome Eric Ford, who'd once upon a time deceived her by pretending to be attracted to her in order to save his sister's husband from her attentions?

They were all worldly and sophisticated people, but even so they stood silent, obviously unable to know what to say to this creature who'd once been the Lady Annabelle, the most beautiful woman in London.

"We can come back later," the Earl of Drummond said gently.

"Yes!" Gillian Ryder, the blond beauty who had married Damon, said too brightly. She turned her head, "Why, listen! They've struck up a polka. My favorite. Come along, Damon."

Since the lady was enceinte and would hardly dance a polka, a shocked silence followed her hastily improvised attempt to give Annabelle some privacy. It was broken by Alyce's cry of dismay.

"Oh my!" Alyce gasped, her hand fluttering to her lips, "Poor Annabelle. Your hair! Or rather what happened to your pretty toque. Oh what a shame, for it disguised everything so well." She raised her eyes to her son. "I didn't know why you two went off alone. But I so wanted to surprise Annabelle with her friends, so I followed. I knew the earl's estate was nearby and could only hope that he'd come to the squire's party tonight. I was delighted to see him, and then to find his houseguests also knew her! I was so elated I couldn't wait. I ought to have, I see it now! Annabelle surely didn't want to be seen in such a state. Can you forgive me, my dear?"

"It's all right, Mama," Miles said patiently, because his mother was now wringing her hands.

"No, it isn't," she declared, "We must give Annabelle time to restore herself. We'll just go now."

"No," Annabelle said, taking in a deep breath. "Good evening," she said calmly, dipping a short curtsy to the new arrivals. When she rose, Miles put his arm around her shoulders, and stood close. She knew he was the only one who could feel her trembling, so she faced the others with as bright a smile as she could muster.

"Yes, as you see," she told them, "you've caught me at a bit of a disadvantage. But there's no need to run away. I've been ill, and the devil is in it, but when I was at my worst, they cropped my hair to fight the fever." She put a hand to her errant cap. "Now look at me! Or rather, don't! I'm not exactly bald as a newborn babe but it's not attractive, unless you fancy the look of shorn sheep." She slid a glance at Miles and added, "Some do, but it isn't quite the style." Then she turned back to the company. "Whatever was done to my hair, they didn't cut my tongue, and I haven't seen any of you since my wedding. So please don't rush away. How are you?"

Miles looked down at her with a proud and tender smile.

Damon's wife, Gilly, beamed. "Bravo!" she cried, "You've got bottom, my lady. But, you know, you wear that cap so well I thought you'd shaved the lot off to start a new rage. Damme if you couldn't do it too!"

The others laughed. "Gilly!" her husband said, shaking his head, 'You're the only female I know who could cause a scandal trying to scotch one. But she's right, Annabelle. That blue cap looks very well on you."

"Even crooked?" Annabelle asked. She still smiled, but her jaw ached because her facial muscles were so tight.

"Especially crooked," the earl said. "Trust Lady Annabelle to start a new fad," he told his wife.

Annabelle's eyes slued to his countess. She had once vied with the woman for the earl, and lost, in what seemed so long ago as to have been another life. But after all, Annabelle realized, trying to subdue a hysterical laugh, she'd tried for each of these men and made a fool of herself each time, hadn't she? That made this hideous moment simple by comparison.

But it wasn't that hideous, after all.

"The headdress isn't meant to be crooked," Miles explained, "I set it askew with my enthusiastic waltzing. Once I saw my mistake I led my bride away to a nice dark corner so we could adjust it. I'd hoped it would look like we were trying to be alone," he said with a glance at his mother. "We are newly wed, you know. Well, actually, I was going to try to take advantage of that too," he added in mock complaint to make them laugh again. "But I was finally trying to straighten it when you came along. As you can see, I'm hamhanded and made it worse."

Drum's lady tipped her head to the side and looked at Annabelle, "Your own hair is lovely and curly, if short, my lady. I think you could dispense with that toque in a few weeks. In the meanwhile, would you like me to set it straight?"

"A good idea," Gilly declared. "I'll help. Eric, if you stand in front of us, no one will see."

"If he stands in front," the earl remarked dryly, "no one will see if we build a barn."

His lady exchanged a merry look with him as the others laughed.

"Absolutely," Eric said, bowing. "I'm delighted

to be of service. I always wished to be of service to you," he told Annabelle sincerely. "So, if you'll pardon my back? I'll just turn around so I can divert the curious while I'm using myself to best effect. You always did want to see the back of me, didn't you?"

Annabelle nodded, trying to smile as the others were doing, fighting back the damnably easy tears she'd been plagued with since her illness. These people had seen her at her worst and were being kindness itself. But what was making her want to weep was the sudden realization that though they had indeed seen her at her worst, and not only once, this moment was not one of those times, after all.

"That ended well, didn't it?" Miles asked as he came into their bedchamber later that night.

Annabelle watched him from bed. He didn't have to explain what he meant. "Better than I'd hoped. Better than I deserved," she added in a small voice. "I . . . wasn't very kind to any of them when I was in London. They have little cause to like me. But they were wonderful." He was smiling as he ambled over to the bedside to turn down the lamp, until she added, softly, "It's astonishing how kind people can be when they pity you."

He turned and stared at her. "Enough," he said abruptly.

She looked up, surprised.

"The only pity I see is your own, Belle. You were very sick, I grant you. But you're mending and you look much better than you think. If you're not as you were, you may be soon enough. No one was about to drop pennies in your cup."

She looked at him through narrowed eyes. His hair was dewed from his bath, his skin glowed even in the dimmed light, he looked strong and fit and virile. What did he know of illness? Or loss of confidence because of loss of looks? She remembered how secure she'd felt in his arms tonight, and found herself strangely angry at him because of it.

"They might not give me charity," she told him through gritted teeth. "But they don't give me compliments either, other than: 'Oh, you don't look so bad.' What else can they say: 'Oh my God, what happened to you?'"

"Life isn't just about how you look."

"Oh, it isn't? So you'd have offered for me if I were plain or wall-eyed or fat? I don't think so. You married a woman you hardly knew, but one you liked looking at!"

He stood still, for what she'd said was irrefutable.

"Ask any woman how much life is about looks, my lord. Better yet," she went on angrily, "ask any man. He may be wall-eyed as a pike and fat as a stoat, but you may bet he's looking for a beauty in his bed."

"Well, then," Miles said lightly. "I am fortunate. I have one."

She reared up on her elbows, eyes flashing, ready to battle.

He didn't want to fight. What she'd said was too true, a thing he wasn't proud of now. He'd have to distract her—and himself.

He put his hands on the sash of his colorful long night robe and paused. "Lord, it's so late and I was so eager for bed that I forgot," he said. "I didn't put on a nightshirt." That was true. But he'd have never made a point of it if he didn't need to divert her. He'd just thought of a wonderful way to do that.

"Would you mind if I came to bed as God made me?" he asked. "It's a luxury to sleep like that after my years aboard ships when I slept in my breeches, ready to spring into action if I had to. But will it trouble you?"

"Not in the least," she snapped, still in a fine rage. "You sleep so far from me you could wear armor and I wouldn't notice."

He chuckled. "Liar," he said, and shucked off his robe. He stepped into the high bed and took her in his arms. "Or did your recent illness damage your memory?"

She muttered something indistinct because his nudity disarmed her. But she didn't resist him; she gingerly laid her head on his chest. It was odd and exciting. He'd only removed all his clothing once before, that first night when they'd made love. Since her illness he'd come to bed dressed in a nightshirt, chaste as a monk. But there was nothing chaste about the feeling of his warm bare skin against her cheek now.

She tried to stay still. She was, after all, very angry at him. But his body was so heated, so hard, so interesting, that she couldn't help but move. It never occurred to her that he'd been holding his breath. She raised her head. He lowered his.

His mouth covered hers, and their kiss was very sweet and comforting. It was exactly what she'd wanted, although she hadn't known it. She sought more. Then the touch of his tongue and the intoxicating taste of his mouth filled her senses and made her long for even more. They parted for a breath of air, and then kissed again. And again.

She rejoiced in knowing she was wanted, and had something to offer him at last. But it went beyond flattery, and she seemed to catch fire from the taste and touch of him. She tried to get closer, fumbling in her efforts to get off her night shift, until he helped her. Then, naked as he was at last, she sighed, tried to encircle his wide, warm shoulders, and leaned into him, skin to skin. She reveled in the feeling of strong arms wrapped around her, the feel of his sex rising against her belly. She felt vulnerable, yet powerful, her breasts peaked against him as a long slow throbbing began in her own sex. Life awakened in her again.

He fondled her, stroked her, his mouth moved from hers to each rising breast in turn. He ran his palms down her body, making her shiver. He cupped her, he touched her, he sought her, and she shifted, parting her legs . . .

He drew away and dropped his hands. "It's still too soon," he said as he lay back down on the bed beside her.

"What?"

He sat up and ran a hand through his hair. "It's too soon. We shouldn't . . . I definitely should not."

She sat up, facing him nose to nose. "I feel fine!"

"We can't risk getting you with child, Belle."

"Oh," she said, and fell back on her pillow, feeling foolish and needy—stunned by her behavior as well as embarrassed that he might think of her as being foolish and needy.

"But," he said thoughtfully, looking down at her, "there are ways . . ." He gathered her in his arms and lay down with her again.

He kissed her. After a second's hesitation, she responded to him again. Their kisses grew deeper and soon he was caressing her as though nothing had interrupted them. His hand went between her thighs, but this time he didn't stop. He parted her and kept caressing her, murmuring soft words of encouragement. She stiffened, then relaxed, then caught her breath as a slow strange stirring began to rise in her. She tried to draw away.

"No," he whispered, "Let be. Just let yourself feel it. This will be fine, this will be for you."

She hardly knew what he was saying because she was feeling so much. His hand dipped deeper; she gasped. Then his fingers went higher, then back, maintaining a steady rhythm that moved her with it. The sweet dark throbbing began to spiral upward, all her senses gathered in that one place, and it was beyond anything she'd known. She was astonished when the delicious thrumming ended in a tumultuous, ecstatic burst of feeling.

"There," he said into her ear as she arched upward and gasped. "That's what I meant."

He held her close as her pulses slowly stopped thundering and the thrilling feeling drained away to a soft, languorous glow of satisfaction.

And though he ached with thwarted desire, Miles smiled with his own satisfaction at having done something right. It hadn't been charity, even though he still longed for physical satisfaction, and had to keep his lower body turned so his questing sex didn't disturb her. But not only was she comforted, he hadn't been acting. Because when he'd held her he'd found firm flesh beneath his hands and a strong response on her lips. He'd been further aroused by the realization that she—the proud Lady Annabelle—had wanted him badly. He was relieved, though his body was still aching. There'd be time ahead for him. A lifetime, now.

He tried to relax, but felt her move restlessly. He'd thought he'd brought her peace. Yet now she raised herself on one elbow and looked down into his face. She was frowning.

Had he shocked her? He'd have to explain that it was no shame, he realized. He'd have to teach her there were still other ways to bring pleasure between men and women, and decent people did practice them. Just as some men preferred quick couplings, he knew many saved their sexual skills for their mistresses. He was trying to frame the words to explain this when she spoke.

"But you," she said, "there was nothing for you in this. What can I do?"

She never stopped surprising him. That she'd even thought of his pleasure gave him deep pleasure.

"Oh, you can do many things, many delightful things," he said, touching a finger to her nose. "But not tonight, I think. You're tired and it is late. I'd rather have us both seeking pleasure at the same time anyway. Otherwise, I'd feel too much like a schoolmaster giving lessons, more of an object than an object of desire."

She settled against his chest again. "Yes," she muttered as she splayed one small hand over his heart, "Just as women so often do."

He covered her hand with his and smiled. So she hadn't forgotten, or forgiven, their argument about women and men, the one that had started all this. Good for her. She stirred against him, trying to make herself more comfortable, and he felt himself stirring again.

"On the other hand . . ." he said slowly, "since that may have to be a while from now, perhaps we might reconsider having that lesson now."

"A while from now?" she asked, suddenly alert.

"Yes," he murmured, as his hand slid down her back to the gentle curve of her buttocks. "When I come back from London and—"

"When you come back from London?!" she squeaked and sat straight up.

He sighed and tried to quell his rising expectations. He'd said one thing too much, or at least at the wrong time, and now he knew there'd be no time for more lessons tonight.

Chapter 15

"I didn't mention it before because I don't want to go and have been putting it off. But I can't any longer. Some things can't be done by letter," Miles explained as Annabelle sat up against her pillow, arms crossed over her breasts, frowning at him. "For example, I've been using my seafaring background to build my—our future. I know ships, as well as their captains' reputations, which foreign ports they go to, and what products can be bought cheaply there. I try to keep up on how high goods can sell here so I can invest in their ventures. And I've sailed enough to know tides and weather cycles, so I can predict when storms are likely to come, and what hazards can crop up to delay any shipmaster from honoring his contracts.

"A letter can't possibly tell me what an afternoon in a tavern by the docks in London can. The gossip of able-bodied seamen becomes news on the financial market in a day. I need that extra day. Because of that, and other business I have in London, I must be there. At least, I can't leave London for so long a time. I never intended to, but our honeymoon took a bit longer than anticipated."

He smiled at her. She didn't smile back at him.

"We'll be going back for Camille's come-out in September," she said angrily.

"Yes, but September's in a week, Belle."

She blinked.

"Time has moved on," he continued carefully, seeing how stunned she was by what he'd said. "You're not ready to go back yet, but I have to, if only for a little while. We may have changed our plans, but some things can't wait."

"But Camille . . ."

"Camille will keep. She can make her bows in the spring."

Annabelle stayed silent. Miles placed a light kiss on her cheek, and lay down again. He pulled up the coverlets and turned to a comfortable position. It had been a difficult thing to tell her, but it was done. "Now go to sleep," he said. "We'll talk about it more in the morning." He closed his eyes and welcomed the drowsiness that would lead to sleep.

Annabelle remained sitting upright. "No," she finally said into the darkness.

His eyes opened.

"I have to go back to London," he murmured sleepily. "I'll come back soon as I can. You'll be fine here. Now sleep."

"No," she said. "I'm coming too. And so is Camille. And that's that."

"Belle," he said wearily, "you were upset by such a small thing tonight, just a matter of your cap slipping. London's filled with unkind people who live on gossip, the more false it is, the better. You look fine to me, but obviously your standards for yourself are higher. How will you cope with that? Better if you leave it until next spring, when everything will be as it was again."

"I promised Camille this autumn," she said. "I lost track of time, but it has marched on, and so will I. I may not look as I'd wish, but I can deal with it. If you can." Before he could answer, she went on, "I won't stay alone here, hiding my head under a . . . toque," she said with loathing.

He chuckled. "You have time. I won't leave for a week. You can meet me in town later, if you wish. You don't have to make any decision now. In fact, it would be better not to say anything to Camille or Mama until you're sure of what you'll do."

He closed his eyes again and was on the brink of sleep when she spoke again.

"I'll pack," she said.

"As you wish," he mumbled. "But do you think you could go to sleep first?"

The room was silent.

"Perhaps it would be best to wait," Annabelle said.

"Whatever," Miles murmured. "Whatever makes you happy."

She lay down, curled up against his broad warm back, and eventually heard his breathing become deeper. He radiated heat, and she was tempted to drift off to sleep beside him. But she had too many questions to think about that no one could answer but herself.

Was she ready to go back?

The thought terrified her. She was no longer beautiful. Gossip about that was undoubtedly already on its way to London. People would certainly hear of her altered appearance. If she returned too soon she'd only give them more to chatter about. But if she never regained her looks, what sense was there in waiting?

Still, though Miles had been joking, the truth was that if she stayed away when he returned, rumor would make people think she'd really become some kind of gargoyle. If she waited, she might be able to make her return a triumph. But she couldn't even be sure of that.

The alternative was to stay here with Miles's distant mother and disappointed sister. Bernard would be gone back to school. It would just be the three of them and the staff of servants. There'd be no pressure on her, and she could continue to recover in peace. Hollyfields wasn't a bad place.

But it would be empty without Miles. And she'd promised Camille her Season. It had already been delayed once before. Camille had done so much for her, she deserved her reward. Moreover, Annabelle knew how she herself would feel if such a treat was snatched from her.

Her parents were in London too. She longed to see them. Her father would know the right things to say, her mother, the right things to do for her. She smiled, thinking about how protective her mother was. If people gossiped, her mother would be there to support her; she'd only have to be careful that Mama didn't call anyone out for saying something rude.

Her grin faded. But they would gossip about her. And Camille could wait until spring.

And meanwhile, Miles would be in London, in a city filled with diversion, parties, balls, plays, concerts—and beautiful women everywhere, highborn and lowborn, with high and low morals too. There were women she'd hear about, many more she'd never know he consorted with. Women who were beautiful as well as discreet. London was filled with demireps and courtesans, actresses and playful wives, all sorts of available women who knew how to keep an affair secret . . .

But the other choice was to let him see those same women, and then look at her and really see how she compared, honestly see what she now looked like. It was one thing to be attractive to him when she was the only available female in sight . . . another to face such competition without anything to wage battle with.

He was right, Annabelle thought. It was a decision that would take time. The only question was: Did she have that time?

Annabelle was pale and heavy lidded at breakfast. She hadn't slept much. Miles said she had a week to make up her mind, but she hated indecisiveness and delay of any kind. One moment she was ready to leave, and the next, she wanted to hide until she looked good enough to be seen. Since her emotions were as variable as a weather vane, she didn't want to speak too soon. Who better than she to know how life could change the best of plans?

She was grateful that she didn't have a chance to say anything, because the family was busily gossiping about the party the night before. They carefully didn't mention Annabelle's accident with her toque or her meeting with her old acquaintances, but they couldn't stop talking about all their friends, or how Camille's popularity would doubtless ensure her triumph when she went to London.

"Now, much as I'd like to linger and keep talking about Camille's prospects, I have go play lord of the manor," Miles said when he'd finished his breakfast. He grinned as Camille stuck her tongue out at him, and rose from the table. "First, I must see Thomson, who has a problem with his roof. Then I promised to stop off at Driscoll's place. He's got a new pair of foals he wants to show me. I'll be back by tea."

"Oh! Can I come?" Camille asked eagerly. "I want a look too. I heard they're showing great potential."

"Good idea," Bernard said, on an exaggerated yawn. "Think I'll come along too."

"Try keeping you away!" Camille laughed. "What he wants to look at is Mary," she told Annabelle. "She's Driscoll's daughter, just turned sixteen, and is showing more than potential—as Bernard just noticed last night."

"Surely you're too young to think of anything serious, Bernard?" Alyce said, looking up from her plate.

"It's the horses I want to see," Bernard insisted. "How can I be serious about them? It's not like I have any money. My allowance wouldn't buy me a flea on a horse," he added, looking sulkily at his brother.

"You have money, and then you had money," Miles said. "That's how it always goes with you. The amount doesn't matter." He bent and kissed

Annabelle's cheek. "Now, I'm off," he told his brother and sister. "If you want to come along, get your hats."

Within minutes, the breakfast room was empty except for Annabelle and Alyce.

Annabelle prepared to make some excuse and leave. She was always uncomfortable with Miles's mother, more so this morning. It might have been an accident last night when Alyce brought Damon and his party to see her at the precisely wrong moment. But Annabelle would never be sure.

"Annabelle, my dear," Alyce said, looking up at her. Annabelle was startled to see tears swimming in her faded eyes. "Can you forgive me for last night? I never meant to hurt your feelings, and I feel so foolish and stupid for forcing those people on you. Please forgive me."

"Of course I do," Annabelle lied. "Please put it behind you."

"I wish I could put so much behind me! Oh, this is so difficult! It ought not to be, and I know that, which only makes it harder. I suppose I could ask you to go for a walk in the gardens with me, or ask you to my sitting room. But I never have done, have I? So that would look peculiar, and I most definitely want our conversation to be natural and easy." She sighed. "That was another mistake I hope you'll pardon me for. You must think me a hard, cruel woman. But my first priority is my children and I realize that in being so involved with them, I've never shown you the true hand of friendship. For that, I also earnestly beg your forgiveness!"

Annabelle spontaneously took the older woman's thin, cool hand in hers. "I'd most earnestly forgive you for that," she said, "but there's nothing to forgive."

"Little you know," Alyce said on a broken laugh. "I, of all people should have realized how it must have felt for you to return to us in the condition that you did. I was once beautiful myself, you see, though you'd hardly credit it now."

"Oh no. What foolishness! You're still lovely," Annabelle said. "Anyone can see you must have been a great beauty in your youth."

Alyce lifted her chin. "So I was. But now . . ."

Annabelle protested again. "You're still a lovely woman," she said, but as she did she felt a queer sensation of having heard it all before. She had, she realized with dismay: every time Miles reassured her that she was still attractive. Every time, she realized, that she insisted he do so, the way Alyce was doing now.

It wasn't a pleasant feeling.

And why did Alyce only apologize for not recognizing how hard it had been to lose her looks? Why not for not helping her get accustomed to her new home? Didn't she realize that a new wife coming to a strange home to start a new life after being so desperately sick had been just as distressing as losing her looks?

Perhaps, Annabelle thought guiltily now, because it *hadn't* been as important to her.

"You're very kind," Alyce said. "And in that spirit . . . Oh dear, how shall I say this? I want to ask a favor of you, but I don't deserve any favors from you."

Annabelle was taken aback. Real tears were coursing down Alyce's thin cheeks now. This was far removed from the woman she'd thought she knew. "Tell me," Annabelle said, leaning forward. "What can I do for you?"

"It's a matter of funds," Alyce said.

Annabelle stared.

"Money," Alyce went on, withdrawing her hand so she could dab at her cheeks with a handkerchief. "Yes. How ridiculous! But you see, last night I did something I never do. Since you and Miles were watching over Camille, I was free to wander. I agreed to a friendly game of chance with some local women. Well! Little did I realize that they were familiar with each other's skills as I was not, and that they'd set out to make money from me. So I lost a great deal. I didn't have that kind of money on my person, of course, and so offered my vouchers. Now, in all honor, I'm expected to pony up, as the gentlemen say."

Annabelle laughed. "That's not such a very great thing."

"Oh, I'm afraid it is. My household money doesn't begin to cover it, even if I include the little bit I've put by. I'd never have lowered myself enough to ask you if it weren't essential—"

"Of course," Annabelle interrupted, because she was becoming embarrassed by the woman's neediness, "I'll give you the money—"

"Loan," Alyce said quickly.

"Yes, but why not just ask Miles? I think he'd be very amused."

Alyce turned pale. "Oh no. Please don't tell him. I know it sounds silly, but I prefer he not know I was such a fool." She looked down and murmured, "As you know, I did a very foolish thing by marrying a man I ought never to have trusted. In fact, that's the reason you're here, isn't it? To help repair that damage."

She slid a glance at Annabelle, who had grown very still.

But Annabelle was caught between unhappiness and confusion. She didn't like being reminded why Miles had married her, and wondered if Alyce was trying to befriend her or alienate her.

"I've spent the last years trying to repair my reputation with my children, as well as the world," Alyce went on. "Not paying what I owe in the neighborhood would be devastating to our name. They'd think I was just like Peter—my last husband—had been. Telling Miles I lost that sum of money through my own foolishness would devastate me. But you hardly know me, so it is easier to ask it of you."

Annabelle was too puzzled to speak right away. This was the strangest interview. The woman was both asking for friendship and holding her at arm's length at the same time. But perhaps that was the only way a woman of such pride could ask for a favor. "Very well," she said. "I'll give you the money. How much is it?"

Alyce named a sum that made Annabelle gasp. "But I don't have that kind of money!" Annabelle said. "Good Lord! How could you lose so much so fast?"

Alyce shrugged her shoulders. "They played for high stakes. And I suppose they thought the lady of the manor could well afford it—although you are that lady now, aren't you?"

Annabelle was doing sums in her head. "I never needed money, every tradesman knew me, and if not, I could sign my name for everything," she murmured. "Of course, I usually had some small sum with me, for this and that. And my mama did give me a neat sum before my wedding day, because she worries about me so much. Well, I have most of what you'll need. But not all."

"Surely you could ask Miles?" Alyce said. "He

owes you a deal of pin money, doesn't he? You couldn't have spent anything while you were ill, and he's a very generous man."

"I suppose," Annabelle muttered, still trying to balance figures in her head.

"Good, then he can give you even more. I knew I could count on you." Alyce rose from the table. She looked down at Annabelle. "I hope you keep faith and don't tell him a word of this. I should know it if you did, you know. He could never keep a secret from me. Oh. And if I could have the money by tonight? Thank you, my dear. I feel so much better now."

Then she wafted from the room, leaving Annabelle to sit baffled and vaguely angry, with no one to tell and nothing to do but swallow her pride and ask her husband for money. She knew it was hers to ask for. But that wasn't the same as making it an easy thing to do. She, unlike her mother-in-law, hated to ask for favors, especially since her husband had been nothing but charitable to her since she'd married him.

"Oho. So that's why you married me," Miles teased when Annabelle, pink-cheeked and hesitant, finally asked him for the money that evening as they were preparing to go down to dinner. "You're a fortune hunter. Don't look at me like that. I'm joking," he said, putting his hands on her shoulders and shaking her gently. "You could have married the Golden Ball and I know it. I've been a dunce. Of course you need your own funds. I should have given you an allowance immediately. As soon as I get to London I'll set up things with Mr. Greer, my banker. Then you won't have to come to me for money. Just apply to him. Now, how much do you need straightaway?"

She told him.

His eyebrow rose. But he cut off whatever she was about to add. "Fine," he said. "Do you need it now?"

She nodded.

He seemed puzzled, but let her go and went to his wardrobe. He opened a drawer and took out his wallet. "No," he said, as he sorted through it, "I don't carry that kind of money, but I do have it in the safe downstairs. You need it tonight?"

"Yes," she said, now ruddy-cheeked. "Please. So I don't have to remind you, or ask you again. This is hard enough for me!"

"I'll go down and get it. I'll be right back. Is that soon enough? Oh, Belle," he said more gently. He came to her and pulled her into his arms again. "Such a proud lady," he whispered into her ear. "Don't look so miserable. I'm the one who ought to be embarrassed for not thinking of it first."

"Do you give your mama and Camille an allowance?" she asked, trying to sound casual about the question.

"I do," he said, and told her how much.

Her eyes widened. She wouldn't worry about Alyce's finances again, though she wondered how such a restrained woman had allowed herself to go wild and play so deep.

"All right? You're assured that everyone in your world is now fiscally sound?" He chuckled. "I'll be right back," he said, released her, and went out the door.

Annabelle sighed. She hated keeping anything from him; it felt like cheating. But she was buying her mother-in-law's friendship. Perhaps one day she could tell him about it, and they'd laugh. Or sigh. As long as they did it together.

Miles returned with the money and handed it to Annabelle. She accepted it gingerly, as though it were tainted.

He didn't know what to say, for she looked beyond embarrassed—she looked ill again. "Here, now," he said softly, putting a finger under her chin and tipping up her downcast head. "Pride is all very well, but I am supposed to support you, you know. I'm the one who ought to be ashamed. I should have made provisions for you immediately. You never should have had to ask it of me."

"Thank you," she said quietly.

"Well," he said, looking uncomfortable, "speaking of funds, I think I'll just go down and have a word with Bernard about his latest requests. They're nothing like yours, my dear. You don't have a heavy hand on the dice and too many on the cards, as he does." He chuckled. "Put away your money and your sad face, Belle; I'll see you at dinner."

When he left, Annabelle went to her bureau and took out the small store of money she'd stowed in a leather purse. She added the notes Miles had given her and closed it. Then she went to the door, opened it slowly, and looked down the hall. Seeing no one, she stepped out, and holding the money close to her breast, she went swiftly down the hall to Alyce's bedchamber.

She tapped on the door. Then she stepped back in surprise, because Alyce herself, and not her maidservant, immediately cracked open the door.

"I saw Miles go down on the way to his study," Alyce whispered. "I've been expecting you. Do you have it?"

Annabelle held out the packet.

"Good," Alyce said, taking it. "Thank you," she said briskly, and closed the door in Annabelle's face.

Annabelle gaped at the closed door, as hurt as she was puzzled. Then she straightened. She took a deep breath, then turned, her face burning, and marched toward the stair.

She'd paid a great deal of money but it was worth it. It had bought her a decision.

* * *

Dinner was even livelier than usual that night. Camille couldn't stop praising the twin foals they'd seen that morning and started a spirited conversation on their merits and prospects. Conversation at Miles's table never flagged, which was one of the things that Annabelle discovered she liked very much about her new family. They talked almost as much as her own mother did.

It wasn't until later, during a brief silence as Camille and Bernard fell on their desserts, that Annabelle could make her announcement.

"Guess what?" she told Camille gaily. "It was to be a surprise but I can't hold it in a moment longer. We're going to London next week! With Miles."

Miles cocked his head to the side and looked at his wife as Camille gasped. "Oh, that's jolly good news!" she caroled, "Isn't it, Mama?"

Alyce looked politely surprised.

Bernard began complaining about being sent off to school with such fun in the offing.

Annabelle shot a glance at Miles. She was delighted to see that he was smiling back at her, looking pleased with her decision.

"I'll need Nancy to come with me, Miles," Camille was saying. "I have to have her. Mama wants to get me a fine French maid, but I'd be lost without my Nancy. She knows my likes, and what I don't like is having to please a new maid as well as the rest of the new world I'll be meeting. At least let me be comfortable at home. Say I can bring her, please?"

"I don't have to be at school early," Bernard was insisting, "I can go to London first with you, can't I?"

"How delightful," Alyce's cool voice cut in. "I must immediately start to get things in train for such an unexpected journey. Bernard, you will certainly go to school. Don't you agree, Miles? Camille, you don't have to bother your brother. I never said you couldn't bring Nancy, only that we will need to have your hair done by someone expert, in London. Oh, and Miles, I shall need extra funds to get such things done quickly. There will be many such expensive necessities, and so I'll require a great deal of money too, I'm afraid."

"You can put it all on my account, as usual, Mother," Miles said wryly. "My credit is very good, even in London."

"But I shall need a great deal for the little things, since there will be a great many of them," Alyce said.

Annabelle shot a look at her, but the older woman didn't acknowledge it by so much as a blink.

"It's all very well that your credit is good, but I shall need cash funds," Alyce went on. "Gratuities for servants, pourboires for dressmakers, incentives for them to get gowns fitted faster. A bit more

money can get one shown the best fabrics, and the
latest acquisitions at any glovers or mantua mak-
ers. Extra bits for extra service, you know the sort
of thing."

"Thank God, I do not." Miles laughed. "But
don't worry, I'll see you well financed for
Camille's assault on the town."

"London!" Camille crooned. "I can't wait to be
there!"

Annabelle gave her mother-in-law a curious
look before she said, "No, neither can I." And
meant it.

Chapter 16

S he couldn't believe she could be so happy
again. She didn't know if she deserved to be
this happy, but Annabelle felt as if she were flying
instead of riding in a coach on the way to London.
She was still alive after being almost dead, and
she grew stronger every day. She'd married for
convenience and to save face, and discovered herself married to a man who was becoming more
important to her every day. He was handsome,
clever, and kind. His touch made her feel things
she never imagined, and his words healed her
spirit. Most amazing of all, it seemed he approved
of her even though she was no longer a beauty or
toast of the town she was now driving through.
And now she was in her heart's home once more.

There'd been a time when she'd thought she'd never see it again.

It didn't matter if she had to hide, this was a place where she could hide and see.

"London!" Annabelle exulted, staring out the coach window. "Just look! Isn't it wonderful?"

"All that enthusiasm! But it's nothing new to you," Miles said with a smile. "That's for Camille to say."

"I'm too boggled to speak," Camille breathed from the other window, watching the traffic, the street criers, the crowds of people, all the bustle and commotion of noonday London.

"I never get tired of seeing it," Annabelle said. "Look! It's just the same, even though I've been gone for what seems like forever!"

Miles's smile faded.

"But it isn't the same now," Alyce told Annabelle gently. "At least not for you, my dear."

Miles's head swung around, he stared hard at his mother.

"My goodness!" she said, one hand to her heart. "What a fierce expression. What did you think I meant, Miles? I was only reminding Annabelle that she's a married woman now. I was not remarking on how her looks have changed, only her marital state. Still glowering at me? Oh my! You never think I'm commenting on her reputation for flirting? I know she'll be the most faithful of wives. Oh dear, I'm only making it worse, aren't I?" Her eyes began to water. "One has to watch one's every word these days," she mumbled into a handkerchief. "And that only makes matters worse. It makes me misspeak. I'd never intentionally hurt your wife's feelings."

Not when you do so well unintentionally, Annabelle thought, as Miles said wearily, "I know, please don't cry, Mama."

"He's right," Annabelle said, "Don't fuss, Mrs . . . Proctor," she said, hoping she'd remembered the name correctly. "I understood exactly what you meant."

The other woman's eyes widened. " 'Mrs. Proctor'?"

Annabelle hid a grimace. "Should you rather I call you Mother too?" she asked quickly.

"Oh my dear, but that makes me feel ancient."

"Then what would you have me call you?" Annabelle asked, wondering if she was the only one to think this was a very strange conversation to be having after three months of marriage to the woman's son. But now she realized she'd never addressed her by name before, or had any cause to do so. Their conversations were brief, impersonal, and infrequent.

"Variations of mama won't do, for you have a mama," Alyce said. "And as you know, my marriage to Mr. Proctor was not the happiest. I should rather you didn't call me that. Alyce would be fine, don't you think?"

"Alyce, then," Annabelle said, privately vowing to go on as she had been, and never to speak to the woman using any name unless she had to. Alyce had accepted the money Annabelle gave her with only a brief thanks. Then she'd said a cool good night. She'd never mentioned the matter again. But if Annabelle had hoped her favor would win favor, she was very wrong. Nothing had changed between the two of them, except their location.

"Is that Hyde Park we're passing?" Camille asked excitedly. "I can't wait to go riding in it. Is it true the best of the bloods can be seen there?"

"Yes, the Corinthians," Miles said, "as well as other fashionable and would-be fashionable men."

"No," Camille said with a laugh. "I meant the horses, not the gents!"

Annabelle and Miles exchanged amused looks, but Alyce scolded her daughter. "The *first* thing you must do is get the right clothes so you can even set foot out the door. We've come to introduce you to society, which was your brother's entire purpose in mar—" She caught herself and, looking at Annabelle, went on, "making the move to bring you to London, after all."

"Well, that's all right and tight," Camille said smugly. "Belle knows all the best places to go to get me spruced up. I'll get togged out like a royal princess in no time. Then can we go to the park, Belle? I don't want to stop our walks even though my rotten brother would only let me take two dogs to London. Both Muffin and Rags will need the exercise as much as we do."

Annabelle didn't dare look at Miles, but knew he must be suppressing a smile too. She wondered what Alyce would say about Camille's plan. A lady could stroll in the park with a pug in her arms or a small spaniel or terrier on a lead. Muffin and Rags were endearing names, but the actual dogs were two big, rangy country-bred retrievers that Camille had saved from extinction. They were too enthusiastic for the hunt and not steady enough for any kind of work. But they were, even so, the best behaved of Camille's kennel.

"No," Alyce said, as Annabelle had expected. But what she said next made Annabelle go rigid. "Annabelle cannot, or rather ought not go with you. The purpose of this visit is to make you acceptable to the *ton.*"

Miles's expression grew thunderous as his mother went on obliviously, "Our Annabelle's appearance will cause so much talk that you will be quite overlooked, I'm afraid."

"Mother!" Miles roared.

Camille appeared stricken and looked to Annabelle for help.

"No, she's right," Annabelle said, putting up a hand to silence Miles. "I agree. In fact, I made my plans accordingly. I want Camille to have the best time of her life and find a good husband too. But if her entry on the scene is in the shadow of the appearance of the once beautiful, now ravaged Lady Annabelle, it will definitely be overlooked. I know," she told him, "I'm not a gargoyle. But I will be commented on, and you know it. It's not something I look forward to, and in truth, I'm not sure I can bear it just yet. Don't worry, I won't go into hiding, at least not for very long."

He stared at her.

She shook her head. "Miles, I wouldn't have come here if I planned to do that. It's just that I'd rather make my grand reentrance after Camille does. I think that would be better even if I hadn't . . . had such an interesting illness. At any rate, I might be myself again by the time we introduce Camille. If so, I'll go with her, and that way I'll squash all gabble about me so people can concentrate on her instead. And if not? Well, whatever I am, and however I look," she said with some of her old arrogance, "I'll deal with it. In the meanwhile, we can do it all anyway. Camille can be outfitted without me being seen with her. The modistes can bring fabrics and patterns to our house, and—"

"But I wanted to go with you to see the shops and the models and everything you told me about," Camille wailed. "The fashions don't mean that much to me. I wanted to have fun talking about it with you! You'd know all the people too, so you could tell me about them, and we'd have such a good time together. Mama, you're game to go, I know," she said before her mother could protest. "But Belle knows so much more about what's fashionable right now."

"I can certainly learn," Alyce said stiffly.

"I have the best idea!" Annabelle said, warding off the coming storm. "I know a woman who knows everything about the latest fashions and is a wonderful judge of style, as well as being good company who knows all the latest gossip too. Not only does she have a lot of time on her hands, but she said she'd like to take charge of your come-out. I planned to see her this afternoon if we came in on time. You can come with me. And best of all," she added as Alyce realized who she was talking about and fell silent, "no one can say my mama will overshadow you."

Camille grinned.

Miles suppressed the urge to applaud.

Annabelle was as nervous about her appointment with Harry Selfridge as she was about meeting anyone she knew on the way to see him. She'd scheduled a time when he promised there would be no other patients waiting. Even so, Annabelle wore a long pelisse and a coal scuttle bonnet that hid most of her face, and she scurried from her carriage to the office in his neat town house. Miles came with her, for he wouldn't hear of her going alone.

Harry's nurse, a tall, thin, dour female, went to tell him of Annabelle and Miles's arrival. The surgeon came out of his office at once and greeted them anxiously.

"My lady," he said, taking Annabelle's hand, trying to peer into the recesses of the shadow of her bonnet. "Please come into my consultation room and tell me what pains you."

"I'm not in any pain," she said at once, then laughed. "Well, perhaps I am, but it's only my conceit that hurts now. I've lost my looks, and I'm such a vain creature that it nearly kills me!"

"Let me see," he said seriously. "If you'd come into my consultation room, take off your bonnet and your coat, so I may?"

Annabelle nodded.

"Miles, would you rather wait outside?" Harry asked.

"Must I?" he asked in return.

The doctor looked at Annabelle.

"There isn't much my husband hasn't seen," she said sadly. "No sense in my hiding from him now."

Harry's consultation room was dominated by a long wooden examining table. It also held a bureau with all his implements on view, and a long cabinet with dozens of bottles of liquids, dusty compounds, and what looked like bits of vegetables and seeds. Sunlight streamed in through long tall windows and a skylight overhead. Annabelle's nostrils pinched at the strong scent of some

herbal potion that filled the room, and her eyes
narrowed at the sight of all the medical tools. But
she let Miles help her off with her pelisse. She took
off her bonnet, averted her eyes from the evil-
looking physician's devices laid out on the top of
the bureau, and then stood, head down, in the
sunlight.

Miles dug his hands into his pockets and
waited, trying to see her as the doctor did. She'd
looked healthier to him these past weeks than she
did now. Now, silent, stripped of her personality,
she looked only as she physically was, with none
of her airs and graces to divert him. She seemed
very different, and he was appalled that he'd allowed her to come to London at all.

Her head still appeared too large for her slender body, and that proud head looked strangely
pathetic adorned only with the meager fleece that
had grown back in. Miles felt ashamed of having
made any kind of love to her. Clearly, she was a
long way from well.

But Harry was delighted.

"Very good," he said, as he circled around her.
"Excellent! Now, if you'd please take a seat on my
examining table, so I can have a better look?"

Harry listened to her heart and looked at her
hands; he had her cough, he made her flex muscles;
he examined her tongue and the soles of her feet.

"Brilliant!" he said at last, with a proud smile.
"Everything is as it ought to be. Continue what-

ever it is you've been doing. I hope Mrs. Farrow sent along a good amount of her specifics for you to take here in London?"

Annabelle laughed. "A satchel full, and almost another filled with her instructions."

"Good. Be sure to eat plenty of eggs and drink fresh milk, get enough sleep and exercise moderately, and never hesitate to send to me to ask any other questions." He cleared his throat, and avoiding Miles's eye, said, "Your courses are returned and regular again?"

"They have, and are," Annabelle said.

"Very well," Harry said. "I think you should keep up the doses of cod's liver oil to give your hair sheen."

Annabelle made a face.

"I agree," Harry said. "Vile stuff, but effective. Your hair's getting thick, so let's give it back some luster. It will take time, but I see no reason why it shouldn't be exactly as it was before, by Christmas, at the very least."

Annabelle sighed. Autumn had only just started, Christmas seemed a long way off.

"But otherwise, avoid drafts, get sufficient sleep, don't skip meals, and have them at the same time every day," Harry told her. "You may indulge in drink, in moderation. In fact, beer and ale will be good for you. And see me again in another month. Now, I'll let you put on your hat again—though letting sun and air on your scalp will do you more good. Miles, I know you've seen all, but at least you can let your lady put herself to rights by herself?"

Miles grinned and went out the door with Harry. Once the door closed, he turned to his friend. "Now, tell me," he said seriously, "is what you told her the truth?"

Harry looked affronted. "I never lie to my patients, unless they're going to die, of course. Doesn't help to tell them that. But your lady is doing wonderfully well."

Miles cleared his throat. "Well enough for . . . marital matters?"

"Oh," Harry said, looking at his friend with an odd expression.

"What's the matter?" Miles asked.

"Nothing to do with your lady," Harry said quickly. "It's just that I've never known you to be so mealymouthed when it comes to sexual matters. And you a navy man! Marriage certainly has changed you."

"If and when you stop chuckling," Miles said sourly, "do you suppose you might answer me?"

"No, I know of no impediments. She was sick, but she's not now."

"Not well enough for childbearing though."

"Oh, you have a medical practice now?" Harry asked archly. "I'd no idea. But no, I never said that. She's healthy, if not in the pink of health as she was when you married her. But if you choose to wait, I don't have to tell you the alternatives that can bring you some surcease, and your lady similar comfort, if she wants that, of course. Otherwise, I'd suggest you find another ... well, never mind what I'd suggest," he added, as Miles's expression grew thunderous.

"Then, too," Harry went on, "often a husband's attentions will do wonders for a woman's spirits. And she did say her vanity was bruised." He looked at Miles. "Shall I spell it out, or would you prefer a book? I have a little volume put by for just such occasions, with illustrations too. It's by an ancient Hindu chap. It's not for the ladies, but it is, in a way."

"Ah, the Sutra," Miles said. "Good Lord, Harry, do you think you had to tell me about that? I read it back at Eton—no—I memorized it then, like most of us. And as you recall, I do have a certain history." He hesitated. "So, such activities won't set back her recuperation?"

"Not if she enjoys them. On the other hand, if she doesn't ... If you'd like, my nurse can speak to her."

"No need," Miles said quickly, "I assure you there's no need for that. Quite the contrary."

Harry smiled. "Very good! There are some physicians who claim gently bred ladies shouldn't be taxed by such things as ecstasy. My wife thinks such men shouldn't be allowed to live. And she is, I remind you, even more gently bred than I am!"

Miles laughed, but not because of his friend's jest. He was so relieved he couldn't stop smiling.

"So, I'm really doing well!" Annabelle exclaimed when she opened the door to see him grinning so widely.

"So you are," he said tenderly. "And so you will continue to be, I promise you."

"Where were you all day?" Annabelle scolded Miles, putting down her hairbrush to glower at him as he entered their bedroom. She tended her newly growing hair with patience and sorrow, brushing it every night, watching to see if it had grown another millimeter during the day. Miles thought it made her look piquant, and told her so.

"You'd say anything to get me in your bed," she scoffed. "But where were you?"

"Business, as I told you. Now, about that business of our bed?"

She held out her arms to him.

He laughed and scooped her up. "Yes, time for Dr. Pelham's miraculous remedy," he said as he carried her to their bed.

In the week since Harry had said she was improving nicely, Miles had come into her eager arms every night. Each night he made gentle, if incomplete, love to her, withholding his own release, but making sure to bring her peace so she could drift off easily afterward.

He hadn't asked her for more, even though there was so much more he desired of her.

Now, laughing, Miles followed her down to their bed. He flung off his clothes and they fell together. As they'd done every night since he'd first touched her again, they kissed and caressed, his hands and mouth eventually bringing her release. But she didn't fall asleep immediately afterward, as she usually did.

"There's more I can do for you," she finally said in a troubled whisper as they lay in each other's arms. "You admitted as much, and so I've heard tell."

"Indeed?" he asked carefully, "And who was it you heard tell of it?" He had a vision of Harry's dour nurse lecturing her and could swear he felt his private parts growing cold.

"At home," she said, avoiding his eyes, "the servants. And at parties, and such, other women gossiping. They spoke of ways in which a gentleman could be . . . made satisfied, other than by doing . . . that."

He grinned, delighted by her question. "So there are other ways," he said, trying to keep his voice as cool as he no longer was. "Are you sure you want to know more?"

She nodded, her short curls tickling his chin.

"What you do for me," she said in a small voice, addressing his collarbone, "I can do for you, can I not?"

"Such an advanced student, or should I say eavesdropper? But yes, you can, in a way. Very well, we'll get on with that tomorrow night if you wish. There's a good deal of anatomy involved, as well as some Latin studies and a soupçon of French, as you probably heard."

She giggled. Nervously, he thought. "Come, love," he said softly, "it's not so bad." He took her hand in his and guided it to himself, closing her fingers over his rising sex for the first time.

It was difficult to say which of them was more startled at her touch.

"There," he whispered huskily. "It can't be so terrible, can it? After all, I have to do the same at least four times a day."

Her laughter relaxed her; her touch became bolder. She explored his reactions with rising interest. He gritted his teeth in rising pleasure. She found it fascinating, his skin warm and smooth, this part of him as strong as the rest of his body, but so much more sensitive.

He kissed her, and drew her close again. "Yes," he said, closing his hand tightly over hers to show her how to set a rhythm. "Like that, and faster, please."

She was astonished and delighted at the pleasure she brought him, and how powerful that made her feel. But she was puzzled. "Miles?" she said later, as his heartbeat slowed again. "Why don't you just come to me? I mean, as you did on our wedding night?"

"Because you're still too weak for childbearing."

"Harry didn't tell me so. Did he tell you that?"

"He didn't have to. When you look ready to fling me over your shoulder, you'll be ready to bear my child. And that will be soon, he said, so I'd better watch my manners."

"Yes, you'd better." She smiled and curled next to him.

An excellent start, he thought sleepily. Amazing, that she was a different woman when they were in bed together, all veneer of social correctness vanished. He was as pleased and proud that she had insisted on reciprocating tonight, all on her own, without him even having to give her a hint or a command. He'd thought a woman like Annabelle would take his ministrations as her due. Instead, she'd asked how to ease him. Had she changed because of her illness? Or because of his efforts? Was it a change at all; would she have been as generous if she'd never lost her looks? He wouldn't complain, whatever it was. And whatever her reasons, this personal form of treatment was a success. She was glowing. As for himself, he'd found some relief, but even so, thought he might die of frustration.

But he couldn't forget how quickly she'd fallen ill, how close to death she'd been. She wasn't ready for his full attentions, and he was resolved to wait until she was. But certainly, there were other things he could find for them to do. He fell asleep smiling at the thought of them.

"She'll be wearing shell pink, which I thought would be unfortunate with her coloring," Annabelle explained as she and Miles strolled along in Camille's wake, as she strode ahead with her pair of exuberant dogs. "But Mama picked the most subtle shade and had them add a silver over-dress to tone it down, and she looks lovely in it. She'll do us proud."

Miles put a hand over the small gloved one on his arm and smiled down at her. He'd insisted on accompanying them on their walks through the park each morning.

"You need more than a footman with you," he'd told Annabelle. "Besides, I enjoy it. It's practically the only time we have together these days," he'd added with a warm look at her.

"What about the nights?" she'd whispered.

They'd exchanged conspiratorial smiles.

He gazed down at her with pleasure now. She wore a bonnet that hid her hair and showed off her charming profile. She always wore a pelisse on these walks, even on mild days, so no one could notice her figure. But each night he saw and felt how it was rounding out again. Soon, he promised himself . . .

He wasn't surprised by his lust for her, but was astonished at the rush of emotion he now felt when he saw her, the surge of feeling that consumed him when she merely smiled at him in public. He'd married for convenience and had gotten so much more than he'd expected, or knew existed. But he wasn't ready to tell her about that, any more than he was ready to really make love to her again. That, however, wasn't only because of her health, but for his own pride's sake.

They were realistic about why they'd married. She couldn't know that his feelings had changed, not when he was just getting used to the astonishing idea himself. Her feelings, however, might not have changed. She appreciated him now, he knew that. She liked him too, he'd bet on it. His physical attentions obviously pleased her mightily. But he wondered if her heart would ever be involved. Because he very much feared he'd lost his, to her.

That was a thing he'd never reckoned on.

She was a constant wonder. Feminine but brave, clever but wise, and with a well-informed mind. He liked to talk with her, laugh with her, in short, he found himself deeply in love with her, to his great surprise. Still, if she didn't reciprocate his feelings, he couldn't blame her. After all, their marriage had been a bargain. She hadn't broken it. He had. By falling in love with her.

"Camille should be ready for presentation now," Annabelle was saying. She laughed. "It sounds like she's a stuffed goose ready to serve up on a platter, doesn't it? She isn't. She's so lively. We've told her not to bounce around as much, and to watch her tongue, because she will speak like a stable boy. But I really do think she'll cause a stir! . . . Why so glum?" she asked, noting his silence.

"Not glum. Awed. You and your mother are like a pair of sea captains rigged for battle. The men of London don't have a chance. As I didn't."

It was a mild enough comment, but he had trouble keeping a bland expression. He was startled to feel the rims of his ears growing warm as he waited for her response. The absurdity of it astonished him. They were intimate and yet strangers in so many ways. He slept with the woman each night and she received his caresses eagerly. Would she take his tentative words about his feelings with the same glad delight?

"You didn't have a chance?" she asked. "But you weren't looking for a love match." He opened his mouth to tell her what he was thinking, when she added, "As I wasn't, of course."

He closed his lips on the words. Just as he was delaying giving her his body again, he wouldn't give her his soul until he was sure of his welcome.

Out of pride, and because he couldn't forget her reputation. They said she'd toyed with men because she couldn't get the ones she really wanted. They claimed she'd had an acid tongue to go with her lively wit, and used it on unlucky suitors. She'd been famous for her scornful, callous treatment of them.

He'd known all that when he'd married her, but it hadn't mattered then. It did now. He was yoked to her for the rest of their lives. He could, he thought, tolerate her not returning his love. He could not, he knew, bear living with her contempt for it.

"So, tell me," he said casually, "what will you wear?"

"Does it matter?"

"To me, certainly."

"I won't disgrace you," she said, opening her parasol, and hiding even her profile from him.

"No," he said softly, "you will never do that."

Chapter 17

"You think so? You really think so?" Annabelle asked.

"I don't say things I don't mean," Camille said.

"Nor I," Annabelle's mama said.

Alyce said nothing.

Annabelle peered at herself in the mirror again. It had been a long time since she'd done so. But tonight she had good reason. She'd given in to Camille's pleas and was making a public appearance in London for the first time since her marriage and her illness. She didn't want to be pitied, but mostly she didn't want to cause any kind of sensation. That was for Camille to do. And she would.

Camille looked just as she ought, Annabelle thought smugly, like a young girl on her way to meet her prince at a ball. She was still too robust for London's exacting standards of feminine beauty, but she was perfectly gowned, her hair was dressed to set off her face, and that face was radiant. She'd do. Now her new sister-in-law would have to do also. Because if she didn't, she'd ruin Camille's great moment.

Camille had argued that Annabelle's staying home would attract as much gossip as her going to the ball, or more. Annabelle had reluctantly agreed. She knew she didn't have to be ravishing, not that it was even possible. She just wanted to look enough like herself to stop any gossip before it started. Because this was Camille's night.

Annabelle kept looking into the mirror. A small slim woman in a simple dark blue gown kept staring back at her. She looked worried, as well she might be. Her figure was acceptable, but not as rounded at the breasts and arms as was fashionable. The triangular face was white, but at least it wasn't wan. The eyes were very noticeable, large and blue. But the hair was startling, short as a lad's, a welter of tight curls circled by a thin ribbon, looking like the carved marble cap on a stone faun in a classical garden.

This woman wasn't the spectacularly beautiful Lady Annabelle, not by a long shot. But Annabelle didn't care. It was only important that she not be considered outrageous.

She turned from the glass and looked at

Camille, her eyes searching hers. "I'd never do anything to ruin this night for you," she said. "My feelings would be crushed more by that than by staying home. So, please, be honest; tell me if you think I ought to stay home after all. Or if you think a turban would suit me better. I wanted to guide you and be beside you all night. But believe me, first impressions are paramount in the *ton*. My mama and yours can show you how to go on as well as I can, and Miles will be there, as well as my father. So you'll have ample support. I'm married to your poor brother," she said on a forced laugh, "so my future is settled. This night is yours. Should I stay or should I go?"

Camille laughed. "You're coming, my dear Belle, if I have to drag you in to the ballroom by your hair, and it's long enough now for me to do it too. And I will, even if you screech like a banshee. Now, wouldn't that be a fine first impression?"

Annabelle frowned, "Are you sure I wouldn't be better off in a turban?"

"Just ask Miles," Camille said smugly. "Belle"—she laughed again—"you're really going to be the belle of the ball!"

"No," Annabelle said solemnly. "Even if I could, I wouldn't be. That would be you."

They linked arms and went down the long stair, their mamas following. Miles and Annabelle's father were waiting for them.

"What have you done with my sister?" Miles

asked Camille when she reached the bottom of the stair. "Beautiful, wicked creature, bring my sister back to me at once!"

"Do you really think I'll ravish London?" Camille asked.

"Consider it vanquished. But what a lot of work you've given me. Now I'll have start beating your suitors back from the door."

He turned to watch his wife as she greeted her father.

"Look at you!" the earl breathed, holding his daughter's hands as he stepped back to assess her. "I confess I was hurt when you sent word that you'd rather wait until tonight to see me. But no wonder. You wanted to dazzle me. You have. You look better than ever." He took her in his arms and hugged her. "Too thin," he said with a frown as he stepped away again. "Not that it isn't attractive," he added hastily, "but I'm used to more of you."

"Oh, too soon there'll be much more." She laughed, wiping her eyes with the back of her hand.

"Annabelle!" he said in delight. "I'm to be a grandfather?"

"Oh! No!" she said, her eyes widening. "I only meant I've been eating everything in sight."

"Well, I live in hope," he said.

She lowered her head and fussed with her gloves.

"As do we all," Miles said smoothly. "But now we have to go and give London a treat by introducing it to two beautiful young women."

Annabelle looked up at him.

"My sister, for the first time," he said with a smile. "And my lady, who has returned."

"Everyone in London must be here!" Camille crowed as she stood on tiptoe in the crowded entry hall, watching the ball and waiting her turn to be presented to her host and hostess.

"No, just everyone who is anyone in London," Annabelle's mama said complacently.

Annabelle said nothing. She stared straight ahead. But Miles held her hand and could feel it trembling. He knew she was terrified; he fancied he could almost hear her pounding heart and was a little sorry she didn't lean on him in some way. But he admired her courage, as always.

She'd given her wrap to a footman, and now stood as tall as she could. She was beautifully dressed, but there was no question she wasn't the same woman who'd left London with him in the early spring. She was no longer the exquisite little pocket Venus everyone had known and admired. Now she looked charming, but in the style of a gamine. Still, Miles believed he'd never seen her looking better. But he knew he'd think that however she looked because he was prejudiced—and unfortunately, wildly in love with her.

It was important that his sister do well tonight, but he had no concern about Camille. She could take the town by storm by the sheer force of her goodwill. It was his wife Miles worried about. These people and their opinions meant so much to her. He squeezed her hand, and she looked up at him in surprise, as though she'd forgotten he was there. That hurt him. More than that, it made him realize that they had a far way to go, however this evening turned out.

He found himself as nervous as Annabelle must be, for her sake. When they were announced, he put her hand on his arm, and with his sister on the other, strolled into the ballroom.

The brilliantly lit room was crowded with people dressed as magnificently as only they could afford to. Warm floral scents from the bowers of banked flowers filled the air, as did music played by musicians high on a balcony overlooking the room. Their melodies competed with conversation and laughter. Miles relaxed; it seemed impossible for one tiny person to make much of an instant impression in this assembly.

But his wife did.

Miles saw all heads turn in their direction. He heard conversation falter and stop. He saw all the avid eyes on her, and in that moment, hated every one of them.

But Annabelle's expression didn't change. She

wore a slight smile as she stared right back. Seeing her, Miles lost whatever remained of his heart to his wife forever.

The first to approach them was Damon Ryder and his wife, Gilly. Miles tensed. Did the man know what he said would have enormous weight with her? Miles almost wished he'd carried out his first impulse, which was to call on all her old acquaintances in secret and beg them to compliment her when she appeared. A lively fear of what she'd say and do if she ever found out prevented him. But now he was more afraid for her.

"My lady," Damon Ryder said, bowing over her hand. "I see you've recovered completely. But you've reinvented yourself while you were at it. You look wonderful."

"I love your hair!" Gilly Ryder said.

Annabelle's hand began to go to her close-cropped curls and then fell back. Miles wondered if she thought she was being patronized, or ridiculed. So did he.

"Hark! What's that I hear?" the lanky Earl of Drummond drawled as he and his countess strolled over to join them. "Why, I do believe it's the sound of dozens of scissors snipping. My lady," he said as he bowed over her hand, "I believe you'll keep the hairdressers of London busy for weeks as every woman in the *ton* starts shearing her hair off. My love," he said to his wife, "kindly inform me before you do, because I think few women can wear the style as this lady does."

His wife smiled. " 'Not to worry, Drum," she said. "I wish I could wear my hair like that, but it wouldn't work for me."

"Yes," her husband agreed, "but it's charming on Lady Pelham. It's an improvement on the classic 'victime' hairstyle of the last generation, isn't it," he asked Annabelle, taking out his quizzing glass for a better look. "What do you call it?"

"Well, I was a victim," she said lightly, "but I'd call it the resurrection, because I got it when they thought I'd die if I did not."

"Half the women in the room will die if they don't get it!" Gilly Ryder vowed. "I wish I had curls, I'd crop my head if I could look like you." She ran her fingers through her cornsilk hair and scowled. "But I'd just look bald. How clever of you!"

"Lady Annabelle is always clever," a red-haired military-looking gentleman said. Annabelle stiffened, suspecting mockery. Rafe Dalton had been one of her flirts. She'd treated him very badly once, in a fit of pique. And then again, to get even with him for marrying another. He was said to be an honorable man, but she braced herself for insult, or worse.

"We worried about you," he told her, his expression sincere. "It's good to see you again."

"Yes, it is," his lovely wife said with a warm smile.

"It's not just the hair," a deep voice commented. The blond giant, Eric Ford, joined them. His eyes were filled with admiration. "She's transformed herself and yet remained exceptional. You're back, my lady, and may I say it's good to see you again?!"

"You may," Annabelle said with a laugh, "but I'd rather you saw who I have with me. Eric, here is my sister-in-law, Miss Croft, who is new to town. My whole purpose in being in London is to keep her from rogues like you."

He put a hand on his heart. "You cut me to the quick. Don't listen to her, Miss Croft. Though I look like an elephant, believe me, I'm a lamb."

"You look very fit to me, sir," Camille said, eyeing him with approval. "But tell me, how heavy do you ride? Seems to me you'd need a stout-hearted mount, at least seventeen hands high."

"I'd rather tell you while we're dancing," Eric said. "Will you save a dance for me?"

"Gladly," Camille said. "If only because a partner your size will make me look wonderfully petite."

Her mama winced as the others laughed. Annabelle smiled a true smile at last.

"And here are our friends Lord Wycoff and his lady," the Earl of Drummond said as a striking couple joined them.

"No need to introduce us," the newcomer, a dark, handsome, middle-aged gentleman said. "Lady Pelham is a distant relative, although more distant than we'd like, at least of late. How are you, my lady? And Miles, you lucky fellow, I see your wife's in fine fettle again. We were concerned," he added more seriously.

"There's no need for that," Annabelle said gaily. "I am myself again."

"We can see that," Eric said.

And so could Miles—to his growing anger and sorrow—all through the rest of that long night.

Miles stood by the back wall, where the light barely reached and the sound of the music was distant. But he could hear and see very well—too well, in fact.

Annabelle was dancing. She'd been dancing from the moment she'd arrived. But she'd danced only once with him. As soon as the music stopped, he'd handed her over to her father. In turn, her father had laughingly given her hand to the Earl of Drummond, and then she'd danced with each of her old beaux in turn. Then she danced with every one of her new conquests, and there were many. She'd made dozens of them tonight.

Miles watched from the shadows as Annabelle danced and laughed, chatted and held court, charming the gentlemen of the *ton* again. She had his ring on her finger, but there was no other evidence she needed anything else from him.

It was true that she introduced each partner she left to Camille, and watched as they very correctly led her sister-in-law into the next dance. But that didn't ease Miles's misgivings. Lady Annabelle was back in her element, and from where he stood he didn't see where she needed anyone to help her navigate them now.

"She's lovely, Miles," a voice said close to his ear.

He turned.

An exotic, dark-haired woman stood smiling at him. Her inky hair was drawn up, held high by an elaborate tortoiseshell comb. A long raven ringlet lay against one of her small, high breasts, easy enough to see, since it barely was contained in her high-waisted, low-cut gown. That gown matched her red lips. Angelica was one of the few women he knew who could wear lip rouge and not be shunned in polite circles, maybe because she knew too much about the other inhabitants of those circles for them to fault her.

Born of an English baron and a Spanish lady, she wasn't careful of her reputation because it never mattered to her, or to her lovers. It was jested that she'd married early, and often. She'd been widowed twice by the time he'd met her in Spain. But though they'd shared much more than a lively sense of humor, he'd never been tempted to become her third husband.

"Angelica!" he said, "I thought you were in Lisbon."

"So I was. But when Sir Frederick died, I came here to see him to his final resting place."

"My condolences," he said, bowing, "I didn't know."

She waved her fan, "How could you? You left months before. Without word. I looked for you, you know."

"I didn't know. Nor did I think there was any need to say good-bye. We'd parted weeks before, when I heard you were going to marry Sir Frederick."

"Oh, Miles, but there was always a need for you. Sir Frederick was, for all his kindness, old enough to be my father."

He chose to ignore the blatant flattery, or invitation. "And where is your little friend Philippe?" he asked instead. "Or are you now too English to wear him as an ornament? I'd think a monkey would enliven this gathering."

"He didn't survive the crossing, poor fellow," she said. "I do miss him." She smiled. "I'm surprised you do too. You always asked me to put him in his cage and cover it when I was . . . entertaining you."

"Angelica, my sweet," he said, forcing a matching smile, "that's not a thing we should discuss any longer. Pleasant as it was for both of us, I'm married now. See the lovely woman in the dark blue gown dancing with that young lieutenant? That's my lady, Annabelle, Lady Pelham. My wife."

Angelica scarcely turned her head to see the direction of his gaze. "I know it," she said simply. "But does she? Come, Miles, the lady's famous, I heard of her even in Lisbon. Now I see she's just as they said, beautiful, witty, and charmingly flirtatious. Why, she's danced with every eligible gentleman here this evening, and quite a few who aren't. I know she's your wife, and I congratulate you for it; she's quite a prize. But she's also quite up to snuff, and very occupied this evening—while you're obviously not."

There was nothing he could say, so he remained still.

That pleased her. "So," she said, nodding her elegant head, "if you'd care to resume our friendship, I doubt there'd be any difficulty—certainly not from me. Or her, I should think," she added, gesturing with her fan.

He turned to where she was looking to see Annabelle leaving the arms of the tall red-coated soldier, who was delivering her to another eager partner, this one a slender, poetic-looking fellow who had more hair than she did.

"Yes," he said with assumed boredom. "And see where the partner she's just left has gone? To dance with the tall young woman in pink? That, my dear Angelica, is my sister. My wife is recruiting for her quite nicely tonight, don't you think?"

"Oh yes. How much sooner the war would have been won if all our recruiters so loved their work," Angelica purred. "Come, Miles, as much fun as this is, we know each other too well for this sort of sparring. It's not my style at all, nor yours, as I remember. But the other kind of tangles we engaged in were very pleasant, as I recall."

She gestured again to where Annabelle was dancing. "What's sauce for the goose is sauce for the gander. I'm the last person in the world to fault your wife's activities, but I do despair of her taste." She stared at Annabelle's partner, and shuddered. "A poet, or a fellow who wishes he were one. How ghastly. Those willowy young men are always concerned more with their own moods and reactions than their partners . . . they might as well be making love to their mirrors. As for her last partner? Those stalwart soldiers, so often, too often, they are absolutely not.

"But some gentlemen"—she paused to look him up and down, and with a slow smile said— "are so capable and competent that they don't have to posture and they don't need a uniform. You still look fit, Miles. But then, you never showed any excess on your person, only in your capacities, thank heavens. Or rather, I thanked heavens then. Which brings me to the point. Are you interested in resuming our friendship? There are no possible strings attached this time, because

I know you can't marry me. But that doesn't mean we can't enjoy ourselves, does it?"

Six months, he thought, as he looked at her. They'd shared six months of carnal bliss. She'd been a generous, inventive lover. Her svelte body was long, limber, and strong, and she used that strength to their delight. She'd never shown shyness or hesitation, and was as comfortable in her skin as any man. She could roam the corridors of her villa clad only in that smooth olive skin, and not be embarrassed, just amused at his inevitable response. He remembered it—all of it—very well.

But he'd been able to leave her without a backward look. And he couldn't stop watching his wife, even now. It was no longer the mode of lovemaking that drew him, but the person making that love with him.

"Thank you, but I think not," he said softly, turning his head back to watch Annabelle as she danced. "You're very lovely, and I'm honored. But it's not possible. It isn't a matter of morals, though it might surprise you to know I have them. It is, my dear Angelica, a matter of simple necessity. There's only one woman for me, you see, and I've found her."

"Indeed?" she said coldly, and he heard a wealth of things in that one word that he'd never heard from her before. Maybe he didn't know her as well as he'd thought. "I do see," she went on. "I also see that love really does cloud the eyes, just as the poets say. How very amusing. Because, my dear Miles, it certainly doesn't look as if your wife shares your most laudable morality, does it?"

He forced a laugh. "Only if the Puritans are right and waltzing is really like lovemaking. But it isn't. Just think, if it was, what a strange world this would be."

"I leave you to your love, and your illusions," she said curtly, inclining her head in a semblance of a bow. "You used to be far more entertaining, sir. I'll just have to go looking for someone as amusing as you used to be. Perhaps I ought to ask your wife? She seems to know every man here."

"At least," he said as coolly, "every man here obviously wants to know her." He bowed. "Good night, Angelica, good hunting."

She turned her back and left him. He stood and kept watching Annabelle. He was, he suspected, a very great fool. Because he never saw her look his way. But she never stopped smiling. And he never smiled again that evening.

Chapter 18

Miles said good night to his sister and mother when their party finally got home from the ball in the small hours before dawn. He remained silent as his sister and his wife laughed together, still burbling with gossip they'd been busy with since they'd gone into the coach to go home. His mother looked weary. His own face was a polite mask.

"It went well, I think," Miles finally commented as he walked them all to the stair.

"Well?" Camille hooted. "Ho! I can't remember having more fun. I danced with every man there, I think. And didn't tread on more than ten or twelve toes in all."

"You were a great success," her mother said.

"As to that, I wonder how you'd know, Mama,"

Miles commented curiously. "You disappeared early on. You must have been very sure of Camille's success. I was told you'd left a message saying you were off playing cards with the ladies. I hope you won."

She smiled wanly. "Not a great deal. But I'm very tired now. Perhaps I've been in the country too long. I'm not used to London's hours and feel my years tonight."

"Better get used to them," Camille said, "because I've been invited to dozens of dances, soirées and balls. And I want to go to every one!"

"Your new sister can go with you," her mother said.

"I will, and gladly," Annabelle said gleefully. "We'll go over the invitations tomorrow and find the best ones!" She stretched luxuriously. "Oh, but I'm tired too! Good night," she told Camille, and kissed her cheek. "You were a complete success. All the fellows I danced with told me they'd call on you. Those who weren't already married, that is. And I told those who were married who asked the same question exactly whom they could call on! I hope they liked the idea of meeting up with all that fire and brimstone." She giggled.

"Good night, Alyce," Annabelle added with more reserve. She started up the stair, and turned. "Coming up?" she asked Miles when she realized he hadn't mounted the stair with her.

"In a while," he said.

"Oh well," she said, "I'm going to bed now. Aren't you tired?"

"I have some things to do before I sleep."

"I can't keep my eyes open a moment longer," Annabelle declared. "Isn't it odd how awake we can stay when we're in the midst of fun, but the second we realize we're home again it's like someone opened a seam and all the stuffings come out?" She giggled. "I told my maid not to wait up for me. So I'll hush now so I don't wake the whole house. Good night."

"Annabelle?" her mother-in-law said when they reached the landing together.

"Yes?" Annabelle said, turning around, her hand on the knob of her door.

"I shall sleep late tomorrow, as should we all. So may I have a few words with you now?"

"Well, I'm for bed!" Camille said on a huge yawn. "See you both tomorrow—after I write to Bernard and make him turn puce with envy!" Chortling, she went down the hall to her room.

"May I come in?" Alyce asked Annabelle softly. "You said your maid is asleep, and I dislike talking in the hall."

"Of course," Annabelle said, opening the door and ushering her inside. She turned and saw that Alyce's face was gray, even in the rosy light of the one lamp left burning. "Are you well?" Annabelle asked quickly.

"Well enough. But embarrassed. You see, I—I

must ask you for funds again. I didn't tell Miles the entire truth. I gamed again tonight, for I was told some of the older ladies were playing for small stakes in the salon. I lost again. I thought I wouldn't, and that it wouldn't matter even if I did. But London ladies' ideas of small stakes are not mine. They play deeper than I remembered, and I suppose it was my pride that insisted that I stay in when I ought to have stopped. But I was trying to recoup. I did not. So may I again prevail upon you for funds? The same amount as last time, plus half again as much more, should do."

Annabelle stiffened, deep in thought. Her eyes were troubled when she spoke again. "I think it's time that you ask Miles," she finally said.

"I can't."

Annabelle cocked her head to the side. "Or won't? I could get you the funds but I'm not at all sure that I should. I asked Miles about your allowance. Without telling him anything, of course," she added when she saw Alyce's face grow pale. "He gives you a generous sum. I'm no one to judge you, but surely this is a problem you need help with."

"Surely I do. But just as surely I can't go to him."

Annabelle frowned. "There's more to it, isn't there?"

Alyce paused, then nodded. "But nothing that I can tell you."

"I think that this isn't a thing to discuss now,"

Annabelle said, rubbing her forehead. "I can't think straight. I'm bone-weary, as I'm sure you are. Tomorrow morning?"

Alyce dipped her head in agreement. "But no later. It's a matter that must be taken care of before another night passes. And again, I ask you not to tell Miles."

"I can't promise you that."

Alyce smiled. "I think," she said with curious dignity, "when you know more, you shall." Then she left the room.

Annabelle undressed, her thoughts in confusion. She couldn't concentrate on Alyce's folly. The night had been too wonderful, exceeding all her expectations. She was herself again! Only now she had all of London at her feet, not just the men. The women had been friendly to her too, for the first time. She'd enjoyed talking to many of them, and none seemed hostile or resentful of her popularity. Was it because they knew she'd almost died? Or because she was married and no longer a threat? Or . . . she paused as she rolled down a silk stocking, struck by a hateful thought. Could it be she was really not so attractive after all, but merely pitiful, and deceiving herself because of so many false compliments?

She wished Miles would come in so she could ask him. He might not tell her the truth for fear of hurting her, but she'd be able to read it in his eyes.

She dropped a night shift over her head, gave a

huge yawn, and climbed up into bed. She lay down, but her thoughts refused to slow. She kept thinking of the party, and wanting to talk about it with Miles. She'd introduced Camille to every eligible man, but it seemed she grew enthusiastic only when they spoke about Eric Ford. Did Miles think Eric was a good catch for Camille? Did he think Eric was interested in her at all, or only being polite? Was he as surprised and delighted as she was that Camille got as much attention from the men as any popular beauty tonight? Did he agree with Camille that the young Thornton girl was terrified of that horrid lecher Baron Manton? Would he know how to help the poor child if he did?

There were so many things to rejoice over, almost as many to comment on. Annabelle made a face. She was getting impatient. Why didn't he come to bed so they could share congratulations for a young miss well launched?

And how did he feel about his wife's triumphant return?

She'd thought he'd be as jubilant as she was. He'd approved the way she looked, she'd heard it with her own ears. Surely he'd seen her popularity; she'd danced all night, been buttered up to her nose with compliments. She hadn't been that lauded in years, especially not after her embarrassing failures with Damon, with Drum, with Rafe . . . Something chilly in her thoughts cooled her pleasure in the night.

Now she wondered again why Miles had danced with her only once. She'd actually danced up to him again later to tease him into another waltz. He'd refused, telling her to enjoy herself, telling her partner—she couldn't remember who that had been, it was hard to remember any of them now—to be careful of her toes. Then for the rest of the night he'd stayed watchful and quiet. He'd been like a clam all the way home . . . She sat up. It was very late and growing later, the house was quiet, and yet still he hadn't come up to bed. Was he ill?

Annabelle stepped out of bed, threw on a dressing gown, and, too unsettled even to put on slippers, went barefoot in search of her husband.

She tracked him to the study, finding him by the only source of real light in the darkened house. The door was ajar, so she could see a fire flickering in the hearth. That plus the lamp on the desk were the sole illumination. Miles sat at the desk, a sheaf of papers before him. But he was looking at the fire dancing in the hearth. He didn't look sick, only infinitely weary.

Annabelle took a moment to watch him, unobserved. She seldom got a chance to do that because he was always so aware of her. She smiled tenderly as she studied him. He wasn't as handsome as Damon Ryder; no man in England was. Nor was he as elegant as the Earl of Drummond; few men were. He wasn't as big and impressive as

Eric Ford, or as lean and spruce as Rafe Dalton. But there was no other man like him, certainly none who affected her pulse the way he did.

His hair was rumpled; he sat in shirtsleeves. The glow of firelight etched that hard profile in crimson, tinting his brush of short, thick eyelashes with gold. Those eyes could be ice or silver blue, but when they looked at her with passion, she shivered with warmth. She thought he was more attractive in his own way than Damon; easily as clever as Drum, and a great deal kinder. He was . . . She paused, realizing she was luckier than she deserved.

She'd married because she couldn't bear facing another Season alone, and in so doing had found a man she never wanted to part from. She'd found a soul mate, and at a time in her life when she'd seriously doubted she even had a soul anymore. But he'd uncovered it for her and to her, bit by bit, with his kindness and cleverness.

There'd been a time when she'd demanded the acclaim and admiration of all men, and even that hadn't been enough to fill the emptiness in her heart. Now she knew she needed only the love of this one man, because he was her heart. She'd set such store by her looks because she'd believed that was all she had. He'd shown her otherwise. Other men had been trophies she'd competed for, even Damon, the great imagined love of her youth. Now she knew what love was and could only marvel at what she'd thought it had been. Love was friendship and desire, absolute trust and elemental need on every level she could experience. For her, love was Miles. She was so very incredibly lucky, she thought as she stood in the doorway, gazing at him.

He looked up as though the force of her yearning had penetrated his thoughts. But he didn't smile. "Annabelle," he said, half rising from his chair, "what is it? Are you feeling well?"

"Oh lud!" she said airily. "Am I going to be asked that for the rest of my life? I'm fine, but I wondered if you were ill. It's late, why haven't you come to bed?"

"I'm not tired yet."

"Oh." She crossed the room and sat in one of the big chairs near the fire. She tucked her feet up under her, grimacing at how cold they felt against her bare bottom. "Well, I couldn't sleep. I'm still too excited about the ball. Didn't Camille do wonderfully? She had every fellow there lining up for a second dance with her. I only had to steer them to her, and they never wanted to leave her. I confess I don't know how she does it. I don't mean that she's unattractive," she said quickly, because he didn't answer, just sat there looking at her soberly.

"She's a very handsome girl," Annabelle went on, "but that's not it. Some absolute diamonds were ignored while the men flocked to her. I confess I was worried when I saw Damon's sister-in-law making her bows. Such a little beauty! And the youngest Swanson girl! Who'd have dreamed the last of that lot would be so attractive? But Camille outdanced them all. She deserves it, and I can't tell you how happy I am!"

He didn't answer, but she was too wound up with the events of the night to stay still. She wished he'd share in her summing up. She especially wished he'd congratulate her on a job well done.

But maybe she didn't deserve it.

She grew thoughtful. "I wasn't responsible for her triumph, though. It's hers entirely. I admit I'm still astounded. Though she's always nicely dressed, she doesn't give a fig about fashion—in any way at all. She doesn't simper like most young girls, she laughs right out loud—if she thinks the jest's worth it, because she'll tell you flat out if she doesn't. She doesn't flatter or make doe eyes the way we're taught to do, but men can't get enough of her company. Oh," she said in a smaller voice, her own eyes growing wide. "that's exactly why, isn't it?

He didn't answer, just watched her, eyes hooded, his face still.

Something was wrong. She sat up straight. "Have I done something wrong?"

"No. Why do you ask?"

"The way you're looking at me." She forced a laugh. "Did I offend in any way? I thought you'd be pleased with Camille's debut, and that I was accepted again."

"I'm pleased. Camille did well, but that didn't surprise me. As for you, you danced all night, and you were the belle of the ball. You obviously had a grand time. What more do you want, Annabelle? Shall I send you flowers? I don't doubt you'll get enough tomorrow. Your dancing partners will all send you tribute. Do you want me to as well?"

She was still a moment, thinking about what he said. Then she realized what had jarred, like hearing the wrong note in a symphony. He wasn't calling her Belle anymore. She uncoiled from the chair and stood up. "You don't have to send me flowers. Yes, I danced. Yes, I had fun. Because I was so relieved."

"Yes, you're beautiful again," he said impatiently. "Surely you know that. Was there anything else you wanted to know?"

"You think that's why I'm here, and why I was relieved?" She raised her chin. "Tonight was as important to me as it was to Camille, if for different reasons. It was much harder for me, though. I have enemies. Deservedly so. If they'd all turned their backs on me it wouldn't have been unfair. I rejoiced because I was received so kindly. If it was sympathy, well, I'll accept that too. But it's done. Camille's launched, I am returned, and I wish you'd tell me what's wrong."

"Nothing," he said.

"I see." She drew herself up and gave him a curt nod. "Very well. I'm tired too—of talking to myself. Good night."

She marched toward the door. He rose to his feet in one swift motion, stepped out from behind the desk, and caught her hand.

"What?" she whispered, looking back and up into his eyes.

He drew her close. "Oh, Annabelle," he breathed, as though she'd wounded him. "What am I to do?"

"What is it?" she asked again.

"Make love to me?" he asked, searching her eyes.

"Oh yes!"

He swept her up into his arms. "You're still too light," he whispered, "and far too cold." He enclosed one icy little foot in his hand. "And it's much too late." But nevertheless, he opened the door and strode out, carrying her into the hall.

They didn't speak as they went up the stair. She didn't say a word as he laid her on the bed, only watching wide-eyed as he stripped off his clothes and joined her there.

"We don't need this," he said gruffly, drawing her night shift off.

She didn't need anything but his arms around her and his lips and body on hers. She didn't know how much she needed that until she

wrapped her arms around his wide shoulders and
pressed against him. He joined her with him in
one smooth movement, and she felt her entire
body meld with his. Only then did she allow herself a long shuddering sigh of relief. He paused,
looking down at her, his own breath stilled in his
chest, though she could feel his pulse beating
wildly.

"Don't stop," she said urgently.

He didn't. He kept his mouth on hers as he cou-
pled their bodies again, and drank in her sighs as
they strained together, feeling the beginnings of
an ecstatic, elusive joy they'd never really shared
before. He'd never known her to show such fire;
she'd never felt such bliss. They were together
mind, body, and soul, for once not plagued by
fears or personal doubts. He caressed her, he murmured to her, she held him tight. And then at last
she shuddered and gasped in surprise. Her body
arced against his; he felt his sex clasped hard as
she pulsated around him.

Then he abruptly pulled away to reach his moment alone, convulsing by her side.

They lay silent for a while, slowly returning to
the world again.

"Why?" she finally asked into the darkness.

He rose on one elbow and cupped her face in
his hand. "I told you. Because you aren't ready to
have a child yet. You're newly healed."

She said nothing. He rose and went into the

dressing room. She heard him pouring water and washing. He came back in moments, his body cool from the night and smelling of soap.

He reached for her, and she settled her head on his chest. He stroked her hair, feeling the buoyant curls under his fingers. He thought she might be sleeping. He hoped so.

He didn't know if he could sleep now, because neither his body nor his mind was sated; he was still filled with longing—not for sex, but for her. She'd returned to her world tonight as naturally as a fish slipping out of his hands would return to the native waters he'd taken it from. He'd stood in the shadows watching her transformation, or rather, her reclamation. The sparkling belle of the London *ton* had returned. Whether she was Lady Annabelle Wylde or Lady Pelham, only her hairstyle seemed to have changed from that first night he'd seen her holding court.

But she hadn't betrayed their bargain. He'd never asked her for a marriage of passion, intellect, love between equals. But now that he had a taste of it, or rather had begun to believe in what love actually could be with her, he was devastated by the thought of the eternity of polite indifference that lay before him. Would he be forced to seek out women like Angelica? There were many like her: lovely, cool, expert, heartless partners of the body, never of the soul. Doubtless his wife wouldn't care. She'd again be the fickle, charming, insincere beauty she'd been. He'd thought her sickness had changed her, but that must have been only a momentary lull in her busy life. She'd been afraid and dependent.

Now she'd changed back again. He'd seen it for himself.

At least she still liked him. But for how long? She was famous for her fickle nature. Even though she obviously enjoyed their lovemaking, that would fade in time as she grew accustomed to it. How could it not? Her heart wasn't involved. They'd never exchanged a word of love in all their lovemaking. He, out of pride. And she?

Because Lady Annabelle was who she was. The prize of the London *ton*. And he'd agreed to marry her only for that.

He heard her breathing slow and felt her relax, her body heavy with sleep. He held her close, filled with the bitter joy of a man who held what he most wanted but knew he could never really possess.

Chapter 19

~~~~~~~~~~~~~~~~~~~~~~~~~~~~~~~~~~~~~

Annabelle woke to sunlight. She stretched and smiled with pleasure. Miles was gone from her side, but he'd be back tonight, and the next night, and the next. She was well and the world was right again, even more right than it had ever been before.

She'd been a success in every way, and her husband was mad about her too. She no longer had to worry about whom she'd charmed the night before. She didn't have to plot and plan and connive anymore. She had London's acceptance and approval again. And she had Miles.

She was out of bed and washed before her maid came to her, and so greeted the surprised Meg with a grin and hurried into her prettiest morning gown. She was spontaneously twirling before the mirror to admire it when there was a tap on her door. She sent Meg to open the door, expecting to see Camille eager to continue discussing her triumph.

Instead, Annabelle was surprised to see her mother-in-law. Alyce didn't look triumphant. She was somber, standing with her hands clasped in front of her. She gazed at her daughter-in-law expectantly. Then Annabelle remembered. Her smile faded.

"You may go," she told Meg. "Good morning," she said after Meg left. "Wouldn't you rather wait until we've breakfasted to have this talk?"

"I'd rather wait until next year, my dear. But I can't afford to. Have you thought about my request?"

Annabelle tried not to smile. She'd had better things to do, so much better that she'd completely forgotten her mother-in-law's uncomfortable situation. Still, she had her answer.

"I wish I could help you," she said. "But I think it's best that I don't. You have a problem, one I can't deal with. If I give you money today, you can't promise me you won't ask for the same tomorrow, can you?"

"No," Alyce answered calmly.

"Well, then," Annabelle said with a shrug. "What can I do?"

Alyce's expression was strained, her eyes watery. "You must give me the money and not tell

Miles. You see, our lives depend on it. Ours, socially. His, in fact."

"What are you talking about?" Annabelle demanded. She knew she should ask the older woman to sit down. But something in Alyce's expression told Annabelle she wouldn't want to hear what Alyce had to say.

"The fact is that I'm not a gambler. Not with cards, at any rate," Alyce said. "I need the money for my second husband. He's demanding it."

Annabelle stared.

Alyce sighed. "He isn't dead, you see." She took a deep breath and went on, "I myself didn't know that until recently. He approached me at the squire's ball, just before we left for London. I received a message and thought it was some cruel joke. I met him in the back garden. It was dark, but light enough for me to see the truth. He lives. Years ago, we'd been informed that he'd perished in a misadventure on the high seas. It turns out he'd sent that word by false sources. He's very much alive. And if I don't pay him, he'll tell that to the world."

"Let him!" Annabelle said, taking a step back. "He'll be clapped in jail the minute he shows his nose. Miles told me about him and the mess he left behind."

"And the scandal of that?" Alyce asked. She watched as Annabelle thought about it. "We'd all be brushed by it. Camille especially. Bernard too.

Miles would say he doesn't care about scandal, but of course he would, for your sake, if nothing else. And as for you, you'd be tainted by it for aligning yourself with us. They'd say you were so desperate to marry you chose a felon's family."

Annabelle straightened her spine, refusing to show how the words stung. "We can weather it. Lud!" she said on a shaky laugh, "I've survived worse!"

"Perhaps," Alyce said, and added, with a bitter smile, "but not the rest. It's worse, my dear. You see, he was never really married to me." Annabelle's eyes widened as Alyce nodded, "Yes. That will put paid to Camille's hopes and our family name. Proctor is not so well known. But if word got out that it was Pelham's mother who was involved, that would be remembered, and it would destroy the name. Which, I remind you, is yours now too."

"But that's criminal!" Annabelle cried. "No one would blame you. In fact, the world will forgive your being so vilely deceived."

Alyce cocked her head to the side. "I think not," she said sadly. "I have always known the truth of that, at least."

Annabelle grew still.

Two spots of high color appeared on the older woman's lean cheeks as she went on, "We were never married. Oh, I told everyone we were. I said we'd gone off and had a quiet wedding, just the two of us, not wanting to cause a fuss. I thought no one would ever know. Well, who inspects marriage certificates or even asks to see one? He told me that, and he was right. But he also said his wife was mad, under lock and key at his remote country estate, dying by degree. And I believed him. He had a way with words, and I never doubted him. As it turns out he had not one but two wives, no more mad or dying than I was, but I couldn't know that then. All he said was that I could either live with him without benefit of clergy, or tell the world we were married, because once his wife died we'd wed secretly and no one would be the wiser."

Annabelle sank to a chair and gaped at Alyce. "How could you?" she breathed.

Now Alyce lifted her head. "Unlike you, my dear, I chose a man out of love, not for the sake of appearances. And unlike you too, I needed a man's love. I had a good marriage with Miles's father, but I was alone, growing older and sadder every year. Peter was a fine figure of a man: witty, charming, full of laughter and compliments. He made me feel young, useful, alive again. He told me if I didn't agree to living together, either with a false marriage or without it, he would move on. He said his wife wasn't long for this world. And so I thought, what's a year or two? Without him, it would be forever, because I doubted I'd ever find another man like him. That," she said with a harsh laugh, "was true enough.

"Would you rather I'd knowingly agreed to live with him in sin?" Alyce asked curiously. "Many women do, even in the highest society. Everyone knows about Lady Bessborough, Lady Melbourne, the Duchess of Oxford and her miscellany of bastards, the Countess of Clovelly and her ill-assorted brats from different fathers. You may accept them, as rackety members of society do. But decent people don't; their very names are filthy jokes. I was also still able to have children then, although, fortunately, I did not. Yes, and think of what such an arrangement would have done not only to my first husband's name, but to his children. At least I did think of that. And so I agreed that a little deception, soon ended, was better than outright scandal."

"But Miles . . ."

"Miles was at school. He never knew, nor did anyone. Nor should anyone. All I have to do is pay." She laughed. "Yes, pay the piper for our dance. He says this is the last payment. He says he has business on the other side of the world he must take care of. I can't say if that's true, but this I do know: if you tell Miles, he'll challenge Peter to the death. Miles is younger and a fine sportsman, and he can fence and shoot better than Peter. But Peter's a cheat, one of the best. I wouldn't care to wager on the outcome of any duel between them. Would you?"

As Annabelle sought words, Alyce added bitterly. "Perhaps you would. But remember, if you were widowed in such a duel, the scandal would also attach to you. Come, my dear, it's simple enough. Give me the money and keep your silence, and so keep your husband and the elevated place in society that you've worked so hard to regain."

Annabelle's eyes were blind with shock. But she knew how to defend herself. She gathered her wits. "Whatever I do," she said with quiet dignity, "I won't decide it in a moment. I've discovered too much at once to take it all in: your sad history—and the fact that you have absolutely no affection for me."

"The one I can't change," Alyce answered, standing equally rigid. "The other, though you may not believe it, is because I love my son very well. And I don't think you do—or at least, I believe you do only so long as he worships you and provides you with what you want."

Annabelle smiled thinly. "He doesn't worship me. Nor would I want him to."

Alyce inclined her head. "Whatever you say, my dear. But woe betide him if he denies you what you desire, which is your place in society." She fixed Annabelle with a steady stare. "I warn you, my dear, if you don't help me in this, that place will be snatched away from you again, and this time you won't regain it. Peter wants the money by tomorrow night. I suggest you provide it. And if you've any affection for my son, I advise

you not to tell him any of this. Because if you
think you can still reign here in London as a merry
widow, that widowhood itself will be tainted by
irreparable scandal if there is a duel. Even if there
isn't, our name will be ruined if Peter doesn't get
the money. He promises it. About that, I believe
him. You should too."

Then, in a swirl of her skirts, she was gone out
the door.

Annabelle stood staring sightlessly after her.
The morning had dawned so brightly, and now
she was plunged into darkness.

When Annabelle finally summoned the courage to go to breakfast, Miles rose from the table to
greet her.

"And how are you this morning, my dear?" he
asked with a polite smile.

She was surprised by his coolness, especially
after his ardor in the night. But his mother and sister were at the table, so she supposed he was being
guarded because of them. She'd too much on her
mind to think about it anyway, so she merely murmured something polite in response. Whatever it
was, it satisfied him. He resumed his breakfast.

Annabelle was spared saying another word,
even if she could have managed one, because
Camille chattered about her grand night all
through breakfast. Alyce sat listening quietly, then
excused herself.

Annabelle kept stealing glances at Miles, trying to read his mood. He too was quiet. Why was he ignoring her? What had she done to offend him? She thought back on their lovemaking and could find nothing that could have displeased him. He'd been a tender, impassioned lover last night. But now she remembered that before they'd made love he'd been quiet at the ball and cool to her afterward. At that, she'd had to seek him out, and then even their lovemaking had seemed to be something he'd done against his will until passion had swept away his reserve. Now it was back. He smiled at some of Camille's comments, then took refuge behind his newspaper, never so much as looking at his wife again.

His mother had just said he worshipped her. If Alyce's sordid story was as true as that, Annabelle thought, then she'd been told a tissue of lies. It was as though her lover of last night had never been.

Annabelle looked at Miles and thought of all he'd been to her since they'd married. She remembered the thoughtful man who'd helped her through her sickness and encouraged her return to London. She remembered the witty fellow who'd cheered her when her spirits were at their lowest, as well as the blithe liar who'd told her how well she looked when she'd been at the brink of death. He was silent, but she recalled the charming conversationalist. Though he paid no attention to her now, she couldn't forget the understanding listener to whom she'd confided her fears and doubts. She saw him lifting a fragile coffee cup to his lips and thought about the tender, unselfish man who initiated her in the arts of love. She shivered, remembering the passionate lover she'd held in the night.

Annabelle was in a breakfast room watching her husband, but the flash of enlightenment she suddenly experienced was so profound, she felt as though she were in a cathedral.

"Are you all right, Belle?" Camille asked, seeing her sister-in-law blanch, then gasp.

Miles looked up, his silvery blue eyes fixed on his wife.

Annabelle waved a hand at them both. "A twinge, nothing more. I'm not used to such late nights. Go on, you were saying?"

Miles rattled his newspaper and went back to reading. Camille prattled on. Annabelle despaired.

Why was it that only when everything was about to be snatched away from her did she realize only one thing mattered? She could and had in her time survived the loss of her looks, her position in society, even her self-respect. She didn't know how she could survive the loss of Miles, or forgive herself if she in any way contributed to danger for him.

But what could she do about his mother's request? She couldn't even ask to speak with him in private to ask what was bothering him. She was afraid that if she did the hateful secret would spill out. She couldn't risk that, not yet, not until she decided on a course of action.

She wasn't a fool. Paying blackmail would only encourage more. And could she even trust that Alyce was telling the truth? She had a real enemy there. Annabelle realized she needed someone she could count on now, someone brave, wise, strong-minded, someone she could trust. She knew such a man. But she couldn't confide in him if there was even the smallest chance he'd be hurt by her doing so. There must be someone else she could turn to. She'd have to find that someone, and quickly. Because she wasn't a fool, and knew she needed help.

Annabelle sat staring down at her breakfast plate and reviewed her choices.

Her mama was her strongest defender. But Mama was too much her advocate. The first thing she'd do would be to try to tear Alyce's hair out. Then everyone would know the secret.

No, Annabelle thought, she needed a person of discretion, not necessarily even someone who loved her, but someone who'd help her if she were in need. And she was. She had to have some time alone to choose that someone.

She rose from the table. "If you'll forgive me? I have a few errands this morning."

"I should hope not!" Camille said, laughing.

Annabelle looked at her curiously.

"You promised to help me again," Camille explained. "Remember? Why do you think I'm all togged out like this?"

Annabelle stared. Camille was wearing a new and especially charming gown.

"You said they'd be arriving before noon," Camille added, looking at Annabelle strangely.

Annabelle put her hand to her forehead. She'd forgotten. Before she could put any plan into action, or even think of one, she had to deal with the morning's callers. Camille had been presented to society last night. This morning, society would be presenting itself to her.

The Viscount and Viscountess Pelham's salon was filled with flowers, conversation, and callers. Camille wasn't daunted. She didn't stammer or shrink from the horde of dashing gentlemen who were bowing over her hand any more than she did from the elegant ladies who'd come to welcome her to their circle.

"Your sister-in-law is a delight," Eric Ford told Annabelle as they stood to the side of the crowded room, watching Camille welcoming her guests.

She looked up at him, wondering if this was the man she could confide in. He was brave enough, he'd been in the army for many years, and it was rumored that he and the Earl of Drummond and their friend Rafe Dalton had been engaged in secret work for His Majesty during the war. That would make any of them a perfect ally, but this blond giant was so large and competent-looking, he inspired confidence just by being near.

"Yes, she is," Annabelle said eagerly. "Have you had time to talk with her this morning?"

"Not as much as I'd wish. I hope to remedy that. She likes to ride, she said." He laughed. "I think she knows more than I do about horses. Now, that's a treat for a fellow like me. I'm more comfortable in stables than on dance floors, and I fit better there too. May I ask her to come riding with me in the park one morning? With a groom in attendance, of course. I'll supply the horses. I've a sweet little mare in mind I think she'll want to take home with her."

"You certainly may," Annabelle said. "But it isn't up to me. She's a strong-minded girl. If she doesn't want to go, be assured she'll tell you straightaway. Camille's blessed with a forthright personality, so she doesn't play games with men, fluttering and fanning herself when spoken to. She's very unlike the flirt I was, you know." She paused, waiting for his reaction.

He looked down at her with such sympathy, she was tempted to drag him from the room and speak to him at once. "As you once were, true," he said. "You and Camille are very different, but both surprising, in your own ways. Your championing her now, for example, is something I'd never have imagined."

His expression was earnest as he went on, "I was glad to hear you were recovered, but now I see you are that in many ways. And so whether you're now the Belle Camille keeps talking about, or the Lady Annabelle I knew, whatever I'm permitted to call you, I call you both generous and considerate in the way you're presenting Camille. As well," he said more softly, "as by the way you, once the queen of flirtation, now honor your husband."

"Time changes us all," she said absently, wondering how to get him alone.

"Time?" he asked with a small smile, "or Miles? I've known him a long time and have been his friend every minute of that time, though we didn't meet as often as I'd wish. Yet I was never happier for him than when I saw you two last night."

"Oh?" she asked, diverted, a bit of the old Annabelle in her mischievous smile, "And not on our wedding day?"

His face became serious. "Not really, no. But last night showed me my mistake in that. Because he never took his eyes off you. Nor did you stop looking at him, except when you had your eyes on his sister. Now I congratulate you on a true marriage of minds, as I couldn't then. You used to love to torment us men, or so we thought. Now you've only got eyes for him. Well done, Belle."

She glanced away and bit her lip. Not Eric Ford, then. A request to see him alone would be too easy to misunderstand.

And not the Earl of Drummond. Because that elegant gentleman took her hand, bowed, and said, "Belle, is it now? So Camille would have it. She's right. You're still as lovely as you were when we first met, only now there's a new light in your eyes, one that only lights, alas, when your husband's near. I confess I miss Lady Annabelle, the coquette. Mind, I only admit that because my Alexandria's not nearby," he said with a chuckle to take the truth from that blatant lie, because everyone knew his devotion to his wife. "But I truly admire the constant Belle. Miles is lucky. And you chose well."

And not Rafe Dalton. He had only a few words for her, though they were kind and she was grateful for them. But he was a terse fellow, and they had a difficult history.

And certainly not Damon, she thought, looking over at him and his beautiful wife. Damon and his Gilly never separated. What a fool she'd look if she tried to get him alone! More than that, how would it look to Miles? Because now she noticed that Miles never did stop watching her. Because she kept watching him? Her head began to ache. She closed her eyes and rubbed her forehead.

"Are you well?" Miles was at her side by the time she opened her eyes again.

"No, not really," she whispered. "It's because I'm not used to all this socializing, after all. Would you mind entertaining our guests by yourself? I'd like to lie down."

"Mind? I insist on it," he said, taking her arm. He led her from the room, his eyes filled with concern. "Would you like me to come upstairs with you?"

"Oh no. I think I need to rest a spell, that's all."

"Don't worry," he said. "I'll send Meg up and I'll be there soon too. The hour for visiting's almost over. Rest now, Belle."

She nodded, though she knew she wouldn't rest. She needed time to think. Any one of the men she'd just rejected in her thoughts might have to be the one she finally chose. She didn't have much time to find the perfect one, so a slightly imperfect choice would have to do.

She paused on the stair, suddenly knowing who it had to be. How foolish of her not to have seen it immediately. There was no more logical choice, no matter the danger. He was a strong man, a clever one, and one she'd always loved, although she still wasn't sure of him and really never had been. But he was the only one she could choose now, after all. No matter their history, he wouldn't let her down.

Miles saw her stop on the stair, and hurried up to join her. "Are you all right?" he asked her again.

"Yes," she said, looking up at him with a real smile. "In fact, Miles, I'm feeling better every minute."

Chapter 20

"I'm sorry, my lady," the butler said, "but he's not in. If you'd care to leave word?"

"When is he expected?" Annabelle said impatiently. She'd lied to get here, telling Miles she was completely recovered from the unexpected bout of weakness she'd experienced in the morning, refusing his escort, saying he should go about business with his man-at-law as planned because she'd do fine by herself. That last, at least, wasn't true. Her hands were icy even in her gloves, and her heart was beating too fast. She had to speak to the man she sought immediately.

"As to when he is expected, I cannot say," the butler said. "Perhaps you should ask your mama. She is expected back at six."

Annabelle already knew that. "I've already

spoken to Mama," she lied again. But it was only a half lie. She'd asked her mother how long she was going to stay with Camille, and had been certain the two planned to spend the afternoon at the dressmaker's before she'd set out herself. She just hadn't spoken to her mother about this errand.

"She knew he was expecting me," Annabelle said haughtily. "If he's not here, I can't see why you won't give me his direction. It's very important." The butler looked uncomfortable. This was such a new thing for the usually taciturn man that Annabelle grew suspicious. "My mother fully expects me to meet with him today," she added with a calm she didn't feel. "So where is he?"

"He's expected back in a day or two," the butler said evasively, and Annabelle could almost feel his anxiety now.

"How tedious," she said, manufacturing a little moue of annoyance instead of shouting as she wanted to do. "I quite forgot, so Mama said this very morning. But it's not surprising. Such a pother these days, what with establishing ourselves in London again. It's been one thing after another; I don't even know how I stole this time away." Then with a smile to remind him she didn't have to give excuses or personal information to servants and was only doing so out of long acquaintance, she added, "So where is he?"

He hesitated.

She drew herself up, and using her most bored and imperious voice, said, "Come, Mr. Dean, time is wasting, and this is important."

He looked supremely uncomfortable now. Annabelle could see drops of perspiration on his high, shiny forehead. He'd been with the family for years and always been obedient to her every wish. Now she was both fascinated and a little alarmed by this bizarre reaction in a man she'd always thought half statue. But none of it showed in her face or voice.

Taking a wild stab at breaking through his sudden reluctance to help her, she added, "Oh, he's *there*! Of course!" She stamped one small foot in a charade of irritation. "Isn't that typical of me these days? I'll forget my bonnet next." She looked blank for a moment and then said pettishly, "I know the address and it simply will not come to mind. I know it's not that far, I know the street but simply cannot recall the number."

He remained silent, and obviously anxious.

She huffed in exasperation. "Is it because I'm alone? Mr. Dean, I'm no longer the child you knew, I'm a married woman now, quite capable of traveling by myself." She inclined one shoulder to indicate her waiting carriage. "I'm eager to do so. So. The address?"

"The countess agreed to this?" he said, clearly wavering.

In for a penny, in for a pound, Annabelle thought and said, "Of course. Why else would I be here now?"

It had been a lucky guess because it really wasn't that far, Annabelle thought as the coachman drove her through London's busy streets. She knew the district by the address but had never actually known anyone who lived there. It was a decent neighborhood on the other side of the park, but people of quality didn't live there. Like birds of a feather, they flocked to the same areas, as though they could only exist in their own well-marked compounds. For the first time Annabelle wondered why that should be so. Were they afraid they wouldn't be accepted or recognized as the elite they were if they lived somewhere else, however pleasant? Yes, of course, she thought, answering her own question.

She looked out at the neat rows of town houses and their small, well-kept front gardens as the coachman slowed, searching for the address she'd given him. This neighborhood was charming, entirely respectable. But she too wouldn't live here because no one of birth and fortune would. So what was he doing here, and why would he be planning to stay for days?

The coach rolled up in front of a handsome four-story gray stone house. Annabelle frowned in puzzlement, but stepped out when the coachman opened the door. "Wait for me," she told him.

Annabelle stood on the pavement looking at the house. It was quiet; the only person she saw was a boy rolling a hoop down the street. He stopped when he came near her, caught up his hoop, and looking back at her over his shoulder, trotted up the steps to the house, opened the door, and went inside.

She looked at the slip of paper in her hand again. This was the house. But surely he couldn't be here. She would, Annabelle vowed, pull every last remaining strand of hair out of Mr. Dean's balding head for this. Still, first she had to make a fool of herself by actually going to that door and asking if the man she sought was there. Then she could kill Mr. Dean with a clear conscience.

She went up the stair, raised the knocker, let it fall, and waited.

The door swung open. She'd expected a butler or a footman, but instead, a plump, rosy-cheeked, middle-aged woman stood there.

"Yes?" the woman said, looking at her curiously.

Odd that a housekeeper would answer the door, Annabelle thought, and said, "I'm here to see Lord Wylde."

The woman's rosy cheeks turned gray. She stared at Annabelle. A flash of recognition crossed her face, and she went ashen. "Oh my!" she cried, one hand on her heart. "What's happened! That is to say . . . who shall I say is calling?" she asked tremulously.

"His daughter," Annabelle said proudly, to cover her own confusion.

The woman stared, then turned, then turned back again, and said, "Won't you come in?" As soon as Annabelle did, the woman, eyes wild, turned away, then again spun around and said nervously, "Here, please, in the parlor."

She showed Annabelle to a room on the right. It was a well-proportioned parlor, furnished adequately, if not fashionably. Closed white curtains gave the sunny room a diffuse glow. A few landscapes hung on the painted rose-colored walls, and several small porcelain figures of children were set on the mantel over the hearth, but there were no other items of particular distinction. The room had several comfortable-looking chairs and a settee. But Annabelle remained standing, looking around, her back rigid.

"Please wait here," the woman said, still staring at her visitor. Then she bit her lip, ducked her head in a jerky bow, and hurried away.

Annabelle stood still, thinking furiously. It might not be as bad as it looked; it couldn't be. She let out a breath she hadn't know she'd been holding in. Surely there was a simple explanation. She mustn't jump to any conclusions. He was obviously here. Visiting? A distant relative? An old friend? Yes, certainly, that must be it, she thought with relief. But she remained standing, facing the door, waiting for him to come to her.

He did.

"Annabelle?" her father asked incredulously. He stood in the doorway looking at her.

"Yes, Father," was all she could say.

He strode into the room and took her hands in his. "What's happened?" he asked gravely. "Your mother? What is it?"

"Mother's fine. I'm not," she said on a shaky laugh.

"What is it then?" he asked again, examining her face, "Are you sick again? Where's Miles? Is it Miles? Why have you come alone?"

"I'm not ill, it isn't Miles, and he doesn't know I'm here. I just wanted to talk with you about something, and you weren't at home."

"I see," he said, with evident relief. But then he realized the situation, and demanded, "Who told you I was here?"

She slipped her hands from his. "Mr. Dean did. But he's not to blame. I lied to him. I said Mama told me you were here." She'd been raised correctly. One did not blame servants for one's own bad behavior. Her voice became steady and cool. "Still, though she never told me that, she obviously knows where you are, doesn't she? The whole household must know. Everyone, except for me."

Two almost identical pairs of brilliant blue eyes

searched each other's. The earl was the first to look away.

He nodded and took in a deep breath, seeming to come to a decision. "Yes," he said. "She knows. Has done, for years. And now since you're an adult, a grown woman with her own household, I suppose it's time you knew too." He put his hands behind his back and paced a few steps. Then he looked at his daughter again. "I live here, Annabelle. Half the time, more now that you've left the house. I've done so for years. This is my other home."

His gaze shifted from her to the floor as he went on. "Mrs. Lund, the woman who admitted you because our footman is on an errand, is my companion. We've been together fifteen years now. When I met her she was a young widow with two children and not a lot of money. Still, she is, whatever you may assume, a moral woman and a brave, great-hearted one. We met through some trifling business; I owned a house she was living in. We talked, I returned to talk some more. In the end, it was I who finally offered her my heart and a home.

"She didn't want to accept, because she's a moral woman, as I said. I persevered. If there's fault in this, it's mine. She loved me, as I loved her, but her scruples prevented her from accepting my offer. My money and my position didn't matter to her. Perhaps the fact that she had those two children and no way to support them finally influenced her, I won't deceive myself about that. But I also believe she truly loved me."

He met Annabelle's shocked gaze unflinchingly as he went on, "She accepted my offer because I promised to never desert her. I never have. Nor have I wanted to. She's my friend and my comforter, and yes, my lover. If we lived in a world where it was possible, she'd be my wife. But if I'd sued for a divorce, even if it were finally granted, it would have taken years and dragged everyone through the mire in the process. Fleeing to the Continent with Elsie and her children was possible, but it would have meant deserting you. That I couldn't do, any more than I could bring shame and scandal to you or your mother, or our name. Elsie accepted that when she agreed to my proposal. And so, here we are."

Annabelle kept staring at him.

"I see," he said bitterly. "But you don't, do you?" He eyed her stiff stance and added, "Would it be more acceptable to you if I'd kept a succession of mistresses over the years, as so many gentlemen we know have done? Would you be more understanding if I'd passed all these years with pretty ladybirds half my age? Or if I spent my time and money with opera dancers, or on 'actresses' who sometimes appear on stage? Perhaps you'd be less shocked if I'd supported a succession of fashionable whores like Harriet Wilson and her sisters? Those are the more acceptable routes. But not for me."

He approached her and took her hands again. His voice softened. "Your mother knows, has always known, and in fact, approves. She doesn't mind my absence in her bed or in her life so long as I'm there to take her to fashionable affairs she can't attend alone. I don't blame her for the way she feels any more than she blames me for my life. We were married because our families decreed it. In those days it was the way of things. We simply don't suit. I respect and honor her, but we don't love each other, nor does she expect love of me.

"Annabelle," he said sincerely, "I live with Elsie because of who she is, and my fondest hope is to grow old with her. She suits my heart and my soul, and yes, my body too." His hands closed hard over hers. "You're a married woman now. Surely you know what I mean. Or at least I devoutly hope so. Please, however you feel, speak to me. Let me at least know, because I do love you very much. That's why I've kept this life a secret, that's why I've lived two lives. It isn't easy, nor is it for the sake of what anyone might say. I don't care about that and have the money and power to be able not to care. My parents are gone, my friends are few, those I have accept me as I am. Still, I denied Elsie the respectable life she yearned for. Because of you, Annabelle, no one else but you."

He gave her hands a hard shake. "Do you understand, do you understand me at all?"

Annabelle opened her lips, but then stopped trying to speak. Her throat hurt too much, her chest felt weighted down. In all the days of her mortal illness, she'd never felt so cold and sick. It was as though something was cracking inside her. It was just too much.

She'd faced disappointment before. Damon's marrying another woman had nearly broken her heart. But not quite. She'd faced up to it and in time had even been able to be perfectly civil to the woman he'd chosen instead of her. She'd been shocked and shamed because of her own foolishness too. She'd thought she'd broken Rafe Dalton's heart, only to discover that all along he'd loved another. She'd been publicly humiliated for that. Then she'd sought a safe harbor and been rejected yet again by the Earl of Drummond. Even the gentle giant Eric Ford had once deceived her. Each of those honorable men had rocked her vision of the world and her estimate of herself. Still, she'd been able to go on, head high.

But this long-standing deception by a man she'd loved more than any of them—this broke her heart. She bowed her head, laid it on her father's shoulder, and finally wept. Even though he'd dealt her this blow, she needed him to comfort her.

"Ah, my pretty Belle," he said, his voice thick

with emotion, "I never wanted this. I spent years trying to spare you this."

After a time she raised her head and stepped back. He dropped her hands and gave her his handkerchief. She blew her nose and wiped her eyes and tried for a smile, but it quivered on her lips.

"I understand," she said. "I was just surprised and hurt, I think, because I never knew. That's why you wanted me married and out of the house, isn't it?"

"I wanted you married to a good man. I wanted you to have a better life. It's true I'm marginally freer now, and I can come and go as I please without fear of your knowing and being hurt. But I'm not free, and have accepted that I never will be, because I don't wish your mother any harm either."

She saw the truth in his eyes, and nodded.

"Now," he said soberly. "Please, Annabelle, tell me why you came looking for me. It had nothing to do with this, did it?"

"No," she said in a small voice, "but it doesn't matter now."

His lips compressed to a thin line. His eyes blazed. "Don't lie. You've never been able to successfully lie to me. It was important, but now that you know the truth about my life you don't trust me anymore, do you?"

She took a deep breath. Her world had been turned upside down, but as the moments ticked by it righted itself again. So her father had a life's companion other than her mother. She couldn't blame him if her mother didn't, and looking back, she knew with certainty that he'd told her the absolute truth about that. But he had deceived her, if only for her own sake. She'd had enough of that.

"I had a problem, yes," she told him. "But now I'm glad I didn't blurt it out. Because now I realize it's something I have to solve myself. I am a grown married woman now. I have to grow up even more and stop running to you and Mama for help."

"I'm still your father," he said. "I'd still lay down my life for you. Are you in danger? I have influence. I like to think I can give you good counsel. I'm still handy with my fists and am accounted a good marksman, if it comes to that. Whatever it is, no matter how difficult, please don't let all this change your opinion of that. Please trust me."

She shook her head. "No, it's better this way, I promise you." He started to speak but she cut him off. "Now, will you introduce me to your Elsie? And her children?"

He hesitated. After a moment, he sighed. "I will, and gladly. But Francis and Belinda are both away at school. He's at university, she's just completing her term at Mrs. Spence's Academy."

Annabelle frowned in puzzlement, remembering the young boy who'd brought his hoop into the house not half an hour past.

"But I'll be glad to introduce you to Sophie and Charles," he said, watching her closely. "They're our children . . . Well, but fifteen years, Belle," he said, in a voice she'd never heard from him. He was pleading. "It's been fifteen years, after all. With all the best intentions in the world, there are some things that can't be prevented."

Her ears buzzed, she felt light-headed. She nodded, dumbly agreeing—until she suddenly remembered how Miles had foregone his own pleasure again just last night to ensure that he didn't get her with child. So it could be done. Couldn't her father have done the same? But then, she thought, her heart lurching, perhaps Miles wasn't as lost in love for her as her father was for his companion. Discipline might come more easily to a man when his heart wasn't involved.

Enough, Annabelle told herself. This was her father's life, not hers. She had her own affairs to put in order. Her every impulse was to turn on her heel and leave as fast as she could. That made her understand she should not. Difficult things must be faced, running never solved anything. Her father had taught her that. Most of all, she knew that if she left now, without a word, the children in the other room would feel the pain of it as keenly as she did. That simply wasn't fair.

As ever, she knew the right thing to do, even if it was the hardest to get through.

"Yes, I'd like to meet . . . your family," she told her father as coolly as she could manage. "But is it wise? After all, I didn't know about them and only learned when you were trapped into telling me. Do they know about me?"

"They've always known. You didn't have to know about them. Given the circumstances of their birth, they had to know about you." He eyed her closely. "They are not to blame. Will you be kind to them, Annabelle? Because if you can't be, it might be better if you left now."

She laughed without humor. "I'm nothing if not socially adept," she said with calm amusement in her voice. It was the voice she used whenever she faced the world pretending she was untouched and unhurt by it. "Nor would I ever be cruel to a child."

"Only to a parent?"

She ignored that. "Now, may I meet my half brother and sister?" she asked briskly. "But no matter how charming they are, I can't stay long. I have a very pressing errand."

"The one you refuse to tell me about," he said with bitterness.

"The one I must take care of myself," she corrected him. "Now please, may I meet your other family before I attend to my own?"

He nodded. "But, Annabelle, remember, if you need me, I am here for you, always and ever."

"Thank you, I'll remember," she said, silently vowing to never do more than that. She'd meet her father's bastards, and she'd smile at the woman he wished could be his wife, and she might perhaps forgive him for all of that in time.

But as for now, she had to find another to confide in, and she had to find that someone quickly.

Chapter 21

❧⟡❧

Annabelle had been drilled in the social graces since her infancy, as certainly her father had been. He'd also had many more years to hone his skills. They were both known to be glib and charming in company. But now neither father nor daughter could find a word to say as they waited for his other children to come into the parlor to meet their half sister.

The boy came in first, hesitant and wide-eyed. His sister crept in after him, looking terrified. Their mama brought up the rear. In that moment not a word was spoken. The earl was watching his elder daughter. She was staring at his other children and their mother. Their mother cast one agonized look at the earl and then looked as though she were about to cry. Her children glanced at

Annabelle, and then away, as though ashamed.

It was that which finally prompted Annabelle to speak.

"How do you do," she said smoothly, bending from the waist to try to meet their eyes. "I am Annabelle, Lady Pelham. And you are?"

The boy hesitated and then said, "I'm Charles, ma'am. Charles Lund." He gave her a jerky bow. Then he prodded his sister. She jumped as though stung. "And this is my sister Sophie."

The little girl dipped a curtsy, then stepped back until she bumped into her mama. Then she stood head down, staring at her slippers.

Neither of them looked anything like her or her father, Annabelle realized with a sudden surge of relief. She honestly didn't know how she'd have gone on if they had. The boy's hair was straight and brown and he had hazel eyes. His sister had the same hair, and her eyes were brown. They were sturdy children, rosy-cheeked and healthy-looking, with snub noses. Like their mama, Annabelle realized after another quick glance at the woman. She couldn't understand how this plain, plump female had captured and held her father's interest for over fifteen years. But shocked as Annabelle was, she didn't study her father's mistress more closely, because her every glance seemed to affect the woman like a whiplash.

Annabelle didn't want to make the scene any more difficult than it already was—if that were even possible, she thought, quelling a bizarre rising urge to giggle, or weep.

"And this is Mrs. Lund," her father said in a strained voice, going to stand beside the older woman. He took her hand. "Here is my daughter Annabelle," he told her.

The woman curtsied. "Happy to meet you," she whispered.

There was another silence.

"Sit down, sit down," the earl said roughly.

Annabelle took a chair, sitting poised on the edge of it. The children huddled together on a settee, staring at Annabelle. Their mother sat next to the earl, then sprang up again. "I'll just go see to some tea," she said.

"Thank you, but I haven't the time for tea," Annabelle started to say, just as her father said, "No, Elsie. Betty can see to the tea. Just sit beside me now."

The woman sat again.

Annabelle could hear the tall cased clock in the corner ticking. She wondered why her father didn't say something. Perhaps he didn't know what to say? The thought both pained and pleased her. She gathered her wits. She, at least, had the courage to speak, because she, at least, was not responsible for any of this.

"I realize these are difficult circumstances," Annabelle said, "but it's past time we met, is it not?"

That statement was met by agonized stares from three pairs of eyes. Her father merely looked beset. Annabelle called on all her training, tried to forget her own distress and think of what to say. A jumble of thoughts came to her. She opened her mouth to say: "I've just returned to London; I was on my honeymoon," when she realized that the children were perhaps her close relatives and yet they hadn't been invited, so that would a rude thing to say. But their presence on earth was an even ruder surprise to her. It was a ridiculous situation. She foundered, then her training won out.

"I've recently returned to London," she said, looking at the boy, since he seemed to be the bravest of his small family. "I missed it very much. Do you like living here?"

"Yes, ma'am," he said.

"But I was raised in the countryside. Do you like to go there too?" she went on doggedly.

"I like the seaside," he said. "Papa takes us there in August—" he stopped and cast a wild glance at his father, as though he knew he'd said the wrong thing.

"So I do," the earl said in an agonized voice. "To Torquay. We have a cottage there, by the sea."

"A very pleasant place, I've heard," Annabelle said. She'd never been there, of course. She'd heard Torquay was a pretty harbor town, very like Portofino, in Italy, built into a cove overlooking the sea. It was popular with families of navy personnel, but not persons of her elevated social strata. Whenever she'd visited the seaside it had been to go to Brighton when the Prince was in residence there. How clever of her father to have found a charming vacation spot for his second family, one where he ran no risk of meeting anyone he knew.

The room was silent again.

Annabelle waited for someone else to speak. So did her father. His second family merely sat there looking at her dumbly.

Annabelle wanted to tell them she didn't blame them; she wished she could tell them not to be afraid of her, because she'd never do them any harm. None of this was their fault. She was the interloper in their home, after all. It suddenly struck her that they might be her father's favored children, and told herself it didn't matter. None of it did, actually.

Annabelle rose to her feet. "I only dropped in for a moment," she said, "and am sorry to have disrupted your day, but I had something I had to tell my . . . the earl. I'd like to stay and get to know you better, but haven't any more than that moment, you see. Perhaps one day we'll meet again."

Her father's mistress shot to her feet too.

"Please feel free to come back whenever you wish, my lady," she said quickly. "You're always"—she glanced at the earl and added wretchedly—"welcome, I'm sure."

"So you are," he said as he stood up too. "I do mean that, Belle."

"Thank you. Good day," Annabelle said, and walked stiffly from the parlor.

The children remained behind with their mother. After a swift glance at his mistress, the earl left the room and went to the door with Annabelle. He didn't speak to her until he'd walked her down to her waiting carriage. Then he stopped her before she could enter it.

"I'm sorry you had to find out this way," he said.

She laughed. "I doubt I'd have found out any other way."

He frowned. "I always wanted to tell you, but the time was never right."

"Better this way," she said in a voice that was much too bright. "The time never would have been right, would it? And as a deathbed confession it would be far too melodramatic, too much like something at Covent Garden, don't you think?" What she'd said reminded her of something, and she felt a lump rise in her throat. She cocked her head to the side. "But how nice for you," she went on, blinking tears back. "You never had a son with mama, and that is the goal of every landed nobleman, isn't it? And now you've remedied that."

He blanched. "You don't have to worry about your legacy, Annabelle," he said. "I will leave those children provided for, but they can never inherit my title or our estate."

She blinked, then laughed again, a little wildly. "I never thought of that. You may leave them everything for all I care. You made a fine settlement on me when I married, and I did marry a wealthy man. I was only speaking about—but that doesn't matter either. Good day, Father, I do have to go home now."

"Annabelle," he said, taking her elbow to hold her back. "Listen. I know how painful this was for you, and I'd have given anything to have prevented it."

"But you did, didn't you?" she asked with a bitter smile. "You did do everything you could to prevent it. I'm the one who should apologize for oversetting your apple cart. Good day. I really must be going."

She wrenched her arm from his grasp, and stepped into the carriage. He saw her in, then turned and walked stiffly back up the walk to his other home. Only then did she sit back, feeling as dizzy and weak as she had when she'd gotten ill those months ago. She didn't allow herself to fully accept what had just happened until her father entered the house and the door closed behind him.

Then she wept a little more.

"My lady?" the coachman asked after a time, when a look assured him his mistress had composed herself. "Shall we go home?"

"No!" she said, but couldn't think of a destination. She wasn't ready to face her world yet. She was no closer to dealing with the problem she'd set out to solve. "Around the park," she told him on an inspiration. "Just drive around the Regent's Park until I tell you where to go next."

But she still didn't know by the time the coach had slowly gone round the park twice. The fashionable of London rode and strolled by her coach window without her seeing them. Annabelle sat back, lost in her thoughts. The day was trickling away. She had to know what to do by tomorrow, and she still had not a hint.

She tried to steady herself. First, she had to clear her mind of the shock it had just received. With effort, Annabelle relegated the astonishing truth about her father to the back of her mind, telling herself there was nothing she could do about that but what she'd already done. She could perhaps learn how to live with it more comfortably and more generously in time, but she didn't have to do anything about it now. That was the past; it couldn't be changed. Now she had to deal with the threat to her new life and family.

She could deal with many things, but she was a realist. This was a case of blackmail by a conscienceless villain, something she had no experience with. She needed an ally, if only someone who could give her another perspective, or good counsel, and still keep the matter secret between them. But who? She knew few women well, so her first instinct had been to run to a strong man. She had a bevy of old flirts and a roster of old loves, but she rejected them all, she couldn't and wouldn't appeal to them. It would be like being unfaithful, and of all the things she was, she was never that.

Then she reviewed the facts again. Not only her father, but her mother had lied to her, and for years on end. That had to be dismissed from her mind as well. *The facts, Annabelle!* she scolded herself. *Only the facts!*

The fact was that there was a man demanding money to keep secret the lie of the illicit life he'd led with her husband's mother. Annabelle shivered when she realized that the scoundrel was, in his way, no different from her own father. No, she decided, at least her own father had only lied to her . . . *The facts, Annabelle!* she reminded herself, only the pertinent facts.

She thought about her mother-in-law's lover for a long time, and again concluded that giving him the money wouldn't solve the problem. Only frightening him would. But what could she threaten him with? He obviously cared for nothing but his own pleasures, and it seemed the foremost of those pleasures was money.

Secrets, she thought, leaning her aching forehead against the cool glass of the coach window. Suddenly her life had become caught up in a web of secrets. Lies and more lies; she'd done bad things in her own life and wouldn't deny it, but she'd had her own code and had never lied, she thought virtuously, and smiled. No, she'd lied too, as many times as she'd thought it would profit her. So she should be able to deal with such a man. But try as she might she couldn't think of any way to do that except either by killing him or by paying him. The one way was permanent. The other was endless.

She knocked on the roof of the carriage. The coachman drew back the flap. "Home," she said. "It's time to go home now."

Miles stopped conferring with a footman and spun around to face the door when Annabelle entered the town house again. He strode to her, his light eyes filled with anxiety as they scanned her. "Are you well? Were you taken sick?" he asked, taking her hand, looking into her eyes.

"No, I assure you, I'm well."

"Then where were you?"

"I just had business to attend to," she said weakly.

His mouth thinned, his eyes turned icy bright. She stepped back in surprise. She'd never seen him in a rage before. But he obviously had only the barest control of his fury. "A word then, my dear," he said through gritted teeth, "in my study, if you please."

That was when she noticed the servants clustered at the back of the hall, looking at her. She glanced at the tall cased clock in the corner and bit her lower lip. She hadn't been aware how much time had passed since she'd left, but now saw she'd been gone for hours.

"Where have you been?" Miles demanded the moment he was alone with her.

"I went to see my father," she said, taking a seat by his desk. She concentrated on removing her gloves to avoid his angry gaze.

"No," he said slowly, "you did not. That was the first place I went when you were discovered missing with no word of where you'd gone."

"Didn't his butler tell you where I was?" she asked, looking up in surprise.

"Mr. Dean was also gone, and no one in the house knew his whereabouts. Your mother's still here. She said she was too nervous to go home until you came back. She's with Camille upstairs, worrying about you. My own mother had to take to her room with a headache." He strummed his fingers on the back of a chair as he gazed at her, obviously thinking about what to say.

"Annabelle, you are . . ." He hesitated and changed his tack. "I'd never leave you without word. I'm a married man now, and I know it's not considerate." He turned his attention to some papers on his desk, but only randomly stirred them with one hand as he added, "Although, I admit, I might not tell you if I was doing something I thought would upset you."

She looked at his rigid back. "And that would be . . . ?" she asked lightly, refusing to let her apprehension show in her voice.

"Seeing another woman," he said as lightly. "So, tell me, what where you doing, and why haven't you told me even yet?" He turned and looked at her, waiting for his answer.

She saw his expression and felt the back of her neck crawl. This was not her easygoing, amiable husband. She'd always admired his firm jaw, but she'd never seen it clenched in rage. There was nothing of love or admiration in those light eyes now, only cold appraisal. He might have been staring at her through glass.

She longed to blurt out everything. She couldn't. She'd endanger him by telling him anything. Because of course, he'd want to know what was so important that she had to tell her father in secret, and she was too muddled and weary now to invent as blithely as she might have done if her heart and head hadn't been assaulted with so many lies and hidden truths.

She hesitated a second too long. She saw it in his eyes.

"I see," he said. He shook his head as if acknowledging a hit. "It's somewhat early in our re-

lationship for you to stray, my dear. I believe the
approved time is after you present me with an
heir or two, not a few months after our wedding."

She shot up to her feet. "I have not strayed," she
cried. "It's cruel of you to say so. You know better,
or at least you should." She collected herself and
said more quietly, "I had a reputation for flirtation, nothing more. You knew about that reputation before we married but you also know I came
to you a virgin, so obviously I'd never dallied before. And I'd hope that those few months of marriage we've shared would have convinced you
that I'd never deceive you . . . unless you deceived me, of course," she said haughtily, "because then I'd fully repay you in kind, my dear."

It was an excellent speech, she thought. But ruined by the tears now spilling down her cheeks.

He moved toward her, and checked. "I apologize," he said, jerking his head in a semblance of a
bow. "So then why won't you tell me where you
went today?"

She took a shuddering breath. She'd believed
him to be an ally, a friend as well as a lover. She'd
thought he was lost in love for her too, but here he
was, believing the worst of her. The profound
emptiness she felt made her dizzy. Foolish Lady
Annabelle, she thought. There was a reason she'd
become a joke, an explanation for why she'd
stayed so long on the shelf. And now she'd done it
again, only this time disastrously. She'd mis-

judged a man again, this one, the most important in the world to her.

It was, all of a sudden, too much. Too much in one day, too much in a lifetime for her.

"You want the truth?" she asked bitterly. "Then beware, because the truth is the worst thing I know. I've heard nothing but truths and I'm sick of them! I did go to see my father today, but he wasn't at home. Poor Mr. Dean wasn't there when you went looking for me because he was probably coursing through London trying to find Mama to tell her where I'd gone."

"He did come here later, asking to speak with her," Miles said slowly.

"Then that's why she's upstairs," Annabelle said. "She doesn't want to face me."

She stood as tall as such a small woman could, head high. She was, Miles realized, the old Lady Annabelle again, filled with pride and so beautiful she made a man yearn to touch her. Even though he knew that if he did he'd find his fingers seared. Her appeal was as strong as before, but the attraction was different now; it was as if her sickness had burned away illusion and her inner self had emerged. She was still beautiful, but even more dangerous. Nothing in her appearance looked soft and yielding now. With her slender form, close-cropped hair, and blazing eyes, she looked like a young St. Joan, proclaiming her mission even as they tied her to the stake.

"I went to see my father because I needed to talk to him," she told him coldly. "I didn't want to wait for him to come home. I wish I had. Because I lied and discovered his whereabouts. He was with his longtime mistress, and their two children, in the house they've shared for fifteen years—and never told me about."

He winced. He made a fist and struck the top of his desk. "Damme! I thought you knew," he muttered. "I'd have given my arm to prevent you from finding out that way—as I'm sure he would have too."

Her eyes opened wide. "You know? Oh Lord!" She laughed wildly. "Am I the only one in London who didn't?"

Now he did reach out to grip her shoulders. "No," he said, holding her at arm's length and looking into her eyes. "I knew because I investigated your family before we married. I wanted you the moment I saw you, but only a fool would plunge into marriage with a stranger with his eyes blinded by desire for her. I investigated your father as thoroughly as he did me. I didn't judge him half as hard as he did me, though, that I do know.

"Belle," he said imperatively, "listen to me. Many men of your father's age and class do as he did, and much worse. At least he found one love and stayed with her. I don't say it was right, or right that he lied. Still, he didn't lie to your mama, but to you, and only to save you pain and scandal."

He was so sympathetic, Annabelle began to relax. Then she thought of why he was so understanding, and her blood seemed to freeze in her veins. She was hurt and angry and frightened all at once. Before she could stop herself, her pride for once forgotten, she gazed into his eyes and spoke urgently.

"Miles. I never asked because I suppose at first I didn't care. But no more lies, please, not between us. I won't live through something like this again. What my father did, what you say so many gentleman do—is that what I may expect from you? Because if it is, tell me now. I've had enough and should at least like to prepare myself so that I'm *never* shocked and surprised like this again. If it is something you intend," she hurried on, "I'll understand. Ours wasn't a love match either. I don't say I'd enjoy it, but—Miles, at least tell me now. Is that what you intend too?"

He pulled her close. "Oh, Belle," he said into her ear, "never, never, never, I promise, never." He drew back and smiled a peculiar tilted smile at her. "Ours wasn't a love match, no. But strike me dead if it isn't one now. At least, it is with me."

She pulled back, and fixed him with a wide blue stare. "Are you saying you love me?"

He smiled. "I am." But he wouldn't say more. He only watched her closely.

She seemed to look inward, considering his words. Then she cast her gaze down. She'd been brave in her time, boldly facing rooms filled with people she knew were whispering about her, mocking her. But she couldn't look at him as she finally whispered, "So it is with me too."

"Are you saying you love me?" he asked.

She nodded.

"You'll have to do better than that," he said softly. Then he laughed, low in his throat. "Lord! What a love scene. Like two wary opponents, circling, each afraid to show the other an exposed throat. Belle, I'll say it loud and clear. If I did not when we married, I do now. I love you: your wit, your charm, your well-informed mind, your bravery as well as your vulnerability, your lovemaking—yes, your body, as well as the soul that lives in it. I found the woman beneath the façade as beautiful as the one who first attracted me. I still have nightmares remembering I almost lost you, but I begin to think that if I had not I'd never have found you."

"Or I, myself," she murmured. "If I hadn't been so sick, I wonder if I'd ever have found you either. And that would have been a tragedy. To marry as we did—oh, we were such fools, Miles."

"No longer," he vowed. "Never doubt it again; I do love you, wholly. Now come, can you say the same of me? . . . Or anything like it?" he added hesitantly when she didn't answer at once.

She raised tear-filled eyes to his. "I can say it better!" she whispered. She flung her arms around his neck and dragged his head down. They kissed, long and deep.

She felt the sigh deep in his chest when he finally raised his head. "Thank you," he said, grasping one of her hands and pressing a kiss in her palm. She closed her fingers over it, as though to keep the sensation close.

When he looked into her eyes again, his own were sober. "And so I must ask again, what is it that you can't tell me? Never was truth so important, Belle. I think love feeds on it; I know it can starve to death without it. So please, tell me. What was so important that you had to seek out your father wherever he was? You said you wanted no more lies. Let's not have any between us."

She swallowed hard. "But if that lie is to protect someone, how terrible can it be?"

"Your father was protecting you. How terrible was that when you discovered it? Exactly," he said, seeing her stricken expression. "A man, or a woman, can deal with anything if it's known. It's shadows we can't fight."

"Yes, of course. You're right," she said dully.

He led her to the settee by the window and sat beside her. She clasped her trembling hands together and spoke rapidly. "Your mother borrowed a huge sum of money from me before we left Hollyfields. She said it was to cover gambling losses."

He frowned. "She doesn't gamble."

"So I thought." She nodded. "But she said she

got in over her head playing cards with some local women at the squire's ball. She was so upset that I agreed. She also begged me not to tell you. I thought it was a little thing to do for her, and I so wanted her to like me. She doesn't, you know."

Now he nodded. "Yes, I know, but she doesn't like women in general, and she wouldn't like anyone either of her sons married. I love her because she is my mother and so I must honor her, but believe me, I know her too. She's only comfortable with men, and was never content with merely flirting. She can't live without their adoration; the lack makes her bitter. My father's doting on her made it worse. Even her second husband, cad though he was to the rest of the world, seemed to honestly adore her, and so whatever he was, she was content with him."

"She asked for more money yesterday," she said quickly. "A great deal more. I refused. Then I learned it wasn't because of gambling, at least, not hers." She closed her eyes and blurted before she could think better of it. "It's for her second husband. She said he isn't dead. He's come back and is blackmailing her."

Miles rose to his feet. "What?" He thought a moment and then laughed. "No. There's a prime lie. If he came back, there'd be nothing waiting for him but dozens of his victims and creditors, a long term in Newgate, and possibly the hangman's noose. He was a very bad man and if he didn't come to the bad end we heard about, turning up alive again in England would ensure he did."

"He's alive, she said. "And what he has to blackmail her with," Annabelle said in a stony voice, "is the fact that they never married."

Miles raised his head.

"Your mother told me that. They couldn't. He was already married, and she knew it." She fell silent. There was nothing more to say. She watched Miles standing, lost in thought.

Eventually, he looked at her again. "Now that, at least, could be," he mused. "It makes a kind of sorry sense to me now. If so, it's bad, but it could be dealt with. And so why didn't you tell me?"

She hesitated. She knew men. Telling him she was afraid for him would surely make him dash from the room, baying for blood. That was exactly what she didn't want.

"I see," he said in a strange voice when she didn't answer. "It was the scandal, was it?" He let out a long-held breath. "So much for protestations of love," he murmured almost to himself. "They are easy to say, living with them is more difficult, isn't it? Well, you needn't have worried," he went on briskly. "It wouldn't brush off on you. You'd be pitied, not scorned. But I forgot, you don't like pity. That is the reason you married me, isn't it?"

She rose slowly to her feet to face him, gripping her hands together hard, so she'd have something to hold. She thought out each word she had to say, because they were vastly important to her now. She had the feeling they'd be the last she'd say to him for a long time. Because even if he didn't die in a duel with his mother's scoundrel of a lover, Annabelle doubted she'd ever speak to him again. What was the point? He was right, protestations of love meant nothing, at least it seemed his didn't. With all she'd done, and no matter how she tried, obviously he'd never trust her.

"You're right," she said with a twisted smile. "It was about the scandal. But I wasn't concerned about myself, because as you say, it had nothing to do with me. I was worried for Camille and her prospects. She's been so excited and delighted by everything that's happened to her here in London, I couldn't bear to see her blighted by a past she had nothing to do with. I know too well what gossip can do. And I worried for Bernard, who gives not a fig for me. Still, it's sad to think of a young man ruined by scandal before he comes of age. Even more than that, I worried for you."

Her voice became as cool as Lady Annabelle of old putting down a presumptuous suitor, as she added, "Because your mama told me that Proctor would kill you in the duel you'd surely challenge him to. You're the better sportsman, she admitted, but he'd doubtless cheat and kill you. That is what ensured my silence."

He blinked. She saw the realization dawning in

his eyes. She waved a hand to silence him before he could speak.

"The past haunts all of us," she said bleakly. "You, no less than I. You married a woman for convenience, for your family's advancement. Maybe you think you changed your opinion since we married. But you haven't. The merest thing I do and you immediately believe the worst of me. Lady Annabelle's returning to form, you think, selfish to the bone again. And do you know? You're right, I haven't changed. I'm selfish. I tried to spare myself the pain of your death. I can face a world turned against me, and I have done," she said proudly. "I can deal with deception and lies from those I thought loved me, and I have done. But I didn't think I could bear your death."

"And you think you can now?" he asked into the stillness of the room.

They stared at each other for a long moment.

Neither knew who moved first. But then they were in each other's arms. They kissed until they had no breath left. Only then did they stop to look at each other. Then they kissed again because there were no words to heal the words they'd spoken, only their silent lips.

"Oh, Miles," she finally wept, "why are we tearing ourselves apart?"

"Because neither of us is used to loving," he said fiercely. "Get used to it, Belle. We'll have a lifetime of it ahead."

"But—your mother's lover, his plans."

"I'll deal with them, and him."

She put her hands on either side of his face and kissed him, this time with desperation. She didn't doubt him, but she knew the fates and the way they had of amusing themselves with her.

Chapter 22

"**N**o more lies," Miles said firmly. He looked at his mother and sister in turn. "That's the whole truth, and we have to deal with it. Belle has said she will. Now the question is whether you can."

"Of course! What do you think I am?" Camille asked, incensed.

"A young woman with the world ahead of her," he answered. "And an impulsive one too. Rein in, Camille, think before you leap. If Proctor tells the world the reality of his ten-year stint with us, you're ruined, tainted with the same brush. Yes, I know dozens of people in the highest ranks of society live together without benefit of clergy, but none that I ever heard of lied about it to their equals. And none did so with a scoundrel like Proctor. Half of

London despises him; the other half will when they hear more about him, which he says will happen if he's thwarted. Those who lied for him will fare no better if his secret's made public.

"How are they to know we didn't know he was already married? Would they believe us? Open adultery is one thing. It takes courage and gall, but it is done. Trying to pull the wool over the polite world's eyes is another. I'm not judging you, Mama, but that's the truth."

Alyce said nothing. Annabelle couldn't tell if she was offended or angered by what he'd said. What worried her was that Alyce had said nothing since Miles called them together that morning to expose her secret behind the locked door of his study. She hadn't apologized or said she regretted anything. She'd only sat silently, staring without expression at Annabelle as Miles talked. Her only sign of emotion was the two high spots of color on her white cheeks.

"I don't care," Camille said firmly. "Even if I did, it would be stupid to try to hide the truth." She shuddered. "I hated him then, I despise him now, but it's ridiculous to pay him to keep the secret. We'd have to keep paying until the end of time. End it, Miles. Don't pay him. If he talks and people blame us for the deceit?" She shrugged. "I'll survive. Living in society's been fun, but so was home. I'll do. Any fellow who doesn't think so is a man I wouldn't want anyway."

Miles smiled, "Practical girl. I agree. Mama? You've said nothing. What do you think?"

"I scarcely have a say in this anymore," Alyce said in a pinched voice. "I kept it from you all these years, and now that you know it's out of my hands. Do as you will. But he's coming here to-night expecting money."

"Good," Miles said as he rose to his full height. "He'll get something else. Me."

Evening came, and the town house was quiet. The servants had been given the evening off. Alyce stayed in her bedchamber, while Miles went to meet her former lover. Annabelle sat in her bedchamber with Camille because Miles wouldn't hear of them seeing the man who was trying to ruin their lives.

"You're both too volatile," he'd said, and laughed. "You'd try to remove his head. I wouldn't mind in the ordinary way of things, but though I'd like to do the same, the best thing is to say no to his demands and dismiss him. He might want an excuse to duel, after all. My job is not to give him that pleasure."

"What good would dueling do for him but risk his neck?" Annabelle asked.

"Who knows what goes through that kind of reptilian mind? But if he threatened Mama with that, it's a risk. The good thing is, he thinks he's meeting her secretly. I'll have surprise on my side.

If he dares threaten me, I can take the matter into my own hands immediately. Don't worry. He's smart enough to know that, and so he won't. He's a coward too."

"So denying him blackmail will make him go away again?"

He cupped Annabelle's chin in his hand and dropped a kiss on the tip of her nose. "That, and a few firm threats. Don't fret. Keep Camille company. She is worried—that she'll go against my orders and come down and kill him herself."

"If you'd only let me!" Camille cried.

He chuckled. "Aye, I know you could. So could my lady. I'm surrounded by Amazons, so I've nothing to fear. Proctor is nothing to your fury. I'll let you know what happens as soon as I can."

He went to the bedroom door and looked back. "And yes, I'll have a footman and a loyal, and armed, friend concealed in the shadows in case he has anything even more underhanded planned."

So now Annabelle sat with Camille and discussed the strange meeting that might be going on in the darkened kitchens.

"What more underhanded thing could he have planned?" Annabelle wondered out loud.

"Proctor's an utter bastard," Camille said in the stable language Annabelle would have objected to if she weren't so upset. "You wouldn't think it to look at him. He looks like a gentleman and he's charming. He had Mama completely fooled. Me too, at first. But that's what a Captain Sharp is like. He cleaned out our coffers and then cleared out himself. Miles found out before he was quite finished with our fortune. He tried to tell Mama, but she wouldn't hear a word against her darling. Miles had to go off to sea to try to repair our fortunes.

"Proctor never hurt me or Bernard, or even Miles personally," Camille admitted. "That wasn't his style. Cheating at cards and horse trading, dirty investment schemes, smuggling, and now blackmail. But he acted the master of the manor at home, and I have to admit that he doted on Mama. He treated her like fine china."

Annabelle opened her lips and closed them again. She'd been about to ask Camille how her mama felt about the man now. But she had the sinking feeling she already knew, as Proctor himself probably did. That might be the reason he threatened to face Miles in a duel if Alyce didn't pay. Because with Miles gone, anything could happen to the new fortune he'd amassed, and if Proctor were free to really marry Alyce . . .

Annabelle began pacing the carpet in agitation. But not for long.

Miles opened the door. "Come out, come out, wherever you are," he said with a smile. "I mean it. Come downstairs, my ladies."

"Is he gone?" Annabelle asked anxiously.

"Did you plant him a facer?" Camille asked eagerly.

"Gone," Miles agreed. "I spoke my piece, and he listened—after he got over the surprise of seeing me there. He heard me out and left quietly. It's over and done. Forever, I think. I offered him money for a passage to the Antipodes. He took it."

"Oh, Miles." Annabelle sighed with relief.

He gave her a hug, "Now, let's go down, shall we? Eric Ford is downstairs by himself, and I'm afraid that if we don't reward him for standing watch, or at least divert him, he'll finish every scrap in the kitchens. He did say he hadn't had dinner yet."

Camille's broad face flushed rosy red. "Just give me a minute to change my gown," she said. "I didn't know we were having company."

"Well, well, well," Miles murmured after she'd hurried out the door.

"What did your mama say?" Annabelle asked, calling his attention back.

He frowned. "I haven't told her yet. I left the worst for last, thank you for reminding me. I'd best do that now. You go down. I'll be there soon. I don't think she'll want to join us, but we'll celebrate."

They did. Miles and Annabelle, Camille and Eric made merry late into the night. Annabelle was too excited to stop talking even after she got into bed. As the night fled, she was still murmuring jumbled congratulations to Miles.

"Yes, thank you, now go to sleep," he told her, gathering her in his arms. "We'll have time to talk more later." And time to make love then too, he thought ruefully. They hadn't, though he'd looked forward to it. She'd been too eager to talk. But he was content. They had the rest of their lives for that.

Annabelle closed her eyes and fell asleep, smiling. But knowing the folly of tempting fate, she'd have woken up screaming if she'd heard him say such a dangerous thing.

The next morning lived up to its name, dawning sunny, a perfect Sunday. As part of their continuing celebration, Miles strolled through Hyde Park, his wife on one arm, his sister on the other. They were dressed splendidly; Miles in a blue superfine jacket and buff breeches, Annabelle a vision in matching blue, and Camille looking very well in a sprigged muslin gown. They greeted acquaintances with smiles or nods, pausing now and then to chat.

The park was crowded. It was inevitable that they'd also run into people they didn't especially wish to meet. Annabelle tensed when she saw her parents strolling toward them arm in arm, for all the world as though they were the closest couple in town. She marveled that they could. But they lived by a different standard, she reminded herself, one she was so very glad she'd never have to try to measure up to again.

Yesterday, after she'd faced her mother with her deception about her marriage, her mama had been defensive as well as defiant.

"There was no reason to tell you," her mother said. "Parents don't confide their liaisons with their children, nor should they. Not mine, of course, I was ever faithful. But as for your father, I've always told you men were different and had different needs. And so if he felt he had to seek his pleasures elsewhere, it was no concern of mine, or yours. It's the way of the world," she said. "You'll see."

Before Annabelle could challenge that, her mother's expression grew worried. "But it oughtn't change anything between us," she said anxiously. "I've always loved you more than anything in life. You do know that, don't you?"

It was true and Annabelle knew it. She had to spend the next half hour assuring her mother of that, and the subject of her father hadn't come up again.

But here her parents were, walking down the fashionable lane together, smiling as though they'd never dream of spending days apart, much less their entire lives.

"My lord," Miles said when they came abreast.

"Give you good day. My lady," he said, bowing over Lady Wylde's hand. "How are you keeping?"

"All's well," Earl Wylde said. "I don't have to ask how you're doing. My daughter is radiant, your sister is blooming, and you look more content than any man in the park, as well you should be."

They spoke pleasantries, and even Annabelle was able to muster an artificial smile. She didn't think she could ever trust her father again, and managed the smile only by remembering that now she had a more trustworthy man to rely on.

Other strollers saw them chatting, and slowed to look some more. They whispered enviously about how the Viscount Pelham had obviously tamed his notoriously flirtatious lady, and how blissfully happy they both seemed because of it.

"Pelham certainly must have something extraordinary about him," one lady whispered, her eyes measuring Miles's shoulders.

"Yes," her escort said, his expression wistful. "He has the Lady Annabelle."

His lady batted him with her fan, but they both found an excuse to linger on the path with the others watching the handsome couple.

If Annabelle and Miles were aware of the comments, they didn't show it by so much as a glance at those who were making them. They simply stood exchanging pleasantries with her father and mother until there wasn't another thing any of them could say about the weather.

Then the earl and his countess left their daughter and her new family with wishes for a good day, and each party continued strolling their separate ways . . .

. . . until a large man stepped in front of Miles and blocked him. The stream of strollers behind Miles had to stop when he did.

Camille paled; Miles's smile slipped. Annabelle was confused. The fellow didn't seem a threat. He was a dark-complected, well-fleshed gentleman a bit beyond middle age, neatly barbered and well dressed. But he wore a sneer.

"Pelham," the gentleman declared in a booming voice, "I find you at last! And God knows how I've tried since I returned to England, but you hide from me. You won't answer my letters or see my solicitors, or let me in your house, even though I'm your stepfather. Is this how I'm repaid for my charity to you when you were a penniless boy?"

"Proctor," Miles said with warning, his voice a low growl.

"I return from abroad to resume my life with my family," Peter Proctor went on loudly as more people stopped to listen and stare. "And what do I discover? You've lied about me to the world. I left my wife and family in order to repair the estate you ruined with your wastrel ways. I slaved and struggled to manage my estates aboard so I could come home and mend all that you wasted. And I did. How do you repay me? I find you've spread lies in my absence and vilified my name! But I'm a fair man. Confess all and I'll forgive all. My love for your mother transcends my need for revenge."

Mile's face seemed stone. "You go too far," he said slowly, stepping away from his wife and sister.

"No apology?" Proctor shouted.

"I will kill you for this," Miles said, low.

"And hear! He threatens my life. But no," Proctor said, stepping back, "I won't let you silence me in some back alley. I'm a gentleman even if you aren't!" He ripped off a glove and flung it at Miles's cheek, then took several more steps back. "You'll hear from my seconds," he cried, turned, and walked rapidly away.

"No!" Annabelle said as Miles, hands fisted, began to follow. She put a hand on his arm. "You can't. If you beat him, he'll have won, it will look even worse. Oh Miles," she whispered, "what are we to do?"

"We will dance to the piper," Miles said tersely, as the watching throng of fashionables tried to listen close. "But he won't like the music, or the payment he gets for it. That I vow."

Chapter 23

❦❦

"**D**ueling is illegal," Annabelle said again.
"I know," Miles answered.

He lay with his arms crossed behind his head.
She sat up, as she'd done half the night until he'd
come to bed.

"It will solve nothing."

"On the contrary, it will solve everything."

"Is that what your friends told you tonight?"
she asked angrily. He'd gone out and come home
late. But she'd known who he was with, because
he'd told her: Eric Ford, the Earl of Drummond,
and a few trusted others he called friends. She'd
rather he'd passed the night with a lover.

"I can't ignore it, Belle. Dueling is illegal and he
knows it. But no gentleman walks away from
such an insult, and he knows that too. That would

be an admission of guilt. I believe he *is* free now, that's why he's showed up again. I think he meant to marry Mama and make our lives miserable as he bankrupted us again."

"But your mama has no money except for the allowance you give her," Annabelle argued.

"Yes, so he's doubtless discovered, which is why he's resorting to the ultimate blackmail now. I can't allow that. Not to mention that fact that if I turned the other cheek I'd be forever shunned as a coward and a cheat. Society isn't very biblical in nature. I deserve better, don't you think?"

Lost in misery, she only shook her head.

"I won't go to the gibbet unless I kill him," he said into the darkness. "I don't intend to do that, though he deserves it. I can wound him and declare honor satisfied. In the meanwhile, my friends are assembling evidence. I promise you he'll recuperate far from England if he values his freedom."

"Then why did he challenge you?" she asked, rubbing her aching forehead. "He means to kill you even if you don't mean to kill him. With you gone, he could marry your mama. She'll need someone to lean on. She's always loved him and he's an excellent liar. Even if he has to flee the country for his part in the duel, he'll find a way back and into her good graces again! With money, he could go anywhere."

"Bernard inherits if I'm gone," Miles said softly.

"And do you think he can resist a man like

Proctor, or his schemes?" Annabelle demanded—
and knew by Miles's silence that he knew that
very well, which was why he'd met with his
friends and allies tonight.

"There are all kinds of dire possibilities," Miles
said gently. "Life has no guarantees. I've chosen
pistols. I'm a very good marksman."

"And he's a good cheat," she said, flinging herself down on her pillow and burying her face in it.

"We have better things to do than to argue
about this," he said, as his hand made slow circles
on her back. "There's no help for it. Trust in me,"
he whispered in her ear. "I'll earnestly try not to
be killed. But I can't promise that. No man can.
Belle, listen to me," he coaxed her. "I could step
out of the house on my way to the duel and be
mowed down by a runaway carriage, couldn't I? I
might cut my hand on a champagne bottle while
celebrating his defeat, have it swell and fester, and
be dead in a week. You could kill me with love,"
he said softly, nuzzling her neck. "I devoutly hope
you'll try," he added. "Belle?"

She rolled over to look at him.

"So with all the best intentions," he said, "I
can't promise you I won't die." He cupped her
breast and leaned over her. "I'll try not to, though.
For your sake, of course."

She met his lips because she couldn't think
what to say, but needed him more than she
needed to speak.

They made love as they never had before, with nothing withheld. Her terror for him released the last fears she had for herself. She tried to memorize his body, finding the courage to explore him with her hands and eyes and mouth, because she feared never being able to again. She found more than freedom from her own shyness. Miles, so strong and powerful, was at her mercy in this. She showed him none. She remembered everything he'd ever done to her, tried the same with him, and marveled at how he caught his breath and groaned and asked for more. Her own body became caught up in his heat and fire.

He let her have her way with him until he couldn't resist what she'd set into motion. Then, astonished by the enormous pleasure of finally being able to freely mingle all the love and passion he felt, he was overwhelmed.

He bored down on her and she rose to meet him. He exulted, at last not worrying about harming her. She was his, and if they could never do this again, he'd at least have left her with all the passion he felt for her. She matched his frenzy. When at last she shivered, gasping, he fled the world with her.

"Miles?" she said later, after their bodies cooled and their wits returned, "Don't leave me."

He drew a long breath. "I'll try not to."

Then, with so much more to say and no way to say it, they made love again.

Chapter 24

Annabelle stretched, reached out an arm—and found only empty space. He was gone. She sat bolt upright and stared into the darkness. She'd feared this. She'd known this. But she hadn't wanted to believe it.

They'd made love last night as they had the night before, all through the night with nothing withheld and nothing left to be desired, until exhaustion had finally let them sleep. Now, this night—this dawn, she realized by the narrow streaks of gray light showing at the margins of the bedroom windows—he was gone.

She knew where, and thought her heart would break. But Annabelle was prepared. She threw back the coverlets and leaped from the bed. With shaking hands, she hurriedly dressed in the clothing she'd laid out in her dressing room the night before. She hadn't wanted her maid to know. No one must know. She was about to break a cardinal rule.

It was not done. She was an ornament of society, knew its every rule and every nuance, and lived by its code. Those rules had governed her life since she could toddle. From nurse to nanny, from governess to her own mama's lips, Annabelle had been drilled in the Right Thing To Do. She knew no other way to behave. Beyond the polite world, she'd been taught, lay only barbarism, disgrace, and exile. In short, it wasn't worth living.

So she knew better than anyone that ladies did not witness duels. They were forbidden. They looked the other way as the gentlemen went out to their killing fields. Then they waited, behind closed curtains, for news of life or death.

But she was Lady Annabelle, she kept telling herself. Nothing had changed that, though something was now trying to. Lady Annabelle had found the love of her life, and nothing would prevent her from being with him. Because what did society matter, after all? Life in his company was the only life she wanted. Any existence without him would be exile and not worth living.

She flung on the cloak she'd left at hand, pulled up the hood, and slipped out into the darkened corridor.

"What kept you?" Camille hissed.

Annabelle staggered. "What are you doing here?" she managed to ask in a harsh whisper.

"The same as you. I heard him leave. Did you think me so poor-spirited? He needs me, but I felt sure you'd be going too. Look," she said excitedly, fumbling in the folds of her own evening cape. She withdrew a long-nosed pistol. "I'm ready!"

"Camille," Annabelle said softly, pushing the pistol until it pointed down. "No. I'd bring an army if I thought I could end it that way. But we can't even try. Not because we shouldn't, but because he'd never forgive us if we got in his way. He can survive the duel, and I pray he will. But he'd never tolerate the disgrace of hiding behind a woman's skirts. Men aren't as reasonable as we are," she said when she made out Camille's sulky expression. "They live or die by their honor. So we'll go. But we can't interfere. Unless there's cheating," she added, gripping the smooth wooden haft of her own pistol in her deep pocket. "Then it's war."

They went down the stair, and tiptoed through the hall. The servants were still sleeping—the fires in every hearth were out, and the kitchen maid hadn't begun to set up a clatter. They sidled out the front door. When they quietly shut it behind them, Annabelle let out her breath and peered into the dim light. She'd hired a carriage; it stood as ordered, waiting halfway down the darkened street. They hurried to wake the coachman and stepped inside.

Annabelle gave him their direction. There was only one place gentlemen dueled these days, on a patch of open land outside the city, on a heath. She'd made sure of it. Footmen were men and presumed to have the same codes of honor as their masters. But maids were loyal to their mistresses and could be reasoned into listening at doors.

"Now," Annabelle told Camille as the coach jolted and started down the street, "when we arrive, do nothing. Don't let yourself be seen. Just watch. But if you must, do everything. And fast."

Miles gazed at the dawn sky. It would rain later today, he judged, but not until noon. The wind was freshening but the sun struggled through the disappearing night's mists. It would soon be light enough to see clearly. He allowed himself a fanciful notion as he waited for his opponent to arrive: Would the duel have been postponed if it had been teeming rain?

"No," his friend the Earl of Drummond commented, as if he'd read Miles's mind as he looked up at the racing clouds. "I've been at these events before. You face each other even if it rains fire. Bow Street, you see, may have been informed, and it's important to get the deed done before they arrive. And I hope they have been," he murmured.

Miles looked at him sharply.

The earl threw up his hands. "Not I," he said. "I dislike this but understand the necessity. But again, be wary of him, Miles. He's got a trick up his sleeve. I feel it in my bones."

"That's all that will be left of him if he does," Rafe Dalton muttered, pausing in the stalking he'd been doing, waiting for the other party to arrive.

"Here comes a carriage," an elderly, sober-faced gentleman said, peering into the lifting mists. "He arrives late in order to increase the tension. Don't let him, Miles. You were the coolest hand when you were in my command."

Miles took off his jacket, handed it to Rafe, and flexed his shoulders. "I know it, my lord. I won't let my anger get into my eyes or my hand."

"Tricks can't sway him, Lord Talwin," the Earl of Drummond assured the elderly man. "He's played too many himself."

Miles grinned at his friend. "And Eric?" he asked softly.

"Where he should be," Rafe reported. "Sinclair's taken the other end of the field. Unless she creeps through the forest to the north or slogs through the stream to the south, she'll be discovered and detained—if she comes."

Miles laughed. "Do you doubt it? You've met her. Nothing but—no, nothing will keep my sister away. So Eric and Sinclair have their work cut out for them."

The men smiled, until they saw the arriving carriage slow to a stop nearby.

Peter Proctor stepped from the coach, followed by two hard-faced strangers. He handed his cloak to one of them, and strolled over to the earl, never once looking in Miles's direction. "Has an apology been issued?" he asked the earl calmly.

"No," Drum said. "Have you changed your mind?"

"Hardly, my lord," Proctor said. "I've been maligned, and I shall be satisfied. Either by apology or this event."

They waited as Proctor took off his jacket. He was a tall man, heavyset but not obese, fit enough looking, but years older than his opponent. Still, they weren't going to be fencing or having at each other with sabers. Pistols erased the years between men; a level head and hand and a steady eye were all that was needed.

"Would you care to inspect the pistols?" one of the men who had come with Proctor asked Drum, opening the flat mahogany case he carried.

"Of course!" Drum said with astonishment. "Rafe! Lord Talwin! Come and have a look with me, if you please."

Proctor laughed. "Come, my lord, do you think I don't know your reputation, as well as that of your fellows? Lord Talwin's widely known as a man of influence in the War Office, and you and your friend Rafe had somewhat shadowy, though formidable reputations in the late conflict. You may believe me to be a villain, but surely you don't think I'd be stupid enough to tinker with the weight of either pistol or set either bore off balance? If you do, well then, sir, when I'm done with your friend, I'd be happy to meet you too."

The elegant earl's long nose lifted. He stared down it at the other man. "I don't expect you'll be able to do that, Proctor. Otherwise, I'd be happy to oblige you."

The pistols were inspected. The seconds nodded to the men they represented. The duelists moved to the center of the level grassy patch, and when they got there, turned and stood back to back. Miles faced north and Proctor south, so neither would face the glare of the rising sun. The surgeon had finished laying out his tools. Drum and Rafe Dalton stepped to Miles's side of the grassy patch. Proctor's two companions moved to his side.

The duelists stood in their shirtsleeves surrounded by their friends, who wore the sober tones of formally dressed gentlemen. The morning was rising dull; thick, dark green underbrush framed the scene. The white of the two opponents' shirts stood out, the only brightness to be seen. Lord Talwin stood beside them, and then backed away. "Fifteen paces," he said. "Ready?"

Both men nodded.

"One," Lord Talwin said.

The duelists began pacing away from each other, as Lord Talwin counted on.

Annabelle, crouched in a thicket on a rise by the killing field, caught her breath in a sob. It wasn't only because she was still breathless from her secret rushed passage through the bracken, it was because she could too easily envision a blotch of crimson staining the white shirt she watched so closely.

"Hold here," she whispered low to Camille as she brushed back another branch and peered out. "We can't go further. Can you see?"

"All too well," a deep voice murmured.

Annabelle shot up to her full height.

"Now, this one I expected," Eric Ford said softly and sadly, shaking a furious Camille by the wrist he held tight in one big hand. "But you, my lady? You surprise me. She had a pistol. What have you got in your pocket? A cannon? Please, if you will, hand it over."

But Annabelle's gaze had already gone back to the clearing. It had grown suddenly quiet. The men had stopped moving and stood still, holding their pistols down by their sides. They looked at Lord Talwin, who had stepped to the side. He withdrew a large white handkerchief from his jacket.

Eric forgot his request and stood as still as the two women, as they waited for the duel to begin.

A bird called. Annabelle heard nothing else but the blood pounding in her ears. She held her breath.

The men raised their arms and their pistols, and looked toward Lord Talwin.

Lord Talwin raised his white handkerchief.

Then everything happened too fast for anyone to see it all—except for those on a thicket on a rise above the killing field.

A man burst out of the thick underbrush at the side of the clearing, raised a long-nosed pistol, and pointed it at Miles. A stray beam from the rising sun sparked on the metal lock of the dark cased pistol. Miles swung his head to the side to see it. His raised arm followed the direction of his gaze, and he fired. A blast, a puff of blue smoke. Another shot fired. The stranger in the underbrush dropped his gun, gripped his chest, and crumpled to the ground. Yet another shot rang out. Another man had appeared to the side of the clearing, his pistol smoking.

Miles swung his head back and saw the back of his opponent disappearing into the thick blue smoke of gunfire as Proctor ran toward a waiting horse. But he didn't reach it. He staggered, stumbled, and fell. He raised his head and tried to crawl. A blooming bloodstain on the back of his shirt showed why he couldn't. He said something that sounded like gargling. And then his head fell and he was still.

The glade was quiet again, for one appalled moment.

Then Annabelle picked up her skirts and scrambled down the rise, shouting, "Miles! Miles!" all the way.

He was kneeling at Proctor's side and looked up to see her racing toward him like a mad thing. He rose and caught her in his arms. She wrapped her arms around him and clung, sobbing.

"Hush, it's all right," he told her. When she steadied, he looked over her shoulder.

"Well done, sir," he said, his eyes grave.

Annabelle lifted her head and turned to see who he'd spoken to. Her father stood there, gray-faced, breathing heavily, dangling a pistol that still bled a thin blue stream of smoke.

"I saw the opportunity and I took it," Earl Wylde told his son-in-law. "He fired at you—as you shot at his accomplice. I suspected he'd try something like that from my investigations." He paused for breath and went on: "I heard his challenge in the park, you see, and took precautions. I'm a very cautious man. I came here in the last of the night, before anyone arrived, to watch, in secret if I had to, and it seemed I did. And I came prepared. If it had been a fair fight, you'd never have known I was here. As it was, I don't say he could have killed you with a direct hit to the heart, since you were turned to the side when you shot at his cohort. But even so, he might have grievously wounded you.

"That would have suited him. Then he could spread more lies or demand payment to stop. You couldn't kill him without even more scandal. Slaying a stepfather, even an evil one, would have been a difficult thing to live down," the earl went on. "Nor could your seconds do it for you. There'd have been a trial and even more vicious gossip if he didn't get his way. He'd have made sure of it. But I could do it, and I had to. I owed my daughter that, at least."

"Yours is a formidable family, my lord," Miles said.

"It's yours now as well," the earl said. "I'm very glad of it. Well done on your part too, lad. You faced the enemy head on, and won. And you won my daughter completely. I believe that was the harder task." Without a glance at his daughter, he went on, shaking his head. "I couldn't believe what I was seeing. My Lady Annabelle behaving in such a harum-scarum way? Risking her reputation for a man, even her husband? Very well done, my boy. Now then," he said, looking at Miles's friends. "We have some cleaning up to do, gentlemen, don't we?"

"The man is dead by misadventure," Lord Talwin said dryly, "shot and killed by his own hired man, who killed himself in turn. We all saw that."

"Of course," Drum said blandly, "That's precisely what happened, isn't it, my friends?"

There was a murmur of agreement.

"Dr. Selfridge?" Lord Talwin asked.

The surgeon at Peter Proctor's side looked up, surprised, then shrugged before he too nodded. "All I have to say is that this fellow is dead, and he certainly deserved to be."

"Mr. Proctor's other hired scoundrel will testify to it too," Lord Talwin added, looking hard at the man Eric Ford held by his side, "before he goes to the Antipodes for life—if he wants to keep that life in order to do so, that is."

The man, pale, wide-eyed and shaking, one hand on his bloody shirtfront, nodded his head. Camille, her pistol restored to her and in her hand, kept it pointed at the quaking man as she looked at him grimly.

"Damn! We never thought he'd have someone hiding in the underbrush all night," a tall dark gentleman said as he trotted up to them, holding a smoking pistol. He stopped, and shook his head. "Sorry, Miles. That's a new one on us, isn't it, Drum?"

"I'll remember it, Ewen," Drum said with regret. "He was as inventive as he was greedy. But he's done, the doctor says, and off to try to outwit Satan now. I wish them both joy of that." He shot a bright look toward Annabelle's father, and added, "In future if, heaven forfend, we ever have to act as seconds for a friend again, we'd be well advised to beat the bushes before we start.

"Well. Let's clear house, shall we?" Drum said briskly. "Miles, go home. Take your wife and your sister with you, if you please. I can't remember them ever looking lovelier, because I can't remember seeing them here at all."

Miles smiled. "Thank you, gentlemen. Ladies, I can't thank you, society forbids. I can only love you. Let's go home. My lord?" he asked his father-in-law, "Would you care to come with us?"

Annabelle's father looked gravely at his daughter instead of answering.

She stepped out of Miles's embrace, but didn't let go of his hand. "Please come with us, Father," she said. "You owe me nothing. Not now, and not then. You were and are a good father, and that's all any daughter can ask."

"Ask more," her father said softly, glancing at her husband. "Be sure, my girl, that you ask much more and give as much as you ask, now and in the future. No man you love will ever mind that."

Chapter 25

Miles and Annabelle lay in their wide bed that night and spoke together in hushed voices. They weren't speaking of love as most people do. But they both knew they were speaking about nothing else.

"You'd have shot him, would you?" Miles asked with a smile in his voice.

"I'd have shot Eric if he'd tried to stop me," Annabelle declared. "That is, if I'd a chance to protect you."

"Your father was very brave."

"No braver than you."

"I had no choice," Miles said.

"Neither did he," she said on a sigh.

They were silent a moment, the only sounds the sheets rustling as Annabelle turned on her side and raised herself on an elbow to look at him in the faint last light of the candle flickering down to its socket.

"Your mama . . . ?"

"Will go to Bath," he said grimly. "I've told her to lease a house. I'll buy her one if she likes. The sea air will be good for her, and there are a great many lonely old gentlemen there. She's too alone at Hollyfields, and now she'd be even more so if we were there. She knows and accepts that.

"Belle," he said more softly, "I don't know how involved she was with Proctor's last plan, and I don't want to know. Our parents have their lives and we can't let them interfere with ours anymore. Some of them pay their debts, some . . . do not, and so shouldn't be part of our future. But I'd like Camille to stay with us. Do you mind?"

She laughed. "I already asked her. Do you mind?"

"That would hardly matter, as she gets what she wants."

"I think she wants Eric," Annabelle said in a troubled voice.

"She gets what she wants," Miles said again, "but she wants different things every other month. Let it go. We can't live her life either. Now, about living ours, do you think we might continue?"

"Again?" she asked with a delighted smile. "Oh yes!"

He stroked a shining curl back from her forehead. "Your hair is growing like weeds. You've come back, Lady Annabelle," he said more seriously. "You're the most beautiful woman in the *ton* again."

"No. I'm Belle now," she said, lowering herself against him. "Belle, your wife and lover, and she doesn't care about such trivial things. Well," she added, "not as much."

He smiled. "Don't change whatever you are, Belle, Lady Annabelle, Lady Pelham"—he brought his lips to hers—"for I love all of you."

"We'll always be here for you," she promised, and then added, "if, of course, you're always here for us."

"A bargain," he said, "a promise and a pledge, gladly given."

"Well, then," she said. "Can we get on with it?"

And gladly, they did.

Love . . . Passion . . . Intrigue . . .
Avon Books brings you everything
you'd want in a romance.

. . . .

DANCE OF SEDUCTION by Sabrina Jeffries
An Avon Romantic Treasure

Lady Clara Stanbourne will *not* let anyone ruin her charitable work, especially not the mysterious Morgan Pryce. He is very much mistaken if he believes her a delicate rose he can wilt with soft words and passionate promises. Now if only Clara can tame the fiery yearning the charming cad ignites within her.

INTO DANGER by Gennita Low
An Avon Contemporary Romance

In a world of secret missions and lethal deceptions, Navy SEAL Steve McMillan has heard all the stories about the "world's most glamorous assassin." He knows that dealing with Marlena Maxwell is like playing with fire, and to trust her would be crazy. Yet perhaps the deadliest mistake they could both make would be to fall in love.

ONCE HE LOVES by Sara Bennett
An Avon Romance

Legendary English knight de Vessey is entranced by the golden voice of a beautiful singer. Who is this angel who melts his sadness with song, filling the proud, haunted knight with warmth and a tender longing he never thought to experience again? The inviting look she gives him is just too tempting to resist . . .

A SCANDALOUS LADY by Rachelle Morgan
An Avon Romance

Faith has survived on the streets of London as a pickpocket, but on this night, her victim turns out to be the handsome Baron of Westborough. Troyce thought to rescue the poor urchin, never imagining there was a golden-haired beauty beneath the rags and grime. And though he knows he must marry an heiress, it is Faith alone who stirs his heart.

REL 0303